P9-DOH-361

Praise for #1 *New York Times* and #1 *USA TODAY* bestselling author Robyn Carr

"The captivating sixth installment of Carr's Thunder Point series (after *The Promise*) brings up big emotions."
—*Publishers Weekly* on *The Homecoming*

"In Carr's very capable hands, the Thunder Point saga continues to delight."
—*RT Book Reviews* on *The Promise*

"Sexy, funny, and intensely touching."
—*Library Journal* on *The Chance*

"A touch of danger and suspense make the latest in Carr's Thunder Point series a powerful read."
—*RT Book Reviews* on *The Hero*

"With her trademark mixture of humor, realistic conflict, and razor-sharp insights, Carr brings Thunder Point to vivid life."
—*Library Journal* on *The Newcomer*

"No one can do small-town life like Carr."
—*RT Book Reviews* on *The Wanderer*

"Carr has hit her stride with this captivating series."
—*Library Journal* on the Virgin River series

ROBYN CARR

one
WISH

MIRA

ISBN-13: 978-0-7783-1772-2

Recycling programs for this product may not exist in your area.

One Wish

Copyright © 2015 by Robyn Carr

All rights reserved. Except for use in any review, the reproduction or utilization of this work in whole or in part in any form by any electronic, mechanical or other means, now known or hereinafter invented, including xerography, photocopying and recording, or in any information storage or retrieval system, is forbidden without the written permission of the publisher, MIRA Books, 225 Duncan Mill Road, Don Mills, Ontario M3B 3K9, Canada.

This is a work of fiction. Names, characters, places and incidents are either the product of the author's imagination or are used fictitiously, and any resemblance to actual persons, living or dead, business establishments, events or locales is entirely coincidental.

For questions and comments about the quality of this book, please contact us at CustomerService@Harlequin.com.

® and TM are trademarks of Harlequin Enterprises Limited or its corporate affiliates. Trademarks indicated with ® are registered in the United States Patent and Trademark Office, the Canadian Intellectual Property Office and in other countries.

www.MIRABooks.com

Printed in U.S.A.

one WISH

One

Grace Dillon's flower shop was very quiet on the day after Christmas. She had no orders to fill, no deliveries to make, and she'd be very surprised if her shop phone rang at all. Most people were trying to recover from Christmas; many families were away for the holidays or had company to entertain.

Grace drove to North Bend to grab an early skate before the rink got busy. Figure skating classes were suspended over Christmas break and people, mostly kids who wanted to try out their new skates, would dominate the rink later in the day. Grace loved these secret early morning skates. She had a deal with Jake Galbraith, the rink owner. She could call him and if it was convenient, he'd let her skate for an hour or two while they were getting ready to open. He didn't want to charge her, but she paid him fifty dollars an hour anyway. It was a point of pride.

He smiled at her when she came in and told her to have a good skate.

She stretched and then stepped onto the deserted ice, closely following the Zamboni ice resurfacer that had just finished. She warmed up with forward and backward crossovers, backward half swizzle pumps, figure eights, scratch spins and axels. She noticed Jake was watching, leaning his forearms on the boards. She performed a forward spiral and a leaning tower spiral. She executed a perfect sit spin next. She circled the ice a few times, adding a jump here and there. She had been famous for her straddle split jump, touching her toes with her fingers. When she looked for Jake again, he had disappeared.

Suddenly, the music started, filling the rink with the strains of "Rhapsody in Blue." She glided into an arabesque, arms stretched, fingers pointed, wrists flexible. She saw that Jake had returned, was watching her every move. She went for a double axel and fell on her ass. She got up, laughing to herself. She glided around the rink a few times, tried the jump again and landed it, but it wasn't pretty. The music changed to another Gershwin tune. She'd practiced to this music as a little girl; it was familiar and comfortable. Her earliest memories of skating always filled her with nostalgia and comfort. That was before the competition got really fierce.

She'd been on the ice for an hour when the music segued into Alicia Keys's "Girl on Fire" and it lit her up. Her signature music. *She* was on fire! She skated like she was competing. When she was fifteen, stronger but lighter and more flexible, she could really catch the air. She noticed other people watching—a guy leaned on his broom and gazed at her, a couple of teenage girls who worked in the skate rental shop had stopped working to watch, the Zamboni driver leaned a shoulder against the rink glass, hands in his pockets. Two hours slid by effortlessly. She slowed and got off the ice when she heard the sounds of people arriving to skate.

"Beautiful," Jake said. "It's been a while since I've seen you."

"Holidays are busy at the shop," she said. She tried to get to the rink on Sunday mornings, but the past month had been frantic—wreaths, center-pieces, two weddings and increased day-to-day traffic in the shop.

"You should spend more time on the ice. I have a long list of people looking for a good coach."

She shook her head. "I don't think I'd be a good coach. I don't have time for one thing. And I'd never go back on the circuit, even with students. I left that world."

"I thought the day would come that you might be interested in going back, maybe not in competition for yourself, but coaching. I think on name alone you'd make a fortune."

"I left the name behind, too," she reminded him with a smile. "We have an agreement."

"I haven't said a word. People ask me, who is that girl, but I just say you're training and asked not to be identified. Some of them guess and would show up to watch you if they had any idea when you would be skating. The ice misses you. Watching you skate is like seeing music."

"Nice try. I don't train anymore. I spent as much time on my ass as on my blades. I look like crap."

"Your worst is better than a lot of bests I see. I've missed you. Maybe you'll have more time in the new year."

"We'll see."

She took off her skates and pulled on her Ugg boots. Sometimes she questioned her decision to leave it all behind, because being on the ice made her so happy. Then she'd remind herself that while a couple of hours felt great, the difficult routine of a competitive figure skater was grueling, exhausting. As a coach she'd never be able to push young girls the way she'd been pushed.

She pulled out a hundred dollars in cash for her two hours alone on the rink. Jake had told her he put the money in a special scholarship fund for young wannabe Olympians who couldn't otherwise afford lessons. She told him however he wanted to spend it was fine with her. As long as he didn't sell her out.

As she left the rink she reflected that her life in Thunder Point was so much more peaceful than it had been in competition and her freedom was hard-won. She had friends now, even if they didn't know who she had been before. At least no one thought of her as tragic or complicated or as one of the saddest yet most triumphant stories told on the competitive skating circuit. No one was threatened by her, hated her, feared or resented her. No one called her a rich bitch or a dirty liar.

Of course, the weight of her secrets sometimes wore on her. Jake Galbraith had recognized her at once. All she had to do was ask the cost of a private rink for a couple of hours and he knew immediately who she was. She hadn't confided in anyone in Thunder Point.

When she got into the van she saw that she had a message on her cell phone. She listened to it before leaving the parking lot. It was Mikhail, her old coach. He still kept tabs on her. They stayed in touch. Often, they left each other a series of brief messages because he could be anywhere in the world. "I am wishing you happy Christmas," the Russian said. "I think I am day late. If so, you will understand."

Grace waited until she was back in her tiny apartment above the flower shop before returning the call. "I thought you had forgotten all about me," she said to his voice mail. "It *was* a happy Christmas. I was a maid of honor for my friend Iris yesterday—that's how I spent the day. I've never been in a wedding before. It was small and intimate, a beautiful experience. And this morning I went skating. I fell three times." Then she mimicked his accent. "What can I say? I am clumsy oaf with no training." Then she laughed, wished him the best New Year ever and said goodbye.

Grace's beloved father and coach died rather suddenly when she was only fourteen and he was sixty. Her mother, once a competitive and professional figure skater, responded by hiring an even better coach, a very short Russian of huge reputation who could take Grace all the way. There was no time for grieving, they had work to do. Mikhail Petrov was a tough, brilliant coach and they were together for nine years. He had been very unhappy with her decision to leave competition and for a couple of years he pestered her to return to the sport. "Before you forget everything I taught you!"

Her mother, Winnie Dillon Banks, who had herself been a teenage skating wonder, was worse than devastated. She was furious. "If you quit now, after all I've invested in you, you are dead to me." After the 2010 Winter Games in Vancouver, Grace walked away from everything and everyone. All she'd ever wished for was to be like everyone else. To not be constantly judged every time she took a breath. She wanted to be normal.

In the afternoon, when Grace was just about to ruin her dinner with a big bowl of popcorn while looking through various online floral arrangements on her laptop, there was a light tapping at her back door. She pulled the curtain to peek out through the window in the door and was shocked to see Iris. She opened the door.

"Don't newlyweds lay around in bed for several days after the wedding? Doing it until their parts give out?" Grace asked, only half teasing.

"Maybe when one of the newlyweds isn't the town deputy," Iris said. "We did eat breakfast in bed and

Seth didn't go to the office until about one. I cleaned the house, thawed something for dinner and…" She paused. "I called Troy to tell him."

"You didn't tell him before, huh?" Grace asked.

Iris shook her head.

Troy Headly, high school history teacher and the fantasy of all the high school girls, had had a very big crush on Iris. They had dated for only a few months last spring when Iris told him theirs would have to be a friendship-only relationship. She was the high school guidance counselor and before getting involved with a teacher in the same school, she had to be powerfully sure. And she hadn't been. But Troy had pursued Iris right up until Seth was in the picture. Even then, it was pretty obvious he still had a serious thing for Iris and wouldn't mind if Seth fell off the face of the earth.

"How'd he take it?" Grace asked.

"Like a man," Iris said. "Is it too early for wine?"

"Certainly not!" Grace pulled a bottle of Napa Cellars sauvignon blanc from her little refrigerator and opened it. "Was it awful?"

"Nah, it was fine. Good, really. He was surprised we got married so soon, but then so was everyone. So were we, when you get down to it. He congratulated me and said he hoped I'd be very happy—all the right things. Then I asked him if he was going to be all right and he laughed, but he didn't sound amused. He said he was surprised to find himself disappointed an old girlfriend got married. It's hard for me to think of myself as his girlfriend—it was

never that serious. Even Troy admits he's not looking for a wife! Not now. He likes the single life."

Grace poured the wine and put the bowl of popcorn between them. "A gourmet treat," she said. "Or
maybe dinner. So, is it different? Being married?"

"Not yet," Iris said. "Ask me again when we merge
bank accounts. We've been solitary, single adults
for a long time. Right now we're each taking care of
our own obligations until Seth either rents or sells
his town house. There's plenty of closet space at my
house, but we could have issues when his manly furniture looks for space among my decidedly female
things."

"You're staying in your house," Grace said in relief.

"It's perfect for us. I like to ride my bike to work
in good weather."

"I love your house," Grace said. "Aren't you ever
going to have a honeymoon?"

"Eventually. We're looking for deals online right
now. We're going to sneak away in a couple of months,
hopefully somewhere warm and sunny, when Seth can
get away from the town and I can escape my office at
school. But what about you, Grace? Why aren't you
seeing anyone?"

Grace burst out laughing. It wasn't the first time
Iris had asked. "First of all, who? Second, when?"

"Don't you ever meet a groomsman at any of the
weddings you do?"

"Never. They all come long after I'm gone and
I'm not invited to the receptions. Besides, isn't that

the kiss of death? Hooking up with someone in the wedding party at the reception? No thanks."

"We have to get you out more," Iris said.

"Right," Grace said doubtfully. "Maybe I could help you chaperone the prom and meet some very promising eighteen-year-old? Nah, I don't think so."

"We'll go clubbing or something."

"Clubbing?" Grace sputtered. "In Thunder Point?"

"Okay, we'll go up to North Bend. And graze."

"I'm sure Seth would appreciate that!"

"Well, I won't take any phone numbers or bring anyone home…"

"Iris," Grace said, lifting her wineglass. "Let it go. I'll handle my own love life. In my own time, in my own way."

"There's always Troy," Iris said, sipping.

"Nah, we're pals. There's no chemistry." *On his side.* "We had a beer together once, followed by grilled cheese and tomato soup. It was swell. Besides, I'm not interested in your sloppy seconds. I read, you know. Rebound boyfriends are not a good idea."

"You can't just work all the time," Iris said.

"No?" Grace asked. "I thought you could."

Growing up, everyone thought Grace was a spoiled rich kid, but she had been raised on hard, committed, constant work. If she took a day off she felt ashamed. Her program would suffer. But her work hadn't been the kind average people understood.

Her full name was Isabella Grace Dillon Banks. She'd given up most of her name and went by Grace

Dillon because Izzy Banks was very well-known in some circles. Probably not among her Thunder Point acquaintances, but for those who watched champion figure skating competitions around the world, Izzy Banks was known, both for her skating and for her involvement in dramas and scandals that rocked the skating world.

Grace's mother, Winnie Dillon Banks, was a wealthy heiress whose grandfather made money in tobacco. She was a well-known skater in her time, though never as successful as Grace in competitions. Winnie's best show as a competitive skater had been second place in Nationals. But she saw in her daughter her chance to win and became the ultimate stage mother.

Grace had a privileged, isolated childhood where skating was everything.

Grace was born to an ice-skating icon and her coach. Winnie Dillon began a love affair with her coach, Leon Banks, when she was twenty-two. Some cynical rivals and professional observers suggested she succumbed to marriage and motherhood when all signals pointed to her competing days being over.

Winnie and Leon had their daughter on skates before she was four years old. They pushed and trained her hard. In those early days, when skating was simply fun, when she yearned to be the best, Grace was happy. She begged to skate and hated her time off. She'd have been on the ice eight hours a day if her father had let her. She was coddled and loved and indulged. She had a few friends, other little girls who were training and taking lessons and part of a skating club, some of them Leon's other students.

Grace loved her parents very much and didn't quite understand until after her father's death that theirs had been a difficult marriage. Her father was much older than Winnie and more focused on his students than his wife. Her mother was a demanding diva and socialite; she dragged a reluctant Leon to charity events and parties. Her parents disagreed on almost everything, especially Grace's training and education. Grace never went to traditional school, public or private—she had tutors. Leon thought this might be a mistake, feared she wouldn't be a well-adjusted child.

At the age of twelve the level of competition turned serious. But Grace was winning everything in her age category and was quickly viewed as unbeatable. She trained on the ice several hours a day, took gymnastics, ballet and practiced yoga. The family moved from Atlanta to Chicago and finally settled in San Francisco, following the best opportunities for her training and education, as well as for Leon's coaching prospects. Her father was diagnosed with pancreatic cancer when Grace was fourteen. Winnie sought a tougher, stronger, more famous coach the moment Leon fell ill. It was almost as if she'd chosen Mikhail before he was needed. Then Leon passed away rather swiftly, within months of his diagnosis.

Winnie and Grace took a few days off, then it was back on the ice. "Your success meant everything to your father," Winnie kept saying. It was true that

Leon wanted the best for his daughter, but it was Winnie to whom winning was everything. No matter the personal cost. And skating became less for fun and more for life. Winnie blew a gasket whenever Grace didn't take first place.

Grace left the world of competitive skating when she was twenty-three, right after the Vancouver Games. She went to Portland to stay with a sweet older couple who had once worked for her mother. Ross and Mamie Jenkins had known Grace since birth. They'd been part of Winnie's staff, Ross a driver and Mamie in housekeeping. They had retired to open a flower shop a few years before Grace quit the circuit. When she needed them, they took her in.

She collapsed. She was exhausted and depressed and afraid of the future. Mamie pampered her and gave her time; it seemed as if she'd slept for a month. Then one evening Mamie spoke up. "If you lay around one more day, you won't be able to walk. You have to do something—it's your choice. Get a job, go to school, something."

Grace didn't want to be around people and she didn't believe she had any marketable skills. So she started helping in the flower shop, in the back, learning to make beautiful bouquets and arrangements. Portland was a funky, interesting, welcoming city— not too big, not too small, not uppity or flashy. Little by little, Grace came out of the back room to deal with customers, sometimes delivering flowers, even helping Mamie and Ross with weddings. No one made a fuss over her or asked her a lot of questions.

Every time a major skating competition was covered by the mainstream or sports networks, Grace was glued to the TV, watching every move. And invariably there'd be some short vignette about Izzy Banks, the girl who had it all and threw it all away. "Izzy Banks, the brat on the ice, the fiercest competitor in figure skating, obviously couldn't take the pressure," one sportscaster noted of her.

Brat. Boy, that stung.

Her mother would usually get in touch, proving that Winnie couldn't ignore the competitions any more than Grace could. She'd pressure Grace to return home, return to skating, and the few conversations they had would end in a fight and they wouldn't speak again for months.

A year before the 2014 Winter Games in Russia, when the dramatic story of her life might be publicly examined yet again, Grace went in search of a new place to settle and tackle life on her own. A little money had been set aside for her by her father and she found Pretty Petals, the shop Iris's mother had owned. She'd been in Thunder Point almost a year when the winter competition took place. When Grace couldn't watch it, she'd record it. There had been the usual newsy dish about the more stunning events of the life of Izzy Banks, but no one seemed to recognize Grace. There were, thankfully, more interesting sports scandals that year. And Thunder Point was more a football than figure skating town.

All she'd ever wanted was a life she could control. A life that didn't include backbreaking labor, cruel rivals, endless travel across too many time zones, the occasional crazed fan or terrible loneliness. She wanted to know what it felt like to have real friends, not a staff of coaches, therapists, a security detail and competitors. She'd never had a boyfriend.

She did, however, have more than one gold medal. She'd won every significant competition in the world.

It drizzled in the days following Christmas, typical Oregon Coast weather in winter. Grace's only part-time employee, a local married woman with a child in elementary school, came into the shop to resign. The woman's life had grown too busy and complex, she complained. Grace knew it was going to create a challenge, even though all the woman had done was manage the front of the store. Grace was going to be back to doing it all, just as she had when the shop was new. She'd had the doorbell installed so she could lock the front door and go upstairs. The doorbell would buzz in her loft. And she could always close the shop to make deliveries when necessary. She'd ask around for a delivery boy.

Business was typically down the week following a holiday and the days were much shorter so Grace closed the shop at four one afternoon and drove out to Cooper's for a beer. She wasn't surprised to see Troy was back from visiting his family in Morro Bay. She was also not surprised that there was no one around the bar. People didn't hang out on the beach in cold, wet weather like this. But she had to admit surprise at seeing a big pile of books and papers beside his laptop on the bar next to his cup of coffee. She jumped on a bar stool. "Welcome home. Did you have fun with the family?" she asked.

"More or less. My sister has three little undisciplined kids and I slept on her couch. It was brutal. What can I get you?"

"Beer?"

"Was that a question or order?" he asked.

"Beer, please." She glanced at the books. "Homework?"

"Lesson plans," he said, closing everything up, stacking it all and pushing it to one side. "We're caught up in a couple of my classes so we're going to have some fun. I'm going to offer them a chance for extra credit if they research the history of something that interests them—like a rock band or in-line skating or maybe a sport like kayaking. I'm writing up a few examples."

"That almost sounds fun, but not enough fun. Did you get in any skiing over the holiday?"

"Nope," he said, drawing her a draft. "We played some golf, but the weather wasn't great. I might make a drive up to Mount Hood before I get back to work, maybe for a day. If I had more time and money I'd check out Tahoe. So, you were the maid of honor."

"I was. Kind of short notice."

"I heard it wasn't exactly planned in advance…"

"That's how I heard it, too. Iris said they decided and just did it. They got a marriage license, called a judge Seth knew, told Seth's family and got it done.

I didn't even have time to order special flowers." She sipped a little of her beer. "How are you handling it?"

"Fine," he said.

"Good. That's good."

He leaned both hands on the bar. "I went out with my little brother and got roaring drunk. Then I bought a Jeep I can't really afford."

"Oh," she said. "Gosh, I hope you don't get your heart broken too often or you'll go broke."

"I'd wanted that Jeep anyway. And I deserved a good drunk."

"Is that what caused…" She reached out toward the remnants of what looked like a healing bruise on his forehead.

He ducked away from her fingers. "I forgot I was sleeping on the couch, fell off and hit the coffee table."

She couldn't help herself. She laughed.

"And my heart isn't broken," he insisted. "Just a little coronary bruise. Gimme a week or two and it'll be like nothing ever happened."

Bullshit, she thought. He looked completely miserable. "You're very resilient," she said. She sipped her beer.

"I guess we've all been there," he said.

"Where?"

"Heartbreak hotel."

"Hmm. Well, I don't think I have. I haven't had my heart broken. Not by a guy, at least."

Troy appeared to be momentarily frozen. "There's no polite way to ask this, but has your heart been broken by a *girl*?"

She giggled. There were times, and this was one of them, that it would feel so good to dump the story on someone, explain how a heart can be broken by ruthless competitors or the media. "No, Troy. I'm perfectly straight. I'm into guys, I just haven't been seriously involved. I guess it's not in my nature to be tied down to one guy."

"No boyfriend, then?"

"Are you fishing?" she asked. "I've had some terrific boyfriends, just nothing serious. No steadies, engagements or live-ins."

"Why haven't I ever met any of them?" he asked.

She shrugged. "I guess you weren't around at the same time one of them was. I have a date later tonight, as a matter of fact."

"Oh? What's he like?" Troy asked.

"He's kind of like a medieval knight, but has a gentle, sophisticated side. Big and brawny, very physical but disciplined. He's also clever. Wise."

"Fantastic," Troy said. "Where are you going?"

"We're staying in, actually. We might watch a movie."

Troy lifted an eyebrow. "If I popped over unannounced, would I meet him?"

"Very probably. He's a little possessive but I completely ignore that. Like I said, I'm not one to get serious. Let's talk about your girlfriends."

"I don't kiss and tell."

She straightened. "Humph. Yet you expect me to!"

"I think you were bragging and maybe stretching the truth. You're a little weird, Grace. The last time we hung out was Halloween and you were a witch, complete with missing teeth. And you put a hex on me."

She smiled, remembering. She'd told him she was going to shrink his thing. "How'd that work out?"

"Turns out you're not much of a witch. So when you say your heart was never broken…"

"Come on, I've had my share of disappointments like everyone else, just haven't had a romance end badly. We can moan about our various letdowns another time, when we're both drowning our sorrows and feeling sorry for ourselves. Let's not do that now, okay? I have a feeling if you get started…"

"Did Iris ask you to check on me?"

"Absolutely not. She said you were very grown-up and wished her every happiness. And I must say, buying a Jeep you can't afford is definitely mature." Then she grinned at him.

"It's a great Jeep. Maybe I'll take you off-road in it sometime. Besides, I only have one person to worry about so if I have trouble paying the bills, it's not like I'm taking milk out of the baby's mouth."

She leaned her head on her hand. "You're all about fun, aren't you, Troy?"

"I work two jobs, Grace. I like to think of myself as active."

"And your favorite activity is?"

"It's a toss-up between diving and white-water rafting or kayaking. One of the things that brought me to Oregon is the great river trips. I was torn between Colorado, Idaho and Oregon. Oregon had the job. In a town on the water."

"And you're a teacher for the time off?"

"And the high pay," he said, smiling.

"Iris says you're the most dedicated teacher she knows," Grace said.

"Iris should raise her standards."

"Okay, so you're still a little pissy."

"I said I'd need a week or two," he reminded her. He lifted his coffee cup to his lips. "What's your favorite thing to do with time off?"

She didn't answer right away. "I need more balance in my life," she finally said. "That shop gets too much of my time. But it's a good workout."

"Flower arranging?" he asked doubtfully.

"I beg your pardon! I stand all day, haul heavy buckets full of fresh-cut flowers in water, deliver hundreds of pounds of arrangements to weddings and other events, get in and out of the back of that van all day, lift heavy pots and props and that's before I have to clean up and do the books. It's not for sissies."

"And for fun?"

"I like to dance," she said. "I don't very often, but it's fun."

"I bet you were a cheerleader," he said.

"I was *never* a cheerleader. I think I could've been. But I wasn't interested."

"You are the first girl in the history of the world, then."

"I'm sure I'm not," she said. "When I was that

age I was into ballet, sort of. They are not the same moves at all. That, like flower arranging, takes strength. Plus, I have a bike."

He raised his eyebrows. "A Harley?"

"A mountain bike. Retired for the winter due to ice, rain, cold and slick roads." She drank the rest of her beer and put her money on the bar. "I'd love to stay and keep you company but I have a date." She started for the door and turned back to him. "I'm glad you're doing well, Troy. I'd like to see what that Jeep can do off-road. Maybe when the weather warms up. And dries up."

"It's a date," he said.

But Grace knew it wasn't a date. She went back to the shop but didn't go inside. She went upstairs to her apartment, put some leftover lasagna from Carrie's deli into the microwave, changed into her soft pajamas and turned on the TV. While her lasagna cooled on the plate she went through the channel guide and settled on some reruns until her favorite shows came on. With her dinner on a tray and her e-reader in her hand, she opened an old and beloved book—*The Wolf and the Dove*—and settled in with Wulfgar, her medieval knight.

She loved him. And she trusted him.

Two

When Cooper asked Troy about his plans for New Year's Eve, Troy agreed to work. He hadn't gone skiing and was getting a little bored—might as well make money. Even though the night was clear and cold, it was a party night and Cooper's wasn't where the party was. Cliff was packing a full house at his restaurant and would stay open past midnight to accommodate his revelers, but Cooper's on the beach didn't have patrons past eight o'clock.

At a little after eight Troy locked up and walked next door to Cooper's house and brought him the contents of the till. Cooper and his wife, Sarah, were bundled up and had been sitting on the deck where an outdoor hearth blazed under a star-studded black sky. "I hear Cliff is going to shoot off some fireworks over the bay if the wind stays down," Cooper said. "If we're awake, we'll have the best seats in town. The problem with having a house like this—you never want to leave it."

"You look pretty comfortable. The fireworks might wake you up," Troy said.

"We had invitations for New Year's Eve," he said.

"I'm sure," Troy said, grinning. "Getting old, Cooper?"

"Oh, yeah, I guess so. But look at you—working tonight and all washed up before nine…"

Troy was ready to move on. "I'm going to stop at the store, grab a six-pack and drop in on a friend."

"Let me save you a trip," Cooper said. He got up, went to the refrigerator and pulled out a six of Heineken bottles. "Will this cut it?"

"I wasn't going to spend that much," Troy said with a laugh. "What do I owe you?"

"Gimme a break," Cooper said, waving him off. "Just get outta here and happy New Year. I hope the friend is female."

"She's female, but just a friend. I hope she's home or I'll end up at my apartment alone with a six-pack like a loser," Troy replied.

"I guess calling ahead didn't cross your mind?"

"I didn't think about it," Troy said. "Like I said, nothing special. Just a friend."

But Troy *had* thought about it. He was completely prepared to find Grace not at home and he didn't really care. Or she could be entertaining, which he'd kind of like to interrupt. Since Grace never brought out these boyfriends, he figured the only way he was likely to get a glimpse of one was to surprise her. What he'd really like to know was if Grace was as lonely as he was. Because two lonely people could negotiate a deal that would get them through. Why not?

He'd been thinking about her for the past couple of days, ever since she stopped by Cooper's while he was working. Grace had been in Thunder Point a little longer than he had, but he was just discovering her. He'd run across her a few times with Iris; she made him laugh. She was cute. Pretty, actually, but not the kind of gorgeous or sexy that slapped him upside the head. If he was honest with himself, women like that made him nervous. Grace had a wholesome look about her, kind of freshly scrubbed and glowing. She was very small, like a woman in a girl's body. But when she started talking, all traces of the girl vanished—she was clever and had a sassy, cynical wit. There was a sharp edge to her, like she'd lived a lot. She was full of the devil.

He privately acknowledged he was looking for a woman to spend some time with. The truth was, he hadn't often been without one. This might be one of his longest stretches; he'd been too damn focused on a woman he couldn't have. He wasn't above brief liaisons but he preferred something a little steadier. For that, he had pretty rigid standards. First of all, appearance was important. Not the only criteria, but someone who made an effort, put her best foot forward, kept up her looks. Next, she had to like to play. Troy loved extreme sports and it was not required that a woman he was dating be into the extreme, but it was important she liked trying new things, liked being outside, enjoyed physical activity. Iris had fit those requirements. She appreciated the outdoors, liked hiking, biking, paddle boarding. And she'd liked watching his videos of his own more adventurous experiences. She'd covered her eyes sometimes, but she'd watched his white-water challenges, rock climbing, diving with sharks, whales, squid.

Troy wanted a woman who was a good sport, at least. Of course she had to be intelligent and have a sense of humor. And since he was on the rebound, it was probably a good idea if she wasn't the clingy, needy type. That made Grace, who didn't get serious, a contender. She seemed to be casually dating someone and that sort of thing was usually a turn-off, but not at the moment.

He knocked on her second-floor apartment door, not really expecting her to answer. He saw the curtain move and then the door opened. She was wearing yoga pants, heavy socks, an oversize, long-sleeved T-shirt and her hair was pulled back into a ponytail. He tilted his head and smiled at her. "You don't have a date tonight?"

"Well, not at the moment."

Troy tried looking past her. "Is the medieval knight here?"

She put a hand on her hip. "Did you want to come in, Troy?"

He lifted the six-pack. "If you're not too busy. I brought beer. Sorry, I should've called."

She held the door open for him. "I'm surprised *you* don't have a date."

"It's not like I'm desperate," he said, entering. He

held out a beer for her, took one for himself, then opened her little refrigerator to stow the rest. "Oh-oh," he said. It was stuffed. Small to begin with, there was no room for a six-pack.

"Here, I'll do it." Some maneuvering was involved in getting four bottles of beer into the little fridge and ditching the cardboard pack.

"You're sure I'm not interrupting anything?"

"Come in, Troy," she said, moving through the dinky kitchen to the couch.

There was a movie on Pause and a plate of something snacky on the coffee table. He peered at it.

"Pizza rolls. I was just watching a chick flick but it'll keep. Now what's up with you? And take off your shoes."

He did as he was told, then sat on the far end of the couch. "Really, nothing. I worked at Cooper's, which is why I don't have a date or anything. It was dead tonight, and it was still early. I had about three choices—Cliff's, Waylan's or your place."

"You could have taken that new Jeep up to North Bend or even Bandon. Found a lively bar. Party a little." She picked up the plate and offered him a pizza roll.

"Thanks." He chewed it and nodded. "Not bad. I didn't feel like dealing with a bunch of strangers," he said. "I just felt like some company before I go home." He grinned at her. "And I thought maybe I'd run into one of your boyfriends."

"Oh, so that's your ulterior motive and the rea-

son you didn't call. I didn't want to go out tonight.
I went for a run."

"A run? You don't get enough exercise?"

"Short hours in the shop today. The nice thing
about being a one-person operation, I can close early
or open late if I want as long as I have a cell number
for the shop. That way I can take orders anytime. In
fact, if I'm available and someone needs something,
I can run downstairs and make up an arrangement.
But I knew there wouldn't be any calls tonight and,
God, it was beautiful on the beach. There were a
few people out there—Sarah Cooper and her dog,
a couple of teenagers, one older couple I've never
met—maybe part-timers. And me. I like to work
out, but there isn't a gym around here that matches
my oddball hours."

"You work out?" he asked.

"Not regularly. Just a bike ride or jog. I don't
lift anymore—my arms and legs get enough of a
workout in the shop. My flower girl calisthenics are
enough. I add cardio just so I can drink a beer and
eat pizza rolls." She offered him the last one. After
putting the empty plate back on the coffee table, she
curled into her corner of the sofa, her knees under
her chin. "Tell me about Christmas, tell me about
your family. Are you close?"

"I guess. As long as we don't have too much to-
getherness."

"What does that mean?"

He took a pull on his beer. "I love my family. I do.
We don't all get together that often and when we're

gearing up for a family thing, I get excited. Then on the third or fourth day I want to kill my sister and shove my brother in a hole."

She sat forward a little. "Really?"

"My sister can be a bossy bitch and my brother is a screwup. Jess was married at nineteen and they started trying to repopulate the world—my niece was born when Jess was twenty. Then came a nephew and another niece and she thinks she runs a tight ship but if you ask me, the ship is sinking. The kids are out of control, my brother-in-law, Rick, works as much overtime as he can—he's a firefighter—the house is upside down and I think Rick likes the firehouse because it's the only place there's enough quiet to watch a game. And my brother, Sam, can be such an idiot. He's twenty-one going on seven and my mother would cut his meat for him if she could. He's spoiled and irresponsible. He doesn't even walk his plate to the sink and he has to eat on the hour. He looks in the refrigerator and sees eight slices of leftover pizza, so does he ask if anyone wants some? Of course not—he eats them all."

Her eyes were large. "Should I be sorry I asked?"

Troy took a breath. "Nah, I'm just coming off another successful family gathering. I should've stayed in the motel with my folks—it gets a little tight at my sister's"

"Your parents stayed in a motel? Why?"

"Because they're smart! But take 'em one day at a time and they're great, they're really great. Jess's kids might be loud and messy and hyperactive, but they're also *happy*! Rick's such a great guy, I don't know how Jess captured him. And when I got moody and wouldn't tell anyone what was bothering me, Sam took me out on the town. Not that it's much of a town. We must've hit three whole bars. Of course Sam wasn't really trying to cheer me up as much as he was hoping to get laid, but then..." His voice trailed off.

"Then...?" she asked.

"When I was twenty-one, that was always fore-most on my mind. No apologies."

She giggled. "And now?"

"Not *always* foremost."

"So you love your family, when you don't hate them?"

"I'm crazy about them all the time—we just get on each other's nerves. We're typical, I think. I'll say this—half the time I want to punch my brother and slap my sister, but if anyone ever laid a hand on either one of them, I'd take 'em out. Really, I don't know how my folks lived through us. What about your family?" he asked.

She didn't answer right away. Instead, she got up, took the plate and her bottle to the little kitchen area, retrieved two fresh beers and returned to her corner of the couch. "There's very little to tell. My father died when I was fourteen and I'm an only child. My grandparents are gone, one set before I was even born and the other set before I was eighteen. There are some very distant relatives, but if I met some of them even once, I don't remember. I did get a letter from someone who claimed to be a cousin or half cousin or something, but he only wanted a loan." She laughed. "He apparently didn't know anything about me."

"How did you respond?"

She smiled. "I wrote back that it was very kind of him to reach out, but I wasn't making loans at this time."

"No one, huh?" he asked. "Your mother?"

"Also gone," she lied, looking away. She just wasn't willing to get into all that. Plus, she'd told Iris that she was alone. "There are friends, but probably not as many as you have. The couple who owned the flower shop in Portland where I worked, we're close and stay in touch. I talk to them every week and visit now and then. They not only trained me in the shop but took me under their wing. Good people. They're in their sixties and never had children, which probably explains why they think of me as family, though we're not. And there are a couple of other friends who also stay in touch—Mikhail, to name one, but he travels all the time so I never see him. That might be one of the reasons I became good friends with Iris—we have that absence of family in common. And there's the fact that I bought her flower shop, of course. Sometimes I look at people like Iris...and...well, you—and I feel a little abnormal, like I should try harder..."

"Iris? And me?"

"You're both so connected to people. Iris doesn't have family, but she has more good friends than anyone I know. The whole town loves her. The school definitely leans on her. And your family isn't around here, but I bet you talk to them every week."

"Pretty much," he admitted.

"You're really involved with people, too. The school, Cooper's, even Waylan's. All over town, people yell hello! But the reality is, I was raised an only child, had a very solitary upbringing and I'm probably a little too comfortable being alone."

"People around here are pretty friendly to you, aren't they?"

"They are. That's what I love about this town. But I'm kind of a loner."

"But you've had a lot of boyfriends," he reminded her.

"This is true. And they've all been amazing. I spend time with a guy who actually owns a plantation in South Carolina, a guy with a British title of some kind—viscount I think. There's Malone—he owns a lobster boat on the East Coast, there's a bar owner, a guy in the ski patrol, a navy SEAL…very interesting, sexy guys. But I own a flower shop— my time is precious."

He tilted his head and peered at her. "I think you're bullshitting me, Grace."

She got off the couch and went to the wall unit, opening a cupboard under the TV and there, lined up neatly, was a tidy row of books—paperbacks and a few hardcovers. Below the books was a similar collection of DVDs. She left the doors standing open and went back to the couch. She gracefully extended a hand toward the bookcase. "My keeper shelves. From medieval knights to navy SEALs. And there's Wrath…I'm afraid he's a vampire, but a very nice and sexy vampire. They're all mine."

"Should we have a little talk about your medication, Gracie?"

She smiled. "I know they're pretend boyfriends, Troy. But they never cheat and I haven't had to get one single screening for an STD." Then she giggled. "I don't have space for a lot of storage and books so I do most of my reading on an e-reader, but I have a special collection there. I can't be without them. What would I do if my e-reader wasn't charged or I lost it?"

Troy felt a tug of some kind inside, somewhere in his chest. He knew it was a warning sign—it was too soon to feel affectionate toward her. In fact, he'd prefer to never feel anything but friendly. But he couldn't deny it felt good to know that Grace wasn't involved with anyone. Her claim to never having been very involved was unusual for a woman her age and beauty. And he liked it.

"How are you fixed for real dates?" he asked.

"I have a very demanding schedule. When you own your own business every day off is a day without pay. I don't have much help at the shop. I've had a couple of part-timers over the past couple of years, but right now I have no one—the last one had to quit. She wasn't that much help anyway, but at least she kept the shop open while I delivered flowers. I have to try to figure that out. Like I said, I need a more balanced life."

"Have you thought about a high school or college student? Or maybe two who could job share, putting together two part-time schedules that equal one full-time employee? There are so many at the high school who don't want to go to college or who do but have trouble affording tuition."

"Good idea, but when I advertise for help, hardly anyone answers."

"You need help advertising in the right place. There's a work-study program at school. If you can train your student-employee in a trade, they'll get a credit toward graduation and get a morning or afternoon off to work. Didn't Iris ever suggest this?"

Grace looked a little excited. "No! Should I ask her to help me with this?"

"Yes," he said. "Not tonight. Tonight we drink beer and eat something. What've you got? I could run out for something…"

"How hungry are you? Because I make some amazing nachos. And since I have some black olives, taco meat left over from taco salad and sour cream…"

"Oh, *yeah*," he said.

"Didn't you have any dinner?"

"I had a couple of Cooper's mini pizzas…"

"And you say it's the little brother who eats on the hour?" She went to her tiny kitchen.

"Are you sure you don't want me to run down

the street for something? I hate to ask you to feed me," he said.

"Don't go," she said. "It's not much trouble and it sounds good."

She bent over to dig around in her little refrigerator and Troy felt a fever coming on. Those yoga pants had a real nice fit. He had to look away, take a breath. Sometimes, he reminded himself, you don't notice what's right in front of you. He'd spent all that time thinking Iris was right for him. Even though she made it clear it was a no-go, he never bothered to get to know any other women and here was Grace, right under his nose. Making him hot.

She was complicated, he knew that. She said her life was boring, not much to tell, solitary…and he knew that was just a cover. And he didn't mind at all.

"Then let me help," he said, joining her.

They put together a fabulous plate of nachos, ran out of salsa very quickly since that little fridge couldn't hold much and cupboard space was at a premium. They spent the next hour talking about the town, the rivers Troy liked to run in the summer, the kids he taught. Every time he asked Grace a question about herself she gave him a brief answer and steered the conversation back to him.

"You know there are dorm rooms bigger than this loft," he said to her. "You live like a college student."

"I know. I'm keeping my life simple and my expenses down until the shop does better, and it's doing better all the time. There aren't that many weddings in Thunder Point, but I get a lot of weddings out of town. They're killers but they pay like mad. Where do you live?"

"In a small old apartment on the edge of town that's decorated with castoffs from my folks. You're saving for the flower shop and I'm saving for travel." He noticed her eyes widened and wondered where it came from. Envy? Longing? Surprise? Something else? He told her about the dive trips in summer, ski trips in winter, hunting trips with old Marine Corps buddies here and there.

"Marines?" she asked.

"I did a year of community college, enlisted, went to Iraq and got out. That's how I finished college—GI Bill. I was a lowly jarhead but I made some excellent friends. There's good hunting in the mountains not far from here. I'll take you sometime if you like."

"Oh, I've never touched a gun," she said. "I couldn't hunt."

"Then I'll take you for the scenery."

Just then, as they were talking about guns, something that sounded like gunshots punctuated the night. Almost as if choreographed, they both turned to open the shutters behind the couch. In the sky above the bay, fireworks blasted the dark sky, exploding into bright fireballs and falling in sparkling streamers.

"Fireworks," she said in a breath.

"The wind has been too high in the couple of years I've been here," Troy said. "I think Cliff hires someone to do it. Not bad, for a dumpy little town."

"This place surprises me all the time."

Troy turned to her and caught her chin in his finger and thumb. He leaned his forehead against hers. "Me, too."

"Listen, Troy," she said, and there was no mistaking nervousness in her voice. "I… There are things…"

He stopped her by kissing her gently. He slid his hand around her head to the nape of her neck under her ponytail. His kiss was soft, brief and gentle. Instinct told him he was dealing with a major unknown emotional situation and should go slowly, carefully. He moved over her lips very tenderly.

"What things?" he asked.

She took a breath. "I didn't exactly tell the whole story about my family, about growing up…"

"I know," he said.

"How? Do you know things about me? Is there something…"

"Shh," he said. "I'm a high school teacher. I can smell excuses and evasion a mile away. It's an acquired skill. So there's more to you? That's okay, Gracie. Don't panic. You'll tell me when you feel safe."

"Okay?" she said, more of a question than a reply.

He chuckled. "Okay. We're just friends. And we're getting to know each other. Take it easy."

Then he leaned in again, taking another taste of her lips as the popping, exploding sound of fireworks provided the background music. Again he was gentle and sweet because the last thing he wanted was to scare her off.

"I'm not experienced," she whispered when their lips parted.

"Well, except for the navy SEAL, knight and vampire?" he asked with a laugh in his voice.

She smiled against his lips. "Yes, except for them there aren't many experiences. I made out with a guy named Johnny when I was fifteen. For about ten hours I think. He was fantastic and turned out to be gay. Such has been my luck."

He gave her a little kiss. "I'm not."

"Yeah, I was afraid of that."

"Don't be afraid," he said. "It's all good."

"Should we be down on the dock, watching the fireworks?" she asked.

"Uh-uh," he said, shaking his head. "We should be right here." Then his arms tightened around her and he covered her mouth again with kisses that had become hot, demanding and promising.

Troy left at around one in the morning but Grace stayed on the couch. She grabbed a pillow and blanket and decided to spend the night right there, where it all happened, where the kissing and snuggling and whispering took place. She was still licking her lips, touching them with her fingertips, contemplating his skill, his taste. The last time she'd been kissed was in Portland by a nephew of Ross and Mamie's. That was over two years ago. His name was Gary, last name long forgotten. He'd attached himself to her mouth like a plunger and attempted a tonsillectomy with his tongue. He'd gotten away with that three times before she finally told him to stop.

There were some things for which she had very little training and one of them was romantic relationships. She hadn't been in a position to have boyfriends. And if she did have a crush, which happened rarely, her flirting felt conspicuous and clumsy. She'd had a crush on Troy, as it happened, but because she was Iris's friend and Troy had been trailing Iris for a year, she never let on. Growing up, she trained mostly alone, the only exception being her father's younger students—almost exclusively girls. There were men on the skating competition circuit and other athletes competing in some of the national and world competitions. Some of the figure skaters she competed against were so much more womanly—tall, with breasts, worldly, sexy, flirtatious. And they hated her. They had plenty of reasons—she was raised with money while many of them had parents who worked several jobs to pay for their training, not that that had anything much to do with one's ability to perform a perfect double axel. She often competed against older skaters because her talent meant she was a force to be reckoned with. But the other girls tended to act as if she could buy the medals.

Her biggest rival was a girl her age named Fiona Temple. Fiona beat her once and only once, but that was all it took for Fiona to believe the only thing that stood in the way of her stardom was Izzy Banks. Fiona hated her and spread rumors about her whenever she could. Fiona's parents leaked stories to the media. Grace would never forget the time, age twelve, when Fiona told other skaters Grace was a rich bitch and how everything was easier for her. Grace had cried and told Winnie all about it. "Never let them see you cry!" Winnie had said. "Never! Lift your chin and beat her instead! Beat the tights off her!"

That's what she wanted to do, but it was so hard not to feel hurt. So she lifted her nose in the air, ignored them, and they started calling her a stuck-up snot who had everything handed to her.

And then she did something that caused a world of trouble. Winnie had warned her to keep her mouth shut, but she couldn't stay silent. She accused a famous skating coach of sexual misconduct with one of his students, a minor. She quickly learned speaking out gets you treated like a leper, even if it's true. True or not, a smarter person would have proof to offer before opening her stupid mouth. When she asked her coach's advice Mikhail had been blunt. "He is piece of shit but it will get you nothing to say so."

That world-famous coach was not prosecuted and ultimately sued Izzy and Winnie. They settled, giving him money. A year after Grace retired from competitive skating the coach was arrested and eventually convicted of sexual misconduct with minors.

She'd been right. Vindicated. For what good it did her.

She hadn't been completely without friends growing up, but her few relationships had been superficial and strained. When the girls doubled up in hotel rooms to save money, Winnie rented spacious quarters for the two of them and Mikhail, removing Grace yet again from her contemporaries. The only skaters she didn't actually fear were on the men's team. And most of them *truly* wanted to be nothing more than friends.

She couldn't look to her parents as models for a healthy, strong love match. Her mother had married her father because she needed a keeper. Her father had married her mother as he had married a young skater before her, one who bore him a child twenty years before Grace came along. As much as she had always adored her father, she understood—he had a *type*. Young, vulnerable, needy, willing to do whatever he demanded because they were convinced he'd help them win.

She could, however, look to her parents to see what she *didn't* want in a relationship.

Her other advisors on romance were in the book-case—the romances and some classic chick flicks. She and Iris had debated them often enough. Some were pure fantasy, some unreasonably coinciden-tal, but some of her favorite contemporary romances revolved around very strong women and men with integrity. And then of course she studied their fic-tional presumptions, mistakes, missteps, blunders, and from them she learned. Or at least hoped she had.

She had been unprepared for Troy. She had wished for someone like Troy for a long time but assumed that kind of man would never happen into her life.

Troy had kissed with such amazing skill and tenderness. And there was passion—hot, deep, panting, groaning passion. Grace wanted to fall in love with him, something she attributed to her lack of experience. But she thought about what he'd said to her. "You aren't with anyone, I'm not with anyone and it seems like we might as well enjoy the moment. Right?"

So. He was just lonely and had finally accepted that Iris had moved on. She didn't care. She loved his mouth, his arms, his hands. She would try very hard not to fall in love with him.

Grace snuggled down into her blanket on the couch and thought it didn't matter at all. She never imagined she'd have this with anyone and certainly not the very guy she lusted after. They had kissed for an hour. He didn't rush her, didn't push her, didn't treat her like someone he was using to pass the time and it was *delicious*! She decided to close her eyes and dream about him, dream about them taking it to the next level. She was twenty-eight; she so wanted to know what that was like.

Instead she dreamed of Mikhail, the little Russian in his sixties with a cane he pounded for emphasis, shouting in half Russian and half English. It was so unfair, she thought, slowly rousing to the sound of knocking that was not Mikhail's cane.

She was suddenly afraid and her heart started racing. Who could be pounding after one in the morning? Then she saw that it was starting to grow light and at just that moment she heard Troy's voice. "Gracie? Gracie? It's me," he called softly.

She opened the door for him. He was holding a bag. "What in the world are you doing here at the crack of dawn?"

He looked at his watch. "It's nine, Grace."

"Nine? It looks like the sun isn't even awake!"

"It's a gloomy day. I brought breakfast and then I'm going to take you storm watching."

"Why?" she said, frowning.

"Because the swells are huge and I think you need me to show you how to have fun."

"I beg your pardon, I know how to have fun."

"Working all the time, then working out for diversion. Nah, you definitely need a coach. We'll start small—just a little sightseeing. There are big swells, the waves will be awesome."

"But it's cold."

He put his bag on the little table. "And it's kind of wet. You should dress warm, but first, breakfast." He pulled some fast-food breakfast burritos and potato pancakes out of the bag. Lots of them. On the bottom were two large coffees.

"Hungry, Troy?"

"Starving." He sat down and peeled the wrapper off one of the breakfast burritos. "Come on, Grace. Let's do it. This is going to get you all excited. Promise."

"I was going to catch up on some paperwork since the shop is closed today. Accounting and stuff."

He shook his head. "See what I mean? This is exactly why I came over. I don't know you that well but I already know you're working too much. I have two jobs and still manage to take some days off." He took a big bite. "It's New Year's Day. It's a *holiday*."

She sat opposite him and reached for one of the burritos. He was right. Not only was he right, she'd told him last night she needed to find more balance. "Do you have an aversion to making plans?"

"No," he said. "I'm usually much more polite— call ahead, make plans, all that stuff that girls like. I'll work on that. For now, I think we should have some fun. Especially today."

"There are lots of football games on TV."

"I'm recording them," he said. "I might not watch them all and I'm not going to sit around inside all day when there are things to do. You'll be glad you let me drag you out," he said.

"We'll see," she said, but she already was.

Three

"The outstanding question is why have you appointed yourself my fun coach?" Grace asked once they were in Troy's Jeep and driving.

"It's not complicated at all," he said. "I need someone to play with. I work a lot. I give a lot to the students. I have a second job at least ten days a month. Between school vacations and weekends, I manage some time off and Cooper is great about letting me put together days off from his place so I have time to pursue my interests. When I'm not working I look for fun things to do. Mostly skiing, diving or river trips, but since there's decent skiing and diving right here, I only take about one big trip every year. There are lots of places I need to see—Costa Rica, Barcelona, Paris, Montreal, China, to name just a few. My real passion is kayaking or rafting and, honey, there are some rivers in the tristate area that can keep me busy through spring and summer. Who knows? Maybe you'll try it sometime, maybe not. But this is a great place, Grace—there's a ton of stuff to do and see and experience."

"You need someone to play with," she repeated as if that was the only thing she got out of all that. But it wasn't what she was thinking. *I've been all over the world. I could almost work as a guide.* Except, Grace had never toured the countries she'd visited, never really taken in the sights. She'd been all over the world to compete. Usually with an entourage. And now, Troy needed someone to play with?

Her heart beat a little faster.

"Well, that's not the whole story," Troy continued. "I'm not shy about doing things on my own. I meet people all the time, great people who have like interests. But, Grace, you're kind of fun. Let's see if there's anything you like better than working all the damn time."

"You have a point," she agreed. "The problem is I have my own business. And every day off—"

"I know, every day off is a day without pay."

"You pay attention," she said.

"It's admirable, having your own business. But I think your business is a ball and chain. It's all about working out a schedule you can live with, Grace. People don't need flowers twenty-four/seven. And I bet you'll be a happier business owner if you get out a little more."

Of course he had no idea how much getting out she indulged in because she didn't talk about it much—her yoga, working out, secret skating. "So that's why you think you can kidnap me like this?"

"Really, Grace? Kidnap?"

"Hijack."

"Look at that coast," he said as he drove north. "Damn, not a day to go fishing, I don't think. Have you seen the coast up this far?"

"Of course," she lied. In fact, she'd driven down the coast from Portland one summer, barely took in the landscape, made a bid to buy the shop and went right back to Mamie and Ross, where she spent a week lost in a panic attack, terrified of being completely on her own. She was so nervous she nearly called her mother! In the end, she toughed it out and when her offer was accepted by Iris, she drove straight to Thunder Point, never really taking in the coastal beauty.

They passed through the outskirts of North Bend and then Coos Bay. It appeared very little was open for business, it being a holiday. There were a few bars and a Chinese restaurant that seemed to have customers. A souvenir shop on the highway had an Open light shining in the door. Gas stations were operational and a firehouse had the big rig doors spread wide. But the traffic was sparse. Everyone was probably home taking in the football games and recovering from New Year's Eve.

"Have you ever seen it on a day like today?" he asked as they drove toward the ocean. He pulled into a small lookout that faced the water. The clouds were dark and the wind was blowing wicked and wet. There were patches of rain over the ocean and the waves were huge. The air was frigid and the fun coach was grinning. "Yeah, this is gonna be *great*," he said.

"What in God's name have I let you get me into?" she asked. He laughed as if he found that extremely amusing.

He put a knit stocking cap on his head and jumped out of the Jeep. When she joined him, he grabbed her hand and pulled her along a path that she knew led to the edge of the lookout because she could hear the deafening sound of crashing waves. When the path crested she stepped back with sudden anxiety. The waves looked like mountains as they crashed against the rocks.

"God," she said, but only God could have heard her above that noise.

"Come on," he said. "They're about a hundred feet in some places, some of the biggest waves in the world. We can get closer. It's safe."

She shook her head. "I can see just fine!"

"What?"

She put her hands around her mouth and shouted in his ear. "I can see fine!"

He laughed. He put his mouth close to her ear. "It's safe. Look, there's a stone wall. Not like we'll slide off. I can see from here that it's dry. I want to get a couple of pictures with my phone."

It was a very low stone wall, about knee-high. She shook her head. A lot.

"Is it scary, Grace?" he asked, shouting.

She nodded.

"I'll go check," he yelled. He let go of her hand

and walked along the path closer to the edge. Waves rose above the level of the ground she stood on, but they crashed to the surf below. The path began to wind downward, which gave her no peace of mind and she hung back. She wasn't sure of herself on high cliffs over rocky shores facing off with hundred-foot waves. Troy continued on, of course.

The waves were magnificent, she had to admit. The power was *stunning*, no other word.

Troy leaned against the wall, his back to the ocean, and waved at her. She waved back. He jumped over the wall and walked a bit farther toward the edge and she felt her stomach clench. There was a sign, for God's sake! Don't Go Past This Point! But over the wall he went. He turned toward her and shouted something that she didn't have a prayer of hearing so she just shook her head. He spread his arms wide and high, as if in victory.

Probably the award-winning wave of the day came up behind him and her eyes grew as round as plates. Her mouth hung open and she watched in awe as the crest of the enormous wave came down on Troy. She screamed in terror, afraid he'd been washed out to sea. As it receded, there he stood, looking for all the world like a drowned rat. With gunk hanging from one shoulder.

Grace grabbed her heart in relief. He just stood there. Dripping. He plucked the gunk off his shoulder and began to climb back over the wall.

After a couple of relieved breaths, once she was sure the fun coach was all right, Grace hugged her-

self and sank to her knees in hysterical laughter. She
could barely see him trudging toward her because
her eyes were watering with tears. His jacket and
pants were heavy from water, making his movements
slow. She wanted to spring into action and tell him
she was taking charge, except she couldn't talk. Instead, she rose slowly to her feet and by the time he
reached her, she was upright again. She took his hand
and pulled him back up the path toward the Jeep.

"Oh, my God," she rasped weakly, still hysterical
with laughter. "Oh, Troy!"

"It's thirty-eight degrees," he said, shivering. "Get
a grip! Stop laughing!"

"I'm sorry," she said, but she couldn't stop. "I had
no idea you could be such a funny fun coach! Get
in—I'm driving."

"It's m-m-my new Jeep!"

"You're shaking. I'll drive, crank up the heater
and you can start peeling off wet clothes. I don't suppose you have a blanket in the car?"

"N-n-no. That was a f-f-freak wave!"

"There was a sign!" she said. "Did you want to
go over Niagara Falls in a barrel, too?"

"Funny. You're so f-funny."

"Oh, God, I wish I'd gotten a picture. Here," she
said, opening the passenger door. "In you g-g-go!"
she said, mocking him. Then she doubled over in
laughter again.

By the time she got into the driver's seat, he had
already started the engine. "Take off that jacket and
throw it in the back. And that stocking cap," she

said, yanking it off his head and pitching it over her shoulder. It took him a minute to peel off the jacket and once he had, she started touching his shirt. "Not that bad, really, but still wet. That was probably forty gallons of water." Then she touched his pants, patting his thighs and knees. "Oh-oh. These are soaked. Hang in there, the heater will get going pretty quick." She put on her seat belt and made a big U-turn, taking off down the road. Hunching up against the steering wheel, she was still laughing. "That was seriously the funniest thing I've ever seen in my life," she said.

"Shut up, Grace."

That only made her laugh harder. "Relax, I'm going to fix this for you. I hope."

"How?"

"You'll see. Don't be so crabby—I'm going to get you dry."

Troy aimed all the vents at himself and turned up the fan. "Lucky I didn't get washed off the edge," he muttered, rubbing his hands together.

"I admit, that wouldn't have been as funny," she said.

"You have a very big laugh for a little girl."

"I know."

A few minutes later, she parked in front of the souvenir shop. "What are you doing?" he asked.

"You'll see." She grabbed her purse and jumped out, leaving the car running for him. She jogged inside and less than five minutes later came running back to the car with a roll of paper towels in one hand

and a shopping bag in the other. "These were donated by the cashier," she said, handing him the paper towels. "And these are for you!" Grinning widely, she pulled a sweatshirt out of the bag—it read My Heart Is in Coos Bay. "I got the largest one. And here are some shorts." She pulled out a pair of women's shorts with eyelet lace sewn around the legs. "They're actually from a pajama set, but they're XL. They didn't have any men's pants, just tops. This was all they had, but they're dry."

"You're kidding, right?"

"It's okay, you have nice narrow hips. If this place hadn't had clothes, I was going to take you to that fire station, but this is better. And you don't ever have to wear them again, just till we get you home." She craned her neck, looking around. They were alone in the parking lot. "Take off your shirt and dry your head and body…"

"In the car?"

"You're a guy! Guys strip on the street if they have to! Guys pee off boats!"

He ripped off his shirt and used paper towels to dry his hair, neck and his damp chest. He put on the sweatshirt. "Good. That's good."

"Pants. Come on."

"They're not that wet…"

"You're soaked. I won't look," she said, turning away.

"I'm okay, but thanks for the thought."

"Your pants are wet and it's cold. You already made the seat wet—get your pants off and sit on a bunch of paper towels. Even if we get it warm in here, you can't be sitting in cold, wet pants."

"It's New Year's Day and nothing is open. How'd you know about this place?"

"We passed it on the way up. I asked myself what would be open on a holiday—the souvenir shop was all I could think of." She smiled. "I almost grabbed you a couple of refrigerator magnets while I was in there." She touched his shoulder. "Put on the nice, dry shorts, Troy. I'll close my eyes. Besides, cold and wet as you are, there probably isn't that much to see."

He lifted one eyebrow. "Did it ever occur to you that's why I'm not undressing in front of you?"

"Fine," she said. "I'll go back inside the store. There's no one in the parking lot. Get it done."

And with that, she was out of the car. She chatted it up with the cashier for a minute, explaining Troy's shyness. She glanced at her watch, supposing enough time had passed. When she walked back outside, what she saw caused her to stop dead in her tracks.

A police car was parked next to the Jeep and an officer had Troy out of the car, standing in his wet stocking feet wearing his ladies' shorts, talking and shivering. *Oh, no!* she thought. He must have been changing when the officer pulled up. Of course he had to take off his shoes to get out of his pants. She could imagine what the officer thought! She took two steps toward them to help, to be a witness to Troy's explanation.

But she started to laugh again and was absolutely no help at all.

* * *

Troy insisted on taking over the driving. He was no longer chattering and shaking. He was, however, a little out of sorts. And he cast glances at Grace, who was looking out the window attempting not to laugh, the attempt causing her to snort now and then.

She turned toward him, her hand suspiciously covering her mouth. "So, how did the police become involved?"

"He snuck up on me as I was changing pants. I was at a disadvantage. My wet jeans were tossed over the seat and these pretty little shorts you so kindly bought me were around my ankles and I was drying off when I looked up and he was staring in the window. He told me to get out of the car. I had barely stopped explaining the situation when you came out of the store and laughed until you almost peed yourself. I'm writing a letter to the city council. I think it's unprofessional for a police officer to laugh until he farts."

Grace quickly looked out the window. She snorted again. She got the hiccups.

"Glad I could be so entertaining," he grumbled.

"Are you going to drop me off at the flower shop?" she asked.

"Oh-ho, no way, Gracie. I might've screwed up my first attempt at showing you how to have fun but I'm not giving up. And I'm not letting you do accounting on a holiday! I'll just clean up and we'll go at it again."

"Really, Troy, I think your work here is done. I

don't think I've ever had more fun in my life." She snickered a little and bit her lip. "Besides, I think you might be mad at me for laughing. And that doesn't sound like fun."

"I'm not mad," he snapped. "I'm *wet*!" He took a breath and said, "I'll be more fun when I'm dry and not wearing girl pants."

"I think you're fun right now," she said. Then she grinned at him.

He parked behind his apartment complex and led her up to the second floor, leaving all his wet clothing outside the door. He unlocked his dead bolt. Once inside, she looked around. "Wow. Nice."

He smiled to himself. It was a crappy old complex on the outside, but Troy had done a little work on the inside. He'd painted, for one thing, and bought a nice, deep and fluffy area rug to put over the old and worn carpeting in the living room. He had some nice shelving and a fifty-seven-inch flat screen. He'd made repairs and improvements here and there, like taking down the shower curtain and installing a glass shower door, sanding and refinishing the bathroom cabinets, scrubbing the place like he owned it. His parents' old leather sectional fit right in. The only things he had that were new were the butcher-block table and high chairs. His bedroom furniture was only a few years old and he had been collecting a few framed LeRoy Neiman prints for the walls. The frames were more valuable than the prints, but he liked Neiman's sports art.

"Make yourself at home. Help yourself to anything—eat, drink, whatever. There's the remote. I have to get a shower. I'll be quick."

He left her standing in the small living room. Once he was under the hot water, sudsing the smell of salt and seaweed from his hair and body, he smiled to himself. Grace was a free spirit. A little wild and uncontrolled with a deep-down joy and playfulness that turned him on. He might've acted a little insulted at her lusty humor directed at him but, to be honest, he wouldn't have it any other way. That was no prissy little laugh the girl had: she laughed down to her toes. There was passion in her.

He revisited his checklist in his mind and moved *She must be a happy person* to number one in his requirements. If that meant laughing at his foibles, he could live with that. Grace didn't come across as whiny, self-pitying, cloying or desperate. If he demanded a woman be a good sport, then he had to be, too. And who forced him to jump that wall? He'd been showing off. He loved showing off.

She might just prove to be a good little playmate.

When he got back to the living room to Grace, she was curled up in the corner of the sectional, holding a cup of something hot with both hands. Her boots were sitting at attention beside the couch and she was wearing bright pink socks. One of the many New Year's Day bowl games was on television. He stood looking down at her, smiling, with his hands on his hips.

"Do you feel better?" she asked a little sheepishly.

"I'm tempted to hold you down and give you

something to really laugh about. You ticklish, Gracie?"

She pulled back a little. "Don't even think about it," she said, holding up the cup. "I'm armed."

"What is that?"

"Hot chocolate. You had some envelopes of mix in the drawer by the refrigerator."

He wrinkled his brow. "That could be very old."

"I don't think dry powders spoil. Want to taste it?"

"Thanks," he said, reaching for the cup. She handed it to him and he put it behind him on the coffee table. Then he tackled her on the couch. While she shrieked and begged and laughed, he pinned her with his body and attempted to tickle her.

"I'm sorry, I'm sorry, I'm sorry," she squealed.

"What are you sorry for, Grace?" he asked, a devilish gleam in his eyes, pinning her to the sofa.

"I'm sorry I laughed and bruised your delicate little male ego," she said, smiling.

"Ooh," he growled, giving her a good rib-tickle.

"Ack! I'm sorry, I'm sorry, I'm sorry! Stop it, stop it!"

"What are you sorry for?"

"Okay, I lost it, I was out of control, I laughed at you when you were vulnerable and I'm sorry. No tickling!"

"A cop was threatening to arrest me for indecent exposure!" Troy said. "He thought I was a parking lot predator!"

A smile beamed across her face. "That was the best," she said. "I'm sorry, but that was the best part.

Although, that wave...I will never see anything like that again in my lifetime! You are an excellent fun coach."

"It wasn't my intention that you have fun at my expense," he said. But he was smiling when he said it. "I was going to show you how to have a good time."

"And so you did," she said, smiling into his eyes. "Think of how successful that might've been if you could *read*. I mean, there was a sign. Can I make you some stale hot chocolate?"

"I don't think so. I think my mother sent me that in one of her many boring care packages. What should we do today? Want to go out? Any ideas?"

She shook her head.

"Let's stay in," he said. "Let's make some game food. I have stuff in the freezer. I have tri-tip and buns for tri-tip sliders. Or we can go with wings or pizza. I have beer but no wine."

"I have wine in the flower cooler," she said. "I just feel like such a slouch, eating so much trash and bar food."

"I'll slice some onion and pickles for your sliders. I have some deli potato salad but I don't know..."

"Dangerous?" she asked.

"By this date, very likely. I don't expect you to be that much of a good sport."

"Oh, so that's your game? You want a good sport?"

He gave her a quick kiss. "I want to enjoy myself with someone who's enjoying herself. I have a feeling, a dark feeling, you don't need my help with that."

"Okay. I'll do one more day of carbs and fats. But the next time we eat together there will be green things."

"I love green things," he lied.

He told her to take the Jeep to her place to retrieve her wine and she brought back a Scrabble game. She also threw in a DVD of one of her favorite non-chick flicks, *Red*. He looked at it and said, "I love *Red*!"

"Just in case your brain goes numb from football," she said. "But I can do football as long as you can."

They had a rousing game of Scrabble, which Troy won by a stretch. They curled up on the couch together to watch *Red*. Every once in a while Troy invaded her space for a make-out session. In midafternoon they worked together in the kitchen to build some sliders, which they ate on big plates in front of the TV. Troy quizzed her about football teams and stats. "You're a big football fan," he said.

"I'm a small football fan," she corrected. "Or maybe medium. I enjoy the game but I don't live for it like some people do. And I have a good memory for football facts."

"And your favorite sport?" he asked.

"That's a tough question. I think I like watching everything competitive."

"I think I'll invite you to my Super Bowl party," he said while they rinsed the dishes.

"You're having a Super Bowl party?"

"Uh-huh," he said, directing her back to the couch, pulling her down and getting her back in his arms. He loved that there was no hesitation from her.

His arms went around her waist, hers went around his neck, lips on lips and bodies pressed together. It being the height of winter, the sun was lowering and the only light was that from the kitchen and the TV.

"Who's coming to your party?" she asked, lips pressed against his neck.

"I'm thinking of a very small party. It could be a private party." He caressed her back, her sides, ran a hand over her butt and down her thigh. "Maybe just us."

"I'm not sleeping with you," she said.

He backed off a little. "Ever?"

"I'm not ready," she told him. "I want to know you better."

"That's very reasonable," he said, kissing her again. "But really, Gracie, you taste so good…"

"That's sweet. I'm still not ready."

"Are you going to be unready for a real long time? Because, honey, you are a turn-on. And I risked my life for you on the cliffs of Coos Bay today. Just to make you happy."

She chuckled against his lips. "You are such a giving man. I'll be sure to let you know when I'm ready."

"Just out of curiosity, Grace, are you waiting for a sign?"

She nodded. "I am. Plus, I'd like to be sure you're all done pining over Iris. That just feels weird."

Troy immediately put a little space between them. He grew serious. "Iris is married, Grace."

"I know this. I was there."

"Listen, here's how it is. I'm crazy about Iris. She's an awesome person and great counselor for the kids. I consider her a good friend. It's true, for a long time I thought if she gave it a chance we might be more than friends, but we weren't on the same page. All right? We were *never* on the same page and even though she told me over and over, I thought she might reconsider. She didn't."

"I know all that, but you have to remember—Iris is my good friend, too. I don't want the situation to be awkward."

"I hope we're all good friends for a long, long time," he said. "When I kiss you, I'm not thinking about Iris. I'm not thinking about anyone but you."

She frowned slightly. "I'm pretty sure you didn't answer the question," she said.

"Iris married the love of her life, her one true and forever love. Even if I did still carry a torch for her, I'd never admit it. Especially to you. But I don't. She's moved on and so have I. Do you believe me?"

She smiled a little bit. Her expression said she didn't believe him at all, but how could she argue without calling him a liar. "Okay, I believe you," she said. "But there are also things about me... I want you to get to know me a little better."

"I'm ready whenever you are. But so far, you're the mystery. You have some pretty vague answers to questions about your life, your family, your friends..."

"I know, Troy. Since I was raised an only child,

isolated in some ways, I tend to be on the private side. If you're just patient…"

He leaned toward her. He kissed her again and she melted into him.

"How do you like me so far?" he asked against her lips.

She smiled without breaking her hold on him. "You're growing on me."

"You can trust me. When you're ready to tell me more, you can trust me. And you can ask me anything."

"Okay. One important question before we go any further. Are you sure I'm not just a booty call?"

Four

On January second, Grace did an inventory of her stock, updated her calendar, cleaned out the flower bin and made herself a to-do list. She had two couples coming in at the end of the month to get estimates for spring weddings. Valentine's Day would be her next major event and she wanted to begin decorating the shop right away. Soon it would be spring, when her stock would be more beautiful and plentiful than ever. The most important thing on her list was to find help for the shop! She really wanted to spend more time with the fun coach.

Being with Troy was intoxicating. They made out like teenagers, but she knew she was going to have to get ready for the next stage. Oh, so inviting! She was amazed he agreed not to rush her.

She heard the bell on the shop door tinkle and looked out of her workroom to see a familiar face as Al Michel stepped into the shop. He had the most handsome smile, a man who seemed perpetually

happy. He was a big man, in his fifties with a powerful physique, who looked impervious to aging.
He wore his blue work shirt, his name embroidered
above the pocket.

"Hey there," she said, coming into the shop. "How
was Christmas?"

"Excellent," he said.

"And what made it so special?" she asked.

"Well, my lady, for one thing, Ray Anne really
went overboard to make sure it was nice for the boys.
We had Christmas Eve at her house and she cooked
most of the food, but I helped a little. She decorated
and wrapped presents for everyone. Christmas Day
was at our house, but she took care of most of the
food. We brought the boys' mom from the nursing
home for a few hours and it was great. Her MS is
under control for the moment, and I could tell the
boys were proud to have her home, if only for a little
while. I think it was the nicest holiday any of us has
had in years, especially the boys."

Grace leaned on her counter and tilted her head.
"I don't have any idea how you got hooked up with
those boys," she said.

"Simple," he said. "Justin, the oldest, worked with
me at the service station. He's nineteen and real private. I found out he was taking care of his mother and
two younger brothers, killing himself to hold it all together while his mom was just getting more and more
infirm. So we teamed up—me and the boys. I'm their
foster father. Their mom needed the nursing home
and it made sense for me to move into their house.

The two younger boys are in school. They're good kids, but they still need supervision. Not constant, but regular. Know what I mean? But just to be sure things couldn't be simple or real easy, I found my lady, Ray Anne, right about the same time I found my family of boys."

He shook his head and chuckled. "Now, Ray Anne is a good woman and I think she loves those boys like they're her own, but she's..." He cleared his throat. "I don't know if Ray Anne even knows how old she is, but she's not as young as she looks. She's probably too set in her ways to live with a man like me and three teenage boys. She's particular and fussy. The way we got it worked out is good. I live with the boys, she lives in her own house. She visits, invites us over sometimes, and then there's the times those boys grant me leave and I visit my lady without them chaperoning. It verges on a perfect life."

"Wow. All that happened at once?"

"Pretty much," he said. "I didn't think I'd ever be this settled."

"In two houses," Grace said with a laugh.

"Aw, it won't be two houses forever. Justin passed his GED and we're looking into college courses. Scares him to death but the boy is smarter than he thinks. Danny's in high school, Kevin's almost done with middle school. Before I know it, I won't be that necessary to them."

"Oh, I bet you'll be the dad for a long time to come. Maybe even a grandpa."

"Hush now," he said, grinning. "We're in the

grandparent prevention program at my house. Those boys don't need any more complications. Now, Grace, I should take my lady some pretty flowers. She worked so hard over Christmas to make sure me and the crew had a great holiday. That woman is a dream come true. What've you got that's perfect for her?"

"I just cleaned out the bin," she said. "Would you like a bouquet or an arrangement?"

"I don't know," he said with a shrug. "What's the difference?"

"The last flowers I sold you in the square vase—that was a bouquet. A table arrangement is like a centerpiece for her table or bedroom dresser. I have some lavender and white roses, hydrangea, lilies—the pretty green and white ones. Next week I'll have a new crop of calla lilies."

He contemplated for a second and she was thinking what a good catch he must be—a man with tender feelings, strong enough to take on a brood of teenage boys and sensitive enough to think of his lady with flowers. "Just make something pretty, Grace. Fifty bucks or so?"

"Wow, you do love that lady."

"Every time I think of her I want to fill her house with flowers. Ray likes pretty things. I waited a long time to find someone like her."

"What's it like, asking three teenage boys if you can go out on a date?"

He laughed. "A lot of monkey business, kissing noises, that kind of thing. Especially the younger two—I can't wait till they have girlfriends. I'm planning to be relentless and obnoxious, they've earned it. So, how much time do you need on the flowers?"

"Thirty minutes, tops. Want to wait?"

"I think I'll go get lunch at the diner while you work, then come back. Can I bring you anything?"

"That's so sweet," she said, shaking her head. A couple of weeks ago she might've said, *Yeah, your younger brother*! But now there was Troy. "I'm good. I'll get right on this. And don't forget to put in your order for Valentine's Day roses early!"

Twenty minutes later the bouquet was finished—white, lavender, dark green and a little blue delphinium. She might've put extra love in the bouquet just thinking about Al and Ray Anne, finding each other a bit later in life. Here she'd been thinking that at twenty-eight she was long overdue.

When Al picked up the flowers they had a brief discussion about her need for help in the shop and he said Justin might be able to run some deliveries for her if he didn't have to pay for gas. Al promised to ask him.

When she was alone, her personal cell rang and she answered.

"Hey there, flower girl. What are you doing?" Troy asked.

"Ah, you do know how to use a phone. I'm doing flowers. Beautiful flowers. How about you? Wanna go see the waves?"

"You're adorable, you know that? I'm going to work for Cooper today and tomorrow, but Sunday is my day. And I go back to school on Monday. The flower shop is closed on Sundays. So—what should we do?"

"This implies you want to have an adventure? Is that it?"

"Let's take 101 south, check out the redwoods, drive into the Humboldt County mountains and maybe break bread with some illegal pot growers. We can have a picnic in the redwoods. We might have to have it in the car—it's going to be kind of cold but sunny. Except back in the trees, it's dark and cold."

"How do you know it's going to be chilly and sunny?"

"My phone says it's going to be sunny with a high of forty-five degrees."

"What did we do before smartphones?"

"Listened to the farm report. So, what do you say, flower girl? Date?"

In all the places she'd been, from China to Charlotte, North Carolina, she'd never been to the redwoods. "I think that could be fun. We should pack extra clothes this time in case you have to show off again."

"Yeah, I'll take that under advisement. So, that's Sunday. I'll be at Cooper's tonight. It's Friday night. A clear and cold Friday night so there will be people. There might be teenagers on the beach with their fires and shenanigans. If you're not tied up with the knight or the vampire or some loser Navy SEAL you could always come out."

"I could, but I should think about it. Ever since I've had a fun coach some of my boyfriends have felt neglected."

"I'll be here till nine or ten, depending on people. I'll follow you home to make sure you get in safely. Because I'm such a gentleman."

"I'm sure you would. Let me see what I have to do."

"You do that, Gracie."

No one had ever called her Gracie or flower girl. She loved it.

She went to Cooper's at almost eight, climbed up on a stool, her cheeks rosy and her fingers like icicles. It was a perfect night on the beach and there were three different fires surrounded by people, mostly young people.

"Hi," Troy said, smiling. He grabbed her hand. "Whew. Cold."

"I walked over," she said. "I might need a ride home."

He smiled wider. "Gotcha covered," he said, a twinkle in his eye.

Troy found lots of things he could do with Grace. She had never dated like this before. They drove down the coast to the redwoods, another day they went up the coast to Ecola Beach. They drove over to Eugene, and they drove up into the snowy Oregon mountains on a clear day. They went out to dinner twice and saw two movies. She went with him to a couple of high school basketball games and she closed the shop early one Saturday so they could drive to the university for a Ducks hockey game and they watched the Super Bowl together—just the two of them. They always ended the dates with more of that wonderful kissing. And with Troy always dangling the suggestion of an overnight. Grace kept pushing that idea back *for now*. But they made out every night. Every. Night. She really couldn't get enough.

She found herself watching one of her favorite comfort chick flicks a lot—*The Holiday*. It was sweet, warm and fuzzy and she thought Troy looked very like Jude Law, except for the dimple. Grace was falling in love.

Because Grace and Troy had been seen around with Iris so often, not much was made of the fact that Iris was now missing—she was a newlywed, after all. In fact, Troy and Grace ran into Iris and Seth at a high school basketball game and they seemed completely unsurprised to see Troy and Grace together.

Then Iris popped into the shop one day after school. She'd been doing that quite regularly since Grace bought the shop. Iris liked to make her own flower arrangements and Grace gave them to her cheap. But, since she'd been married, the visits had become rare. Grace already had the workroom cleaned up. "I haven't seen you in a while," Iris said. "Are you anxious to close?"

"I'm in no great hurry, but no one will be by now. People who want flowers after five call ahead—they know I'll stay open for them to pick up if I can. This

married business—I don't see that much of you anymore!"

"Because now I go home and cook! If I don't,
Seth's mom will try to feed us every night and we
can't have that. And I run errands and do laundry and
get caught up on my homework before Seth comes
home."

"*You* cook? Oh, God, has he filed for an annul-
ment yet?"

"Very funny. I'm getting better, but sometimes
he cooks. Have any flowers you can spare? I could
use something cheery in the house—this weather
can be a downer."

"Oh, I know exactly how to perk you up," she said,
going into the cooler. She brought out a bottle of nice
sauvignon blanc and two icy glasses she kept in there
for just such an occasion. "Ta-da! You can pick your
flowers while I get the corkscrew out of my desk."

"You are a good person, Grace," Iris said, approv-
ing of the wine and going into the cooler. Grace had
the wine poured by the time Iris returned with a selection of flowers. Iris knew exactly where to get
clippers, tape and a vase. She chose a very attractive oval vase to hold the bouquet. "I'll return it, of
course," Iris said.

Grace passed her a glass of wine and lifted her
own. "To your new status, Mrs. Sileski."

"Thank you, Grace," she said. "And should we
toast a new relationship for you? You seem to be
spending a lot of time with Troy."

"You left him lonely," Grace said with laughter in her voice.

"Oh, please don't tell me he's complaining that I'm off the market! I thought we had that all taken care of!"

"He's not complaining, Iris," Grace said, taking a sip of her wine. "But we're just friends."

"Are you sure about that?"

"Oh, yes. I asked, as a matter of fact. He said he needs someone to play with. And so do I, since you decided to get married!"

"There's no question about it—Troy is fun."

"The fun coach," Grace said with a laugh, then she told Iris about the giant wave until both of them were laughing hysterically. Grace told Iris about some of their fun dates, but she didn't mention the more personal things, like all that wonderful kissing.

After a glass of wine and a very beautiful bouquet were both done, Iris said it was time to get home.

"I bet Troy's not just looking for fun," Iris said.

"Oh, I bet he is," Grace replied. "But so am I."

Grace locked the front door behind Iris, lost in thought. *Why can't I let myself lean on Iris, give her the whole story? She might know how I should guard my heart because I'm starting to fall in love and Troy isn't looking for love. Especially from me.*

She went back to the workroom, put the cork in the bottle and heard a light tapping at the back door. She looked up and smiled.

"Ah, I see you've been working hard," Troy said, pointing to the wine bottle.

"I was about to put this back in the cooler. Iris came by to make herself a bouquet," she said. "You just missed her," she added, watching his expression.

"I saw her earlier," he said, picking up the glasses. "I'll carry these up for you."

"You saw Iris?" she asked.

"I see her at school every day, Grace. Want to go out for Chinese?"

"I need a shower," she said.

He reached for her. With the wineglasses in one hand he lifted her chin with the other and put a sweet kiss on her lips. "Want to have a shower and I'll go get takeout? Or, if you need help with that shower…"

"I'll manage," she said. "So, you're hungry for Chinese?"

"I am. And I want to ask you something. Want takeout or should I wait for you to have a shower?"

"What do you want to ask me?"

"Hold on. I'm going to soften you up first. Is there a beer upstairs?"

"There are two," she said. "You go get dinner while I wash off the flowers. How long will it take you?"

"Forty minutes, tops," he said. "You okay to lock up?"

"I do it every day, Troy. Just get going."

This was what it was like to go steady, she thought. Just a couple of small things missing. Like, there was no future and he wasn't falling for her. Well, if nothing else, it was good dating practice. Troy was a great date, after all.

Troy's question was a simple but difficult one. The high school was having a Valentine's Day dance and he wanted her to be his date. He was going to chaperone. "Oh, God, that's almost the busiest day of the year for me!" she exclaimed.

"How late do you stay open?"

"Just till six, but I will be toast! I might be the worst date of your life."

"I can help you after work, help you clean up the shop and lock up. How about deliveries?"

"I have a little part-time help with that. Justin Russell, Al's boy, is running some flowers for me before he goes to work at the station and he's going to be sure to help that day—I already told him it's madness, but there could be good tips. Oh, Troy, what if I'm no fun? And it's a dance! I love to dance, but I might be knee-walking tired."

"The next day is Sunday. You can sleep all day," he begged. "Come on. I want to take the prettiest girl in Thunder Point to protect me from all the teenage girls."

"Really?"

"You are the prettiest girl in—"

"No," she said. "To protect you?"

"Okay, I can handle them," he said with a laugh. "Come with me, Gracie. We'll dance. Put a sign on the shop door. Closing promptly at six on Valentine's Day so make arrangements to get your flowers early or ask for delivery. The flower girl has a date."

Grace couldn't resist him. And while everything else felt casual, even the kissing part, this felt like the real deal. She asked if the right dress was going to be an issue.

"Not for you," he said. "All the high school girls are competing with each other and trying to impress their dates. But you already have me. You can wear a barrel if you want to." And that was exactly the right thing to say, but she warned herself not to get too excited. At least not until he said something that sounded like *we're more than friends*.

Valentine's Day met all of her expectations for craziness. Grace started early and made up as many bouquets as she could ahead of customers. The pre-ordered roses had been ready the day before and by the end of the day every rose in the shop was gone, along with many other arrangements. Justin started deliveries early and continued right up till five o'clock. Without him, she'd have been lost. She tried to stay ahead of the mess but in the end she left a lot of it—she could give the shop a good cleaning on Sunday.

She would have liked a little extra time to get dressed, but even rushed as she was she went to more trouble than usual with her hair and makeup. Grace wore her maid of honor dress, a sleek little black number and the only fancy dress in her arsenal. She usually pulled her hair back to keep it out of the way of the stalks and stems, but for this date she wore it down. It had grown long, past her shoulders. She even used the curling iron!

"Wow. You clean up good!" Troy said when he picked her up.

Grace expected to stand around a punch bowl with a bunch of teachers while the high school kids danced, but it was so much more than that. She was immediately enchanted. The high school gym was beautifully transformed with painted murals, twisted crepe paper streamers, snowy scenes, balloons, glitter balls, white and colored twinkle lights. The bleachers were pushed all the way back and the gym floor was circled with small round tables covered with long white tablecloths. Candles and little centerpieces decorated each table and there was a disc jockey at one end of the dance floor. To enter the gym the couples walked through a heart-shaped arch decorated with hearts, clouds and snowflakes and their pictures were taken as they appeared. The chaperones hung back and chatted among themselves; only a couple had brought dates or spouses. As the music played, almost everyone danced, and refreshments were being served by volunteers.

It was magical. Grace had never been to a high school dance. She'd never been to a high school!

Iris was at the dance, of course. "No date tonight?" Grace asked.

"My date is patrolling the parking lot and looking for trouble. I'm sure he'll cruise through the dance once in a while."

"Are police necessary?" Grace asked.

"Seth is a little overprotective. He likes to feel the kids are as safe as possible. And since I have to be here anyway..." Iris was pulled away by another chaperone with a question.

A young man approached Grace and Troy. "Is this your girlfriend, Mr. Headly?"

"Yes, this is Grace Dillon, Ms. Dillon to you."

He gave a short bow. "Would you like to dance, Ms. Dillon?" he asked politely.

"Ah, I…ah…"

"It's entirely up to you, Grace," Troy said. "Jerome here won't put any moves on you because he knows I'd have to kill him."

"Is it all right?" she whispered to him.

"No slow dancing. Those are mine," Troy whispered back.

Grace began what became a series of dances with a variety of young partners who were funny and charming and devilish. It was obvious they thought it was a real hoot to get Mr. Headly's girl on the dance floor. Whenever the music slowed Troy was instantly at her side, cutting in, holding her as closely as he dared at a high school function. It seemed as if all the slow dances were crooned by Michael Bublé, but she was surprised by the wide variety of music, from oldies to current rock. There was even a line dance performed to the strains of Aretha Franklin singing "Chain of Fools." It took Grace about two seconds to learn it and Troy joined in. "Am I dancing with students too much?" she asked.

"I love watching you," he said. "There's one small problem—I can't wait to get you alone."

"Are you dancing much?" she asked.

"Very judiciously and as little as possible. Giggly high school girls are just not my thing. Besides, I'm supposed to be keeping an eye on things, make sure the kids aren't getting into trouble."

"What kind of trouble?"

"Oh, you know, sneaking out to the parking lot to be too alone or to get a bottle or smoke a joint or get in a fight over something, like a girl. You know."

That was the point, she *didn't* know. "Really?"

"Been a while since you've been rockin' the high school dance?"

"You could say that," she said. "I thought this would be boring. I can't remember when I've had so much fun."

"Just remember, don't fall in love with anyone because you leave the dance with me." He grinned at her.

She noticed that Troy danced with Iris. Not a slow dance, but not so fast, either. He twirled her around and they laughed. She had no worries that Iris would invade her territory, none at all. But did Troy still wish that romance had worked? She forced herself to look away. When she looked back, Iris was talking to her husband. Troy was nowhere in sight.

He was right behind her, claiming a dance. It was an old tune with a good beat—"Knock On Wood"— and Troy improvised, moving her two beats left, two beats right, a little twirl. She'd been very impressed by his dancing tonight. And it was sexy! Then the tune segued into a bebop beat and she noticed a few kids getting together for another line dance, but Troy pulled her back from the crowd, gave her hands a little shove and made a jitterbug move. "Huh?" he asked, lifting his eyebrows.

She laughed at him. "As long as you don't slide me between your legs or toss me onto your hips and over your shoulder."

"Aw," he said, then led her into a really good jitterbug, so good that kids stopped what they were doing to watch. *This guy knows what he's doing*, she thought.

When the song ended, there were a few claps from the crowd. Grace heard a teenage girl say, "Oh, God, why can't he just *marry* me!"

Five

Four hours flew by and at almost midnight they were on their way to Grace's place in Troy's car. She was completely amazed by the variety of music, from oldies to current rock to hip-hop and even country. And now that she thought about it, Troy was up to speed on all of those dances, even picking up the line dance steps quickly. "Care to explain that dancing, Fred Astaire?" she asked.

He laughed. "Short story. I dated a dance instructor. Not like Arthur Murray—she taught little kids. Her sister was getting married and she wanted someone who could dance to go to the wedding with her, so she taught me a bunch of moves, including the tango. It was fun, to tell the truth. She broke up with me the day after the wedding."

"Aw, was your heart broken?"

"A little bit," he said. "I didn't think I'd ever have fun dancing again."

"Well, you wowed 'em tonight. I even heard a marriage proposal."

He laughed.

"Does that ever become…you know…difficult?"

"What?"

"The girls," she said. "They crush on you! And some of them are beautiful! And look older than me, by the way! Does that ever worry you?"

"Worry me in what way?" he asked, his brow crinkling.

"What if one of them got the wrong signals? Thought you were romantically interested or something?"

He chuckled. "They do all the time, but not because of anything I do—because of their imaginative, nubile young minds mixed with the irresponsibility of raging hormones. Grace, teachers have to play it real safe or find themselves in a bad place."

"What does that mean?"

He shrugged. "There are very specific guidelines. We don't touch the students, except maybe a hand on an arm or shoulder to say, 'Wait up a second.' We can never have private conversations with students with doors closed. We don't give them a lift home even in a nice little town like this. We don't make gestures that could be interpreted as seductive, and we don't respond to such gestures—the list is long. And it's not just for young male teachers but for all teachers—young women, old women, crusty old codgers, guys like me. Counselors like Iris. If she closes her office door, the door to the main hallway is closed to the passersby, but all the offices are internal cubicles that share a common hall between them so that a conversation can be private but if someone yelled or called out, it could be heard. Counselors, principals, nurses—they have to be afforded a degree of privacy to do their work. Students need to feel safe. I, however, am always seen in a crowd. During my private conversations with students, the door to the classroom is open. And we're on opposite sides of the desk."

"But has it happened, Troy? That some girl takes her crush too far?"

"You understand that I like women, but women my own age, right? I'm not tempted by children. High school students are minors. And our school system forbids fraternization with students even of legal age, like eighteen-year-olds. There is absolutely no compromise there."

"Of course," she said. "But…"

"To a certain degree, there are some normal feelings in the mix for the kids. Little girls sit on their daddy's laps and promise to marry them and the fact is, they probably will marry a man just like their father. Crushing on teachers is not unusual, but they're children and it's the adult teacher's job to keep that from escalating. You get to be good at recognizing the signs and creating appropriate distance and barriers before…" He stopped. He pulled up behind her building and parked. He turned to her. "Gracie, why are you asking me this?"

"I just thought it must sometimes be challenging."

He rubbed a knuckle along her cheek. "Honey,

were you molested? Assaulted? By an older man or teacher? Someone in a position of authority?"

"Me?" she asked, genuinely shocked. "No! No, of course not."

"Then you knew someone who was," he said matter-of-factly.

Boy, did she! Years ago, and it all ended so tragically it marked one of the most traumatic experiences of her life. But that was not the direction Grace wanted this conversation to go. Not tonight. So she smiled gently.

"You must either be a very wonderful teacher or so intuitive it's scary," she said. "Once, I thought someone I knew was a victim, a younger girl, but even though I had suspicions, I never had proof. She wasn't a good friend of mine, just a girl I knew. Seriously, I didn't bring it up to discuss that—that was so long ago. I really was curious about how you manage the situation with the students. I'd have asked Iris all the same questions if it had ever come up. It was the dance that brought it to mind. Some of those girls are gorgeous. And you do kind of make them giggle."

"The really scary part is I don't have to do much to make them giggle. There's a real dearth of young teachers in Thunder Point. Another one who gets their constant attention is Coach Lawson. But he doesn't have female students." He leaned toward her and put a small kiss on her lips. "You must be exhausted."

She gave him a little smile. "Would you like to come up?"

"If you think you can stay awake awhile…"

"Come on up," she said. She hummed under her breath all the way up the back stairs to her little loft, and right inside the door, she turned to him and, for once, she made the advance. She put her arms around his neck and kissed him like she really meant business.

"Whoa," he said.

"Would you like a glass of wine? I think we should have a little talk."

He paused for a moment. "Should I go down to the flower fridge for the wine?" he finally asked.

"No, tonight is this very special Shiraz. I hope you like it." She picked up a bottle from the counter and handed it to him so he could look at it.

But Troy frowned, as if he was worried about what was coming. "Let me open it for you so we can get to the talking part."

She turned to grab the corkscrew, then picked up the two glasses that she'd set out earlier.

"Where are we talking?" he asked as he shed his coat and tie.

"How about right in here?" she said, carrying the glasses to the little living room. She put the glasses on the coffee table, kicked off her shoes and got comfortable. "Why do you look worried?"

"Because this seems planned and I have no idea what's coming. I hope it's not bad news."

"I hope so, too. Open that wine and let it breathe." While he did that, she took a deep breath. "Troy, I've never been to a high school dance before tonight."

He stopped twisting the corkscrew for a second, then looked at her. He pulled the cork. "A lot of kids don't go to the dances, Gracie."

"I bet you did," she said.

"I did," he admitted. "But by now you know me— I'm a flirt. I get along with everyone. I'm the fun coach. I almost always had a girlfriend or at least a date. I didn't date just anyone, though—I'm no man whore. I'm not a screw around kind of guy."

"Troy, I never went to a high school dance because I never went to a high school."

He seemed to be momentarily confused. "Boarding school? Some private academy?"

She shook her head. "Homeschooled. With tutors."

"And some classes here and there?"

"Some," she said. "Small groups of tutored kids, now and then. Mostly independent study with guidance and lots of tests to track my progress."

"Wow. You'll have to share that study plan with me someday. It seems to have worked. You're very accomplished for someone who never went to high school."

"I didn't say they were lazy tutors," she said. "I learned things a lot of high school students wouldn't even get to. But there's a reason I'm telling you this, Troy. I've also never had a boyfriend."

He chuckled. "That's very hard to believe. You're beautiful."

"Oh, I had a couple of bad dates, but that's about all. I just wasn't in the mainstream of life like other young women. See, I said my parents were gone and that's true, sort of. My father died when I was only fourteen and my mother and I fell out five years ago. We had an argument about what I wanted to do with my life. She comes from money—she's very spoiled and demanding. She's a diva, that's the only way to describe her. The very thought of me in the back of a florist's shop, filthy, lifting big pots, driving to residences to deliver flowers, being *the help* at weddings and funerals..." Grace shrugged. "She was mortified. We had a standoff. She wanted me to live at home with her, follow in her footsteps, plan charity events, travel with her, let her... Well, she probably had some guy lined up for me from somewhere. We never got that far in a discussion. I wasn't interested. I wanted my own life and I wanted it simple. We haven't spoken in years. It's very sad. It's for the best, I think."

By his expression, he was stunned. He reached out and grabbed her shoulder. "Grace...I'm sorry."

"Thank you. Maybe someday it will sort itself out. What I really want you to know is..." She lifted her chin bravely. "Troy, I'm not like Iris. I'm not like other girls. I'm probably less experienced than some of your students. I've never had a guy I really liked before. I'm pretty lame at it."

"You're doing very well," he said with a smile. He poured them each a glass of wine.

She took a sip. Then a breath. "Well, even though you're probably going to figure it out anyway, I thought you should know—I don't know much about men. Just what my boyfriends in my romances told me. That's it."

He raised one eyebrow. "And how am I going to figure that out?"

"When you realize I don't have any idea what to do! You're going to guess, if we do decide to do it, that I've never done it before. You will be my first unless you run for your life right now." She grinned at him. "No pressure."

He grinned right back. "I'm not worried, Gracie. Are you?"

She nodded. "Maybe a little," she said.

"Want me to tell you how it's going to be?"

Again she nodded.

"The first time it's going to be very slow and safe. We're going to kiss until we're steamy. We're going to touch and get so close we can feel each other's heartbeat." He leaned over and gently kissed her cheek and her throat and she let her head drop back and closed her eyes. "We're going to lie down together and lose some clothes... We'll discover each other. I'm going to touch you in all your special places and you're going to touch me when you're ready. We'll ease into things slowly and carefully, but the most important thing is, you can say no or stop whenever you don't want to go any further. Even if we're naked and breathing hard, if you say stop, we stop."

Her eyes were still closed and she whispered into his cheek. "I don't use anything..."

"I do," he said.

"When is this going to happen?" she asked.

"In a hurry, Grace?"

She shrugged. "Well, when I make a decision…"

"We're going to enjoy a glass of wine. Then, if you're ready, you'll let me know."

Troy hadn't been prepared for this—a twenty-eight-year-old woman as beautiful and funny as Grace, a virgin. He would have expected her to have sexual history, like most women her age. Some had a lot of notches, some only a few, but he'd never encountered *none* before. Even his first girl, his first experience, wasn't a virgin. She'd had a serious boyfriend before him. Of course, just because he was a flirt and liked to have girlfriends didn't mean he'd been a sexual prodigy. He had sex for the first time at nearly the end of his first year of college. At eighteen, he was the last among his buddies, unless they were lying.

They were probably lying. Of course they were lying. At least mostly lying.

He took this very seriously, making love to Grace. It had to be a good experience for her and he was definitely eager to take on the challenge. He just hoped there wasn't some virgin consciousness that would have her leaning toward true love and marriage because of sex. He wasn't opposed to that in the long run, he just didn't want it all to happen in one night. He was crazy about her, couldn't wait to get inside her, didn't see any red flags that would warn him to get out of this relationship—he just needed time to get more serious. *This is how grown-ups court.* They have dates, they discover common interests, they examine their rapport, they go to bed together, they ask, *Does this have staying power?*

They kissed and whispered their way through a glass of wine, then Troy took hers out of her hand and put it on the coffee table. He stood and pulled her to her feet and led her toward the bedroom, which was only about ten feet away. When they stood beside the bed, he took her gently into his arms and kissed her some more, drawing deep sighs from her. Then she turned in his arms and presented her back, pulling her hair away, and he saw the zipper for her dress.

He drew it down slowly, taking a taste of her neck in the process. He pushed the dress off her shoulders and she let it fall, leaving her in a silky black slip. She stepped out of the dress and bent to pick it up, but he took it from her and turned to drape it across the only chair in the room. He got rid of his belt and shirt and when he turned back to her, she had removed her hose and kicked them aside. She was a determined little thing; he wasn't going to find going slowly an easy thing.

When she sat on the bed he withdrew a couple of condoms from his pocket.

"Do you have to put them out now?" she asked.

"Believe me, I do," he said. He let the pants drop, kicked them off and they joined the clothes on the chair. He sat beside her, embraced her, pulled her down beside him and rolled a little, adjusting till their bodies were flush and tight. "There," he said, feeling every curve of her against him. "Perfect."

And he was ready.

"I can feel your heart," he said. He ran his hands down her back and over her butt. She was so firm and solid. "The flower business must be good exercise," he said, chuckling softly.

Her hands were on his chest, caressing every inch of him, kissing his chest, his neck, his mouth and all the time wiggling up against him. He still wore his boxers, but they were doing nothing to keep his secrets. He pushed himself between her legs without really meaning to—he was on automatic pilot.

"Let's get rid of this," he said, pulling a strap of the slip down over her shoulder.

She sat up and drew the silky garment over her head and tossed it aside, leaving her in nothing but a tiny thong. And that, he thought, wouldn't get in his way for a second. But to level the playing field and give her a chance to get used to him, he shed his boxers. There they were. In all their basic glory. He pulled her hand, drawing it to him. She didn't hesitate; she put both hands on him and hummed softly as she figured him out. "Easy does it," he said.

There were so many things he wanted to do to her, but not the first time. He'd like to lick her whole body, make her come before she even knew what hit her. He'd like to lift her onto his lap and watch her ride; he'd like to take her against the shower wall. *Not this time*, he told himself. He had promised it would be slow and safe and he never broke a promise. He slid his hand under her thong. "Open for me, honey," he said, giving her thighs a nudge. He slid one finger into her silkiness. Then two fingers. *Wow*, she wasn't going to need much warming up. He massaged her for a few seconds and she was squirming against his hand, almost whimpering. He slid a finger inside.

"You okay?" he asked in a whisper.

"Okay," she whispered back.

"This has to go," he said, pulling her thong down. She kicked it away as he turned to the bedside table and retrieved a condom, quickly rolling it on. If he didn't suit up, she was going to climb all over him. She was straining toward him, making beautiful little noises. He turned her on her back, spread her legs with a knee and placed himself in the zone. Leaning down to her lips once more, he whispered against them. "Ready to see how this works?" he asked.

"Yes," she whispered back, her eyes closed.

"Look at me, Gracie." She opened her eyes. "I want you to go limp…relax everything. It's not going to hurt."

"Are you sure?"

"I'm sure." He pressed himself against her. "Nice and easy," he said. "It's okay. It's good." And he pressed into her very, very slowly. He kissed her deeply as he went all the way. She moaned. "Okay?" he asked.

"Mmm," she murmured. "Okay."

But damned if he was! This was the best place he'd been in a very long time. And she hugged him like a velvet vise. A quivering, soft, slick vise. He was dying. He started to move, slowly, looking for that sweet spot, pressing deeply into her, listening to the sounds she made, trying to judge them for the right spot, the right friction, the perfect stimulation for her. As for himself, if he unclenched his molars for one second, he was gone.

"Oh." She sighed. "Oh! Oh! *Oh!*"

"Oh, yeah," he said.

"Please," she said, gripping his shoulders. "More. Please!"

He moved a little harder, hanging on for dear life. He took her mouth again, kissing her deeply as he moved inside. "You're beautiful, baby," he whispered. "You're perfect."

"I think maybe you're perfect," she said.

"Only with you," he said. "With you I feel perfect." And he followed that with a kiss. And a thrust.

She came apart. She clenched him inside her body, drawing on him, leaving him to wonder if it was his expert moves or the words. Then thinking stopped. She closed her eyes, tilted her head back and her pelvis forward, upward, bit her lip and if he could see, he'd bet she curled her toes. So he did what came naturally, thrusting a couple more times and having the best orgasm of his life, right then, right there, with her. His eyes teared; his brain clouded over and he wondered if he lost consciousness for a second. He pulsed until there was nothing left in him. Even his brain was empty; her body was still holding him for so long he was amazed. She rode through it with him, the whole way.

He pressed his lips softly to hers, kissing her gently. She didn't move. He gave her another kiss. She still held him in a beautiful, delicious, unimaginable grip. "Gracie," he whispered. "Breathe."

She let out her breath in a slow *whoosh*. "Holy shit!" she said.

He smiled. "Nice?"

"Mmm," she said, her lips curving into a smile.

He chuckled. "Just when I was wondering what to get you for Valentine's Day..."

"Oh. My. God. Do it again."

He laughed. "Maybe in a little bit," he said, but there was really no maybe about it. "No regrets?"

"You're kidding, right?"

"I might not have figured it out," he admitted. "Except I also might not have tried so hard to go slowly and patiently. Because, really, Gracie, you had me in a real vulnerable spot there for a while."

"I did?"

"You did. We came together like old pros."

"If I hadn't told you, what would you have done?"

"I think I'd have just gone for it. I think first, to be sure you had everything you deserved, I'd have licked your whole body. Then I would have just gone for it."

"Okay. We'll do that next time!"

He couldn't help but laugh at her, she was so damn cute. "You like sex, don't you, sweetheart?"

"I like sex," she admitted, smiling. "Oh, God, is that a slutty thing to say?"

"No, Gracie." He brushed her rich brown hair back from her brow. "It's the perfect thing to say."

They made love again and again. Troy knew he was screwed, and not in the usual way. He had himself a beautiful young woman who thought he was pure magic, who would do anything he wanted to do, bring him greater satisfaction than he could remember having and...and he didn't know anything about her. Added to that, he wasn't sure what had caused it, but being the first man to ever get inside her like that really did something to his head. A kind of possessiveness consumed him; he couldn't even think about letting her go. But who was this young beauty who hadn't been properly loved until now? Who asked questions about whether it was difficult being a young male teacher surrounded by teenage girls with crushes? Who was this young woman who'd never been in a traditional classroom yet who seemed to be smarter and more worldly than other women her age? And did mothers and daughters really part ways over the choice to own a flower shop?

He was lying on his belly in her bed, thinking about how he was going to get the answers to these questions when he felt her small hand, slightly calloused from hard work, slide over his buttocks.

"You have the nicest guy booty I've ever seen."

"Roll me over and see what else I've got that's nice," he said.

"I'm afraid to," she said with a laugh. "I think you've had enough. And I've definitely had enough!"

"Feeling a little tender?"

She nodded and blushed.

He laughed. "After the gymnastics of last night, how can you blush?" he asked her.

"It's daylight," she said.

"Better yet," he said, rolling over to show off his rather impressive morning erection.

"Oh, my," she said. "Keep that thing away from me!"

He ignored her and pulled her into his arms. "Let's talk about how to have fun when we're feeling a little...delicate." And he began kissing his way down her body, over her belly, between her thighs. Just a few minutes later he had to say again, "Gracie. Breathe."

"Oh, God," she said weakly.

His pleasure couldn't have been greater.

"Is it my turn now?" she asked.

"Not this time, honey," he said, hoisting himself out of the bed. "Much as I'd like to lie around in bed all day, I have things to do. I have to get ready for classes tomorrow and I'm working at Cooper's all afternoon and evening. You should nap, rest up. If you want me to drop by later to make sure you're okay, just say the word."

"The word," she said with a smile.

"Would you like me to take you to breakfast at the diner before I start my chores?" he asked.

"Would you?"

"I definitely would. You make a man hungry, but I have to go home first and, you know...freshen up."

She laughed softly. "I guess it wouldn't do to go out to breakfast in last night's clothes. Not to mention…"

"Don't mention it," he suggested, knowing where that was going. The scent of sex was all over them. Even without that, anyone who saw her this morning was sure to know. She was wearing a very fetching whisker burn on her pink cheeks, her lips were bright and rosy from a night of kissing and that sleepy twinkle in her eye said everything. Here was a very happy, satisfied lady. "I'll be back in thirty minutes."

Six

An hour and a half later, breakfast done, Troy was back in his apartment, where he was not planning to do any school preparation. Instead, he got on the internet. He had a couple of hours before he had to be out at the beach bar. He didn't expect to find anything, unless perhaps there had been some kind of molestation and charges were filed, but if Grace had been a minor, her name wouldn't have been included. He typed her name into the search bar and the italicized question popped back:

Do you mean Isabella "Izzy" Grace Dillon Banks?

Just for grins, he clicked on the name, expecting to see the picture of a sixty-year-old opera singer.

"Are you shitting me?" he asked the empty room.

Figure Skating Gold Medalist walks out of the Vancouver arena and doesn't look back.

It was *her* in the picture. *Izzy Banks? Gold medalist? Retired at the age of twenty-three?* It just didn't compute. Was that something you didn't think to mention? Although Izzy apparently issued a statement, she refused all interviews. He read her statement.

"The figure skating community and competition has been very good to me and I'm tremendously grateful to my family, my mother, the intrepid Winnie Dillon Banks, my coach Mikhail Petrov, U.S. Figure Skating, and every friend and competitor I've known over the past twenty years, but this is my time to exit. There are so many wonderful athletes prepared to have their chance and, believe me, I won't be missed for long. I crave a quieter life."

Troy was stunned. He almost couldn't inhale. How was this possible?

There were a number of articles and much conjecture, comparing Izzy to other athletes who, exhausted and overloaded, perhaps depressed, crashed after a big win and retreated. She wasn't the only story, for sure.

There were a few differences that stood out to him, maybe because of their conversation just the night before. A grievance was filed against her with U.S. Figure Skating by figure skating coach Hal Nordstrom, a world-famous coach whose students had won many medals. He alleged slander and defamation of character. The direct quote seemed to be well-known but wasn't in the article. Apparently when a fifteen-year-old student of Nordstrom committed suicide Izzy Banks, then eighteen, commented that he mishandled his students and drove them to tragic ends with his sexual misconduct. No

charges were filed against the coach, no corrobora-
tive complaints emerged, no other students stepped
forward and there was no evidence against the man.
The grievance was dismissed; Izzy had uttered an
opinion in the presence of other skaters in training,
their coaches and parents—it didn't say how many.
There were comments from Nordstrom's other students that had nothing to do with sexual misconduct.
They claimed he'd taken his student, Shannon Fields,
out of his number-one slot and put another skater in
it and some believed she was despondent with disappointment and jealousy after so many years of hard
work. No one seemed sure why she took her own life.

But Troy knew. He knew Grace. If she said a younger
skater had been molested, she thought she knew something. It didn't mean she was wrong just because she
had no evidence.

Nordstrom sued Izzy and her mother in a civil
court. There was an undisclosed settlement.

He read other articles. Grace had been trailed by
not one but three stalkers. She was hardly the only
internationally known athlete with this burden, but
she was one of only a few who had actually been kid-
napped. It wasn't for more than a few hours, but he
couldn't imagine how terrifying it must have been.
That particular stalker was captured, arrested, prosecuted and hospitalized. His name was Bruno Feldman and he was schizophrenic and delusional, which
made him ill but no less frightening or dangerous
because of his illness.

He typed her name into the search box again.

There were over five thousand hits. As far as he knew, no one in Thunder Point had any idea who she really was. His little flower girl had accomplished things most people never dared dream of and, apparently, the price had been high. He had an overwhelming urge to run to her, take her into his arms and tell her she was safe now. Instead, he took his laptop with him to work at Cooper's, where he planned to read more on the sly when he wasn't too busy.

He was at the bar by noon. There were ten people, all inside. Cooper and his young brother-in-law, Landon, were behind the bar. Troy was barely in the door when two patrons left. He hung up his coat and put his backpack under the bar.

"If the weatherman is right, it shouldn't be too busy today. Just the occasional Sunday driver," Cooper said.

Sunny Sundays were typically pretty busy. "What's the weatherman saying?"

"Guess? Wind and rain. The baby's trying to get a tooth so we're going to look at a couple of cars for Landon," Cooper said.

"Trucks," Landon corrected.

"*Maybe* trucks," Cooper clarified.

"I thought you had a truck," Troy said.

"It pretty much bit the dust and has been retired," Cooper said. "Landon needs some reliable wheels so I don't have to drive to Eugene every time he feels like a weekend at home."

"And this has what to do with a tooth?"

Both guys winced. "You have no idea how hard it

is to get a tooth," Cooper said. "Apparently she has to work on it twenty-four hours a day and it makes her very pissy."

"She's not happy about anything right now," Landon said. "We're getting out of there."

Troy laughed. "Poor Sarah."

"I did my shift last night," Cooper said. "If it's stormy and empty, close early. Six or so?"

"I'll stay as long as you want me," Troy said, but he knew if the weather was bad, the bar hardly ever saw business after sunset and sunset came early in February. In football season, there'd be people inside watching the game, but that was past.

"You decide," Cooper said. "Let's go, Landon. Have a good day. And thanks."

By midafternoon there was just one couple in the bar, drinking Bloody Marys and eating sandwiches at a table by the fire. Troy checked the kitchen and dishwasher, but as usual Cooper had left the place spotless and organized. In winter this was a one-man operation, but in summer it took a full crew—there were lots of people on the beach, renting paddleboards and kayaks, eating and drinking, enjoying the bay and lighting fires on the beach at night, a constant flow of customers, sometimes until after ten.

He brought a stool behind the bar and opened his laptop. There was enough information about Grace to fill a book. She even had her own Wikipedia page, as did her wealthy mother, Winnie Dillon Banks, a champion figure skater before her. There was a half brother, twenty years her senior, a child of her father's by a previous marriage. One article explained the many ways people managed the expensive training without being wealthy, but such sponsors were difficult to come by before the athlete had at least come very close to winning major competitions. And to his surprise, the number of moneyed US and world medalists was quite small. Most of them, in fact the best known among them, had hardworking parents who got up at four in the morning to drive them long distances to rinks where the best coach could be found. Some moved to accommodate their young champions.

By late afternoon the rain hit the deck outside and the last couple left, and he could get back to his research. Grace and her parents moved a few times; her father was sought after and drew a handsome coaching salary. He did not train Grace's competitors, however. His income and notoriety, in addition to Winnie's old family wealth, was a huge advantage for her. She didn't make the cut for the 2006 Winter Games and there was some talk of moving her to another country. Obviously they hadn't moved.

Lord, who was this girl?

He looked up Winnie Dillon Banks. There were dozens of pictures and all Troy could surmise from them was that she looked rich and cold. Many pictures of her watching her daughter skate in competition had her with a frozen face, wearing furs and diamonds.

That's when he knew they hadn't exactly fallen out over a flower shop. His best guess was that Winnie disapproved of her daughter leaving competition while she was still young enough to train and win.

He looked up figure skating training. It was typical to be on skates by four years old. Six hours on the ice every day, endurance and weight training, ballet and gymnastics, school or, in Grace's case, tutors. Add in travel to every competition that would take her—first Nationals and then World Championships. He looked up international ice-skating championships. Jesus, she'd been to almost every country on the globe.

He watched a couple of YouTube videos of her skating, a long program and a short program, one when she was only sixteen and competing in Seoul. It was the most amazing thing he'd ever seen. She looked just the same. Did no one ever remark on her likeness to a women's figure skating champion? Her skill and beauty on the ice was nothing short of breathtaking.

Next on his list to research was sexual misconduct by coaches. He felt his heart race. It was everywhere. There were some horrifically wrong allegations. One female coach had her life nearly ruined by an accusation that never even went to court as her alibi was actually on film, placing her far from the alleged victim at the time; yet, years later she was still banned from certain gyms, even after the child finally recanted. It sent shudders through him. He thought a person had to be crazy to leave their child in the hands of a stranger even if he or she was a renowned coach.

To get a reality check, he searched the same subject with teachers and it was just as shocking, some cases getting national attention and being made into television movies.

I just thought it must sometimes be challenging...

He closed the laptop and turned on lights around the bar, though if anyone was out in this storm, he'd be amazed. He had a lot to process. It was almost five and the sun might just be on its downward path, but with the clouds it was already dark. He got himself a beer.

He'd known Grace for a year, maybe a little more. He only knew her superficially—he had gone into her shop to buy flowers for Iris twice and once to pick out an arrangement to be sent to his mother for Mother's Day. He'd seen her at Cooper's with Iris. He didn't even really think of her as a friend but rather as one of Iris's friends. He'd liked her but never thought about her—not before Christmas. He'd been looking right through her. He had no idea there was so much to Grace. She was amazing and complicated, part heroic, part tragic. And after last night, more woman than he ever imagined. Little virgin flower girl, a little shy, a little curious and cautious and, oh, God, so willing, trusting and sensual. So loving and innocent. She asked him to take her there, to sex and passion, then put herself in his hands. And man, what a ride.

"She's an athlete, you dope," he said to no one in the bar.

"Who's an athlete?" Sarah Cooper asked, just coming in the door. She shook off her slicker.

"Jesus, you scared me to death!" he said. "Where's the baby?"

"Finally sleeping. Ham's babysitting."

"Sarah, Ham's a dog."

"Best babysitter there is, trust me. He's barely left her side since the day she was born. Don't worry—she's in the crib and the bedroom door is closed, but I trust Ham more than most humans. And I only came over for a second. You should close the bar. You're wasting your time out here. This deluge isn't exactly welcoming customers. Is there anything you need before you go? Besides to finish your beer?"

"I'll just make a quick phone call, maybe take a couple of little pizzas from the cooler—I have a date tonight, I hope. Thanks, I think you're right. No one has come in since two."

She grinned at him, looking at the laptop. "Get your homework done?"

"I sure did," he said. "And it was a load, too."

"Thanks for helping out, Troy. Stay dry." She pulled the hood of her slicker over her head and went out the back door.

He picked up his phone. "Gracie," he said. "Thanks to the weather, I'm closing up early. Would you like me to bring you dinner?"

"I cooked! I cooked, hoping you would come here for dinner!"

"Your kitchen is the size of my closet. What did you cook?"

"Crock-Pot chili. A brick of cheddar and crackers. If I had a fireplace up here, it would be perfect."

It's already perfect, he thought. "I'll be there in a little while. It sounds great."

He wasn't going to tell her what he knew. He decided right then, he was going to wait for her. When she was comfortable, when she trusted him to know that part of her life, when she finally confided in him, he might tell her he'd known for a while. *Might*.

A week later, when Troy was just packing up his papers to take home, he caught a flash of color out of the corner of his eye and turned to see Iris leaning in his classroom doorway. She was wearing a sly grin. "I saw you and Grace at the basketball game last night," she said.

"We said hello," Troy said, frowning slightly, not understanding.

"I was too busy in the concession stand to chat, but not too busy to notice."

"Notice what?" he asked.

"You are officially completely over me."

He smiled and put his papers in his backpack. "I'm over you," he said. "I hope you're not offended. You are married, after all."

She walked toward him. "I saw the way you looked at Grace. I was glad you and Grace were hanging out, but it's a lot more than that. Troy, this makes me happy. Grace is wonderful and I love her. And you're one of my best friends." Then she laughed. "There's the final proof! You didn't wince when I called you a best friend!"

"There's a lot more to Grace than meets the eye," he said, zipping the backpack.

"I think you're falling in love, Troy."

"Easy, Iris. That's a powerful diagnosis. And I don't think you can make it." He picked up the backpack. "My complexion has cleared up, that's all."

She laughed at him. "I hear the hearts of dozens of sixteen-year-old girls breaking."

"Don't even joke about that," he said, suddenly very serious. "That could be a world of trouble a teacher doesn't need."

"Oh, Troy, you haven't had a problem in that area, have you? No one's making you nervous, I hope."

He didn't want to explain the situation with Grace, that her questions on this issue combined with what he thought he'd learned from his research brought the whole thing closer to the surface of his thinking. "No, not at all, it's just that it's a real slippery slope, that relationship. Sometimes I'm afraid to make even the most innocent joke. Know what I mean?"

"Listen, your behavior has always been above reproach, but if you're ever worried about the smallest gesture or comment, come to me immediately. Don't take a chance on seeing where it goes. We don't fool around with that stuff."

"Good. That's good to know because—" He ran a hand around the back of his neck. "I read an article over the weekend about a coach whose life was nearly destroyed by accusations of impropriety with a youngster and she wasn't even in the same city at the time. It filled me with cold dread. Made me think way too much."

"I understand. I get the willies about similar situations in counseling now and then. All I have to do is hear about a terrible counselor, one who does grave damage, and I don't sleep for a couple of nights. But if you're not facing any problems, try to relax and be yourself. The kids love you. And you've been consistently great with boundaries. And now you're in love on top of everything else."

"Don't get ahead of yourself, Iris," he said, but he smiled when he said it. "I've only been seeing Grace for a couple of months." He was suddenly aware that he'd dated Iris for months, thought they were a perfect couple and yet had never uttered those three important words. "When did you know you loved Seth?" he asked, suddenly curious.

"When I was about four, but he was busy playing the field all through high school. Since he never noticed me as anything more than a buddy, an outfielder or tutor, I hated him."

"You're married to him. I guess you got that straightened out."

"Yeah," she said a little wistfully. "Luckily." She collected herself. "Well. If you can be half as happy as I am, you won't know what to do with yourself. Want to go get a beer?"

"I can't," he said. "I'm going to mind the flower shop while Grace meets with some couple about their wedding flowers. Grace has Justin doing some deliveries but no steady part-time help yet. It's just Grace, sometimes closing the shop to deliver flowers, unless I can help her."

"She told me. We talked about student help for her, but it's kind of late in the year to start any kind of work-study situation. I posted an after-school help position on the bulletin board, but…"

"I hope something turns up for her. Hey, tomorrow I'll be out at Cooper's—come on out. I'll treat. Bring Prince Charming. I'll even buy him a beer."

"You're on," she said.

Troy drove to the flower shop, parked in the alley right behind the Pretty Petals van and went in the back door. Grace was finishing the creation of an arrangement at her big messy worktable, but he didn't care. He grabbed her around the waist and pulled her against him, kissing her hard.

"Troy, stop it, I'm filthy."

"I know. Filthy is good. We can get a little filthy later if you feel like it." He picked up her hand and looked at the green and brown fingers, ick under her nails. "Jeez, this is ugly work. Who knew? You'd think working with flowers would be more attractive. Are you sending me home after I help here?"

"Do I ever send you home?"

"What do you want to do for dinner?"

"I grabbed one of Carrie's meals from the deli— teriyaki chicken, rice, asparagus and cheesecake. Will that do it for you?"

He kissed her neck. "For my first meal. Then I'm having you."

She laughed, pushing him away. "I have to run

upstairs and scrub up a little bit," she said, taking off the green apron. She hung it on the hook by the door. "If the Jackson-Paulson couple comes in before I'm back, just put them in my office, will you? I'll be right back."

"Sure," he said. When she'd gone upstairs, he looked around at the mess. Miss Gracie had had a busy day at the flower shop. The big worktable and floor were covered with clippings, stems, florist's foam, tape, all manner of rocks and a couple of glue guns. He put her arrangement in the cooler, picked up the glue guns and swept off the debris on the table onto the floor. The second he'd done that, he realized he was an idiot. Now the rocks and in some cases what looked like flattened marbles pinged around the floor. If he wasn't pretty quick with a broom, someone could break a hip.

He immediately started sweeping a path away from her office door. It could be unpleasant if her customers fell and broke their backs. He was quick about it. He liked it when Gracie thought he was the perfect man and really didn't want to expose himself as just another stupid guy who didn't think.

It didn't take him long to have a nice pile of trash between the back door and the cooler. Just in time, too. The bell on the door tinkled and the couple came in.

"It's just bullshit, Janet. We don't need all this," a man's voice said.

"Maybe I need it," the woman said, her voice watery. "I haven't asked too much and I work for every dime."

"You want a house?" he asked meanly.

"Yes, but not a new truck!" she threw back.

"You want a baby?" he flung.

"When we can afford it, but I don't want to just skip the wedding! I know you don't care, but I care! My mother cares!"

"Then your mother should pay for it!"

"You know my mother has *nothing*!"

"And that's what we're going to have! Nothing!"

"I thought you wanted a wedding?" she said in a near sob.

"I thought so, too, until I saw the list of things we have to buy! I wanted a band, a keg and a good party! Now I'm buying a goddamned coronation!"

The back door opened and Grace stepped in looking completely refreshed in a crisp white blouse, a little shine on her lips and her hair brushed. He wanted to eat her alive, gobble her up. "They're fighting," he whispered.

"Happens all the time. Weddings are famous for it." She looked around. "Oh, Troy, you cleaned up." She took a closer look at the table and floor. "A little..."

"You want me to mop?" he asked.

"No, but thanks. Just mind the front of the store for me, and if someone comes in and needs something, please interrupt me. I can take two minutes while my clients look at pictures, run a sale, get back to them in no time."

"I work in a bar, Gracie. I can ring up a sale. If there are price tags."

"Everything is priced. Let any calls go to voice mail." She kissed him real quick on the lips. "Thank you."

"You are so hard to wait for," he muttered under his breath as she walked away. He watched as she approached the tortured couple.

"Mr. Jackson? Ms. Paulson? Hi, I'm Grace. Would you like to come back to my office and talk about your wedding flowers?"

"We're *fighting* about the wedding," Ms. Paulson said.

"Well, I'm here to lessen your wedding tension and help you find very practical and affordable options in the flower department. Don't worry— looking at pictures of bouquets and arrangements carries no obligation at all. I only want to help. Come with me. Would you like a cup of coffee? Tea? Bottled water?"

"How about a beer," the groom said testily.

"I had to stop stocking beer," Grace said with a laugh. "Too many stressed-out, drunk grooms left my flower shop! Come right in here, let me get a couple of waters." She put them in the chairs in front of her desk and when she walked through the workroom to her cooler, she rolled her eyes at Troy, smiling a little.

Troy went to the front of the store to stand sentry while Grace had her meeting with the bridal couple. She usually met with couples like this at six or later, after work for them, after closing for her. This particular couple had to schedule something a little earlier, so she'd invited them to come at four, which was how Troy got this babysitting job. He positioned himself behind the small counter. There by the computer lay two phones—her personal and her work phone. Everywhere she went, two phones. When the shop was closed and they were together, she rarely answered the work phone. And the personal phone rarely rang. She'd gotten calls twice since they'd been a couple and both times it was Iris.

He heard her tell the couple to "start with this album."

"There aren't any prices," the man said.

"Jake!" the woman said.

"That's a reasonable observation and question. Every bouquet and arrangement can be downsized or enlarged, depending on personal taste. For example, see this beautiful arrangement of roses, fern and calla lilies? I had a bride want a much smaller version of this with just the dusty miller and lilies plus a little baby's breath. I'll be glad to itemize everything with cost per stalk, stem and vase."

"I don't know why we're making it so fancy," Jake muttered.

"It needn't be," Grace said. "Small weddings can be elegant, classy and memorable. In your life together there are going to be many moments you're going to want to capture in pictures. You'll be amazed when you get to your thirtieth anniversary how many boxes or albums or disks of pictures you'll have—every camping trip, T-ball game, graduation, every family celebration. One of the first will be the day you marry. It doesn't have to be any certain kind of wedding, just the one you both want. And done the way you want to remember it."

"And there's the problem," Jake said. "Janet wants a big fancy wedding and I don't."

"I don't need a big fancy wedding," she argued. "I just want it to be beautiful!"

"Completely doable. When you talk it over, you'll find a reasonable compromise. I'll do whatever I can to help with that. I've had couples who ordered so many flower arrangements and bouquets I thought I was outfitting the Rose Bowl. There was a recent wedding where the bride and her attendants each carried a single calla lily. The good news is…for a spring wedding literally every flower will be available and the prices will be more reasonable than at other times of the year."

"This is beautiful," Janet said, looking at a photo. "Isn't this beautiful, Jake?"

"I bet it cost a fortune," he snorted.

"Hmm, if I remember, that wedding ran about twelve hundred dollars."

"Are you freaking kidding me?" Jake said.

"Flowers were very important to that couple, but they didn't have a fortune. Now, there are ways to bring the cost way down, to less than half of that, and still have a beautiful display. Bows instead of flowers on the ends of the pews, smaller altar arrangements or larger fluffier flowers and table centerpieces, less fussy bouquets for the attendants."

"That's still a lot of money," he grumbled.

"When is the happy day?" Grace asked.

"June twentieth."

"Perfect. A great month for flowers and flower prices. And do you have a budget?"

Just as Janet said six hundred dollars Jake said fifty. Troy made a noise as he tried to cover his burst of laughter.

"Let me start by asking you to select your favorite wedding photos from this book. It will help if you can come up with at least three you love and figure out why you love them. The particular blooms? The shapes? The arrangement of the flowers? The colors? Once you do that we can find the wiggle room in the ideas and the price, something that better fits your budget. You're going to buy a lot of flowers in your lifetime, Jake. These flowers are going to live on forever in your wedding pictures. I'm sure you and Janet will find exactly the right ones. I'll leave you to look through the pictures. Just call me if you have any questions. I'll be right out front, ten steps away."

Troy was smirking as she walked out of the back room to where he stood behind the counter. He put an arm around her waist and whispered in her ear. "That's not going to work," he said.

"You'd be surprised," she said. "I think I can handle things if you want to leave."

"Nah, I'm not leaving you with this. I think I'll go get my backpack and start on those papers I have to look through. Then tonight I don't have to spend all my time on homework."

"Let me wipe down the worktable for you."

For about twenty minutes the only sound in the shop was the soft murmuring of the bridal couple as they went through the albums. The loud and snappish remarks had stopped but when Troy glanced into the office, they really didn't appear happy. In a very short time they thought they had selected a few pictures and Grace sat at her desk once more.

"Very good choices," she said.

"I'm sure they're out of the question," Janet said. "They're just too beautiful to be affordable."

"Well, let's see," Grace said. She sat at her computer and, after looking at one of the selected photos, she went to work. She began to type in numbers. "And how many parents and attendants?"

"Four parents, six grandparents, two ushers and four bridesmaids and groomsmen. This has been so stressful," Janet said. "We can't afford a lot. The reception will kill us if we can't figure out a way to get our mothers to stop adding people to the guest list!"

"Happens at absolutely every wedding," Grace said. Then she turned the screen toward the couple. "Here's the package you like the best—it includes everything from bridal bouquets to altar arrangements to centerpieces for a reception that seats one hundred and forty. Even flowers for the mothers and boutonnieres for the men are included. The cost is steep—twenty-four hundred fifty dollars."

"Jesus," Jake said, running a hand over his head.

"Now, let's take a closer look. Tell me your favorite things about these flowers?"

Janet pointed to the screen. "I love this lavender color, this fullness is so beautiful, the lavender roses, oh, my! And this kind of faint green with the white. This altar arrangement is so rich looking and huge…"

"Watch this," Grace said.

Troy was too curious just sitting there. He wanted to see what she was doing and her back was to him. She was literally pulling flowers from the bottom of her computer screen and positioning them together. "For the altar arrangements, a different flower, same color, the hydrangea for color, take out the expensive orchids, three or four lilies with two to five blooms per stalk, baby's breath rather than fern and pale green dusty miller, some carnations for fullness and maybe accented with this white stephanotis. I can use a disposable paper pot that won't be visible under the draping flora instead of the square glass vase, or I can rent you the vases and you can return them reducing the cost. Voilà! The cost is cut in half. Now, look at the bridal bouquet—once again, take out the big orchids but look what I can do with cymbidium orchids, a few lavender roses and daisies. Less expensive flowers, but still very beautiful, very appropriate in a summer wedding. If you don't love the daisies, I can use carnations or even white tea roses. And the bouquet is a bit smaller. The one you liked was three hundred. This would be one hundred. I can add roses pretty inexpensively if you want it bigger."

Troy was astonished. Whatever program she was using—amazing. He had no idea this business could be so complicated or high-tech.

"Let me show you something I've used very successfully for table centerpieces." She clicked on a picture. "A clear glass cylinder vase, flowers, white rocks, greenery at the base—I can do this for forty dollars per table. Or, I can tell you where to buy these glass vases and rocks very inexpensively and you can put the girlfriends to work and make it happen for less than twenty per table."

"They're beautiful," Janet said.

"How'd you do that?" Jake asked.

"I buy in bulk, June prices should be good, I thinned the flowers and I know what everyone else charges. You can't do better and I'll make that a guarantee. I'm going to suggest you get your bridesmaids or mothers or both together to fashion big white or lavender tulle bows for the pews. Skip the flowers, though they are so pretty. You can buy the tulle at a fabric shop like Jo-Ann's and save at least a couple hundred dollars and still have the decor of a fashionable and classy wedding. If they don't show you how to make the tulle bows, I'll be happy to. Now, those pew stands with candles are pricey—they have to be rented and you can probably live without them if you're cutting costs. The things that really show in a wedding are the altar flowers, bouquets and table arrangements. I can work up an estimate for this package and email it to you if you like, but I'm guessing this selection will be in the neighborhood of six to eight hundred. Plus delivery, which I do myself. I want my flowers presented perfectly. And, of course, I guarantee everything."

"Can we look at the next one?" Janet asked, opening the album to another page.

Troy smiled to himself and moved away. An hour later the couple was leaving with a contract in their hands and an official estimate on the way via email. And they were *kissing*.

Grace turned the sign on the front door and locked it. She was closed. Her meeting with the bridal couple had lasted almost two hours.

"I don't know how you did that," Troy said, stacking up his papers.

"I was taught," she said. "The couple I worked for—they were so perfect at pleasing people."

"When I first met Jake and Janet I thought they were headed for divorce. When they left, I thought everything would be fine."

"This is so typical. They think they have a budget, but what they really have done is run out of money after the dress and reception and pictures, but they still want flowers."

"For fifty bucks," Troy said with a laugh.

"You have exceptional hearing."

"Yeah, it's a teacher thing."

"They'll probably argue about the expenses several times between now and the wedding and they'll spend more than they plan to because it's always more. But I use all the flowers I order so the bouquets and arrangements will be stunning, and that's a fact. I'm very good at this."

"Where'd you get the program that pulls the flowers together?"

"Mamie and Ross, the couple I worked for, daydreamed about something like that. We could make up sample arrangements and bouquets, photograph them and load them on the computer, but this is state-of-the-art. I worked on it with a nerdy girl I met in Portland. I admit she did most of the program work, but I designed the site and loaded the flowers and arrangements. Isn't it great? It's like creating an online greeting card. Mamie and Ross sold it to a couple of noncompeting florists. I think they got a good price."

"Did you get a good price?" he asked.

"More than that, I got my future."

Seven

For Ray Anne Dysart, life was more productive and satisfying than ever before, at least as far as she could remember. She had her real estate business, mostly property management, small but respectable. She owned her own home, something she had worked hard to make happen as a hedge against retirement, even though she had no intention of retiring until she had no other option. She had her best friends, Lou McCain Metcalf and Carrie James. And she had Al.

Dear Al. He was hardly her first steady man. She was a little afraid to think about what number he was in a long line of previous beaux and lovers; in fact, she had been married three times. All water over the dam. Al was the most special man she'd ever known and completely unlike her usual type. He was a mechanic for one thing—grease under the blunt nails on those big calloused, gentle hands. He was physical, rough and ready and the best-natured man she knew. Plus, he had those three foster sons. Yes, there was a time Ray Anne had wanted children but she'd gotten over that a long while back. The boys, Justin, Danny and Kevin, were nineteen, fifteen and thirteen respectively. Good boys and Al kept them in line, but Ray Anne didn't feel equipped to be a parent to boys, foster or otherwise. She was a girlie girl. Yet she couldn't help but admit she enjoyed them and got a kick out of the way Al was able to manage them.

She felt she was thriving with Al and his family of boys. Of course, most of the time it was just Al she was with. She saw him every day. She would swing by Lucky's, the service station where he worked. Or he would drop by her house before or after his shift, provided his boys were taken care of. Sometimes they met at the diner for a quick meal or Cliffhanger's for a drink. Cliff's was the only restaurant in town with tablecloths. Sometimes they managed a whole evening or day off together; sometimes she joined Al and the boys for dinner. And if they planned carefully, she and Al could get naked and have some real quality time. Once or twice a week.

Like now.

It was Sunday, early afternoon. Al had the day off. The boys had driven to the nursing home where their mother resided. They visited her at least once a week, such devoted sons. Ray Anne took complete advantage of the opportunity when the boys were otherwise occupied.

She stretched out in bed. She smiled. She could hear the shower running. Al had spent the morning in her garage, changing the oil in her car, checking her brakes and such. He wanted to clean up before joining her in bed. She wore one of her sheer lacy, seductive little nighties, waiting. Her cell phone chimed and she frowned. *It better not be important*, she thought. She'd been looking forward to a little time alone with her man.

It was her cousin, Dick. Ray Anne had very little family, but she and Dick had been close growing up and kept in touch. She picked up. "Dickie, let me call you back in a little while…"

"It's important, Ray," he said. "Call me back right away, okay? As soon as you can?"

"What's so important?"

"It's Ginger," he said. "She's just not doing well. I don't know what more to do. Me and Sue, we're out of ideas. She's had counseling, talked to the minister, her friends have tried to boost her up. We thought maybe if she went to stay with you for a little while…"

"Honey, I don't know what to do, either."

"Could you think about it? Even if it's only a few weeks? Because we worry about her and she just won't help herself. We thought maybe a change…"

"Do you have any idea how gloomy it is here in winter? I wouldn't expect it to lift her spirits any. And besides, I'm in a… Well, I'm in a relationship and it's hard enough finding time."

"Ray, it's almost spring and you always got a relationship, don't you? Girl, I think I need help this time. Could you just think about it? See if you get any ideas that could help us out? Because we don't want to lose her. Ain't we lost enough?"

She took a deep breath. "Sure. Of course. Let me think about this. Let me ask some of my close friends for ideas. They know a lot more about kids and family stuff. I love her, you know that." The shower stopped. "I just don't know anything about how to help in a situation like hers. And God, I'd hate myself forever if I just made it worse. You know I'm not much of a mommy kind of girl."

"You were her fairy godmother," he said. "Just the sight of you made her happy."

"Well, the sight of me is damn hard to fix up these days. I'm not young anymore."

"Neither am I," he said. "And she isn't that young, either."

"I'll call you later, okay?"

"Thanks. Anything you can do. Thanks."

She clicked off and sat on the edge of the bed. Thinking. Dickie had always been there for her. He was a hardworking trucker who'd ended up with his own company and any time Ray Anne had a problem—a man, a big bill she couldn't pay, a need to move, a co-signer, a shoulder—he never asked a single question, never hesitated. He was there. His wife, Sue, wasn't quite as warm and loving toward her, but she sure accepted her and never balked when Ray and Dickie got together or when Dickie helped Ray Anne out.

And they'd never asked much of her.

Al came out of the bathroom, towel wrapped

around his waist, rubbing a smaller towel over his short hair. His arms and shoulders were muscled, his belly flat, a body that usually filled her with all kinds of dirty expectations. But she was distracted.

"Did I hear you talking?" he asked.

She still gripped the phone. She lifted it and showed him. "My cousin, Dickie. Remember, his daughter was the one whose baby died—crib death."

"Yeah," he said, kind of wearily. He sat down beside her. "I wasn't likely to forget about that." In fact, way back in Al's youth when he was a young husband, he and his wife had lost their only child the very same way. Al had spent decades trying to run away from that sorrow. "Poor thing."

"Well, she's not good. She's not getting better. She's grief stricken and they've tried everything from medication to counseling and Dickie wants me to take her in for a while, even if it's only a few weeks."

"Why?" he asked.

"Because she was my little princess and always loved staying with me. But she's not a little princess now—she's a thirty-year-old woman whose baby died and I don't think I can help her get over it with facials and mani-pedis." She looked up at him. "I wouldn't have the first idea what to do. I might just make it worse."

Al shifted into the bed, stretching out his long legs as he leaned against the headboard. He pulled her back into his arms. "Ray Anne, just being you puts a smile on most faces. You're kind and sweet and funny—maybe that would lighten her spirits a little bit. You could let her talk about it."

"Ugh," she said before she could stop herself.

"I know, I know. But they know you're not a professional counselor. I mean, your cousin and his missus. They don't expect you to cure her or anything, right? They just want her to have a safe place to go, right?"

"I think so," she said. "The poor thing. Her marriage was breaking up when she was barely pregnant, so she was alone. Had the baby alone. She moved back with her parents so she could take three months off work and she never went back because... How do you get someone over something like that?"

"Honey, you don't," Al said, pulling her closer against him, holding her in the crook of his big arm. "You can't get someone over something. All you can do is give 'em a little love and space and pray. You pray, baby?"

She laughed in a short, sarcastic huff. "All my damn life, but my prayers weren't very holy. 'Please God, let that big stud buy me a drink.'"

He laughed at her. "I think you should let her come."

"You do? Like we don't have enough complications..."

"I think if you don't, you might not get over it later. Sometimes we have to do things like that just to keep from having too many regrets." He kissed her forehead. "Might have to get a room at the Coast Motel again." Then he laughed.

"She doesn't work," Ray Anne said. "What am I going to do with her?"

"You should talk to your girls—Lou and Carrie. They've been through some rough times. So have you, for that matter."

Indeed, she had. An abusive husband, a couple of acrimonious divorces, getting financially wiped out by at least one of them. That was just for starters. She'd learned a lot, been around the block a time or two.

She'd even lost a child, but hardly anyone knew about that. And her baby hadn't died the way Ginger's had. Hers was a secret teenage mishap that ended sadly and she'd never talked about until very recently.

"I'm not smart or wise enough," she said.

"You're the smartest woman I know. And you're so full of love I can't even hold all of you."

She turned her head to look up at him. "I've never had anyone like you in my life before. Really, I haven't. You're the best thing that ever happened to me."

"I feel the same," he said.

"We've got an awful lot on our plates," she said.

"Bounty," he said. "That's what we call a full plate. Bounty."

"Hope it doesn't kill us," Ray Anne said.

Al planned to take his two younger boys to the high school basketball game on Friday night. Lou's husband, Joe, was a trooper who worked the swing shift four nights a week and Carrie didn't open the deli early on Saturday mornings. Friday night was a perfect night to get together with her girlfriends, so Ray Anne reached out to see if they felt like a little hen party at her house—a little wine and whine.

"Come to my house, instead, and I'll put out some snacks. You bring the wine and I'll invite Gina," Carrie said, including her daughter, who was also Lou's niece-in-law. "If Mac is working or something, she'll just sit around at home. If that's okay with you."

Of course Gina was a welcome addition, anytime. For a woman under forty, she was very prudent in the ways of the world. When Ray Anne arrived at Carrie's, the others were already there and Rawley was just leaving. "You're not staying for the hen party?" she asked.

"I ain't no hen," he said, pulling down his cap. "Thought I explained that."

"Rawley is babysitting tonight," Carrie said from behind him. "Cooper and Sarah want to go out without the baby."

"Really?" Ray Anne asked. "How are you with babies?"

"Perfect," he said. "If they go to bed and stay there."

The women had gotten used to having Rawley in the background of their little gatherings, silently serving them, saying nothing unless specifically asked, hiding out in front of the TV when sports were playing while they gathered in the kitchen. "We'll miss you," Ray Anne told him. "Having you around at a girl's night is kind of like having a butler—there to serve, but not there at all."

"I reckon you'll have to get your own food and drink and do your own dishes tonight," he said. "Don't wear yourself out." And with that, he was gone.

The women were sitting around the kitchen table where Carrie had put out a selection of her best hors d'oeuvres. As Ray Anne moved toward the table, Gina held up an empty wineglass, more than ready for Ray Anne's contribution to the party. She quickly uncorked one chilled white and one red.

"Will Rawley come back?" Ray Anne asked Carrie. Carrie merely shrugged and reached for a crab ball from the platter in the center. "Does he stay over?"

"Sometimes," Carrie said. "If he doesn't want to drive all the way to Elmore, to his house."

Ray Anne put both bottles on the table and sat down. She lifted one of Carrie's amazing crab balls and raised her eyes heavenward. "I have such a hard time picturing you and Rawley together. Romantically, that is."

"Then don't," Carrie advised.

"But seriously, are you a couple now? I mean, I know he's been around for months, like your boyfriend and partner, but…"

"Not everyone is as comfortable talking about the personal side of things as you are," Carrie said.

"He has his own room," Gina pointed out. When everyone stared at her, including her mother, she added, "Well, he does! He has my old room. Which doesn't mean anything, just that it's the way they want it! But believe me, I knock before walking in now."

"Seriously?" Lou said. "His own room? Jesus, are you set in your ways or what."

"Very much so," Carrie said. "Rawley is, too. I've gotten so used to him, I don't know what I'd do without him. He loves to cook, clean up, shop and run errands."

"Very exciting," Lou said.

"That's all the excitement I can stand."

The women were incredibly different. Just a look at them would make anyone wonder what they could possibly have in common. Carrie was plump and grandmotherly; she had never colored her short, steel-gray hair. She nurtured with food that was lovingly and thoughtfully prepared. Lou was small, trim, fit, kept her shoulder length auburn hair free of gray and looked younger than her sixty-two years. Gina was lovely, blond, midthirties with an eighteen-year-old daughter and three stepchildren and had been working at the diner for years and years, yet she looked like a girl.

And then there was Ray Anne. She teased her blond hair, wore her clothes on the tight, short, sexy side, her heels as high as possible. Well, she was short. But that had nothing to do with it, really. She liked them. She'd always worn more makeup, long nails, fancier and, for lack of a better word, *spicier* clothing. Lou called her a Dolly Parton knockoff and Ray Anne was not offended.

The women weren't alike in many other ways, either. Lou was an educator who had raised her nephew Mac and then helped him raise his three children after his wife left him. Carrie had been a single mother and small business owner—the deli and catering. Gina had only married Mac a year ago or so and became the instant mother of a big crowd. Only Ray Anne had been this solitary, childless woman. But somehow they understood one another.

"Remember my cousin Dickie?" she asked, sipping her wine. "Remember his daughter, Ginger, whose baby died a while back?"

"Terrible," Lou said, shaking her head. "Was that almost a year ago?"

"Almost nine months. Last summer," Ray Anne said.

"Nothing could be harder than that," Carrie said.

"Poor thing," Gina said.

"She's coming to stay with me for a little while," Ray Anne said. "And I'm terrified."

"You?" Lou asked. "Terrified? I didn't know anything scared you."

"This does. Her daddy called me—he said she was still in a world of hurt. I knew she wasn't getting better. She's been so depressed she can't work and can hardly get out of bed, lost a ton of weight and is so pitiful she can't talk to anyone for five minutes before she just has to go someplace to be alone. She's still in terrible pain."

"How sad," Carrie said. "Are you going to try to cheer her up?"

"Oh, Lord, what do I know about that kind of grief?" Ray Anne said. "If her daddy hadn't asked me, begged me really, I never would've signed up for this. I have no idea what I'm supposed to do!"

"Has she had counseling?" Lou asked.

"Yes, they've tried that. She even took antidepressants for a while. And I know there was some grief group at the church or something. That didn't go well, either."

"We can look around here for a counselor or grief group. Wouldn't hurt to try again," Lou said.

"I thought she was your niece," Gina said.

"She's like a niece. Dickie's like a brother. He and Sue had two little boys then along came Gingersnap and I was in heaven! A pretty little thing who could have fun spending the night at my house— we'd curl our hair, paint our nails, cream our faces, shave our legs…we shaved when she was a little older. We watched musicals and Disney shows together, dressed up, went shopping. I drove to Portland to help her pick out a prom dress, and I helped her stage her wedding—I was the official bridal assistant. Got way under Sue's skin, I'll tell you that, but my little Gingersnap was so happy!"

"She's married?"

"No," Ray Anne said. "No, her marriage only lasted a couple of years and was falling apart right as she realized she was pregnant and her husband, the bastard, didn't even try to give it a chance to help raise his own baby. So Ginger did it on her own. At the end of her pregnancy she moved home with her mom and dad. They'd fixed up the upstairs for her so she and the baby had rooms of their own and she could save some money. She worked right up till she started labor. Four months later her little baby boy died in his sleep."

"What did your cousin ask you to do for her?" Gina asked.

"Nothing," Ray Anne said with a helpless shrug. "He said the change might help, but he didn't ask anything specific of me. I think they're worn-out, that's what I think. It was Dickie and Sue's loss, too. They have other grandchildren, but this little one lived with them—their baby's baby. And I suppose the others can't get any attention because everyone is busy grieving." She rested her head in her hand. "I'll be useless. I'll probably just sit around and cry with the poor thing."

"For an hour or so, maybe," Carrie said. "Then you'll be done with that."

"Listen, I don't have any natural parenting skills. None. God knew what he was doing when I didn't get to have children."

"You'd have been an ideal parent," Lou said. "God's mistake."

"Me? Oh, believe me, I know nothing about being a parent and even less about what I can do to help my poor little Ginger while she goes through this terrible time. This is the worst idea Dickie has ever had, and he's had some real stinkers."

"No, this is perfect," Lou said.

"She's right," Carrie agreed. "Won't be so easy on you, but then when our youngsters hurt, it's awful. Worse for us, I think. But of all the people I know… yes, you're the one to do it."

"How can you say that?" Ray Anne demanded.

"I know about some of your tough times," Carrie said. "I've seen you through a few of them since you came to Thunder Point. Money trouble, broken hearts, struggles… There were a couple of times that were pretty awful. You had a mean son-of-a-bitch husband stalk you and you had to run and hide. You had a good friend die—what was her name?"

"Marisa Dunaway," Ray Anne said, and tears instantly sparkled in her eyes. "She was a good friend for twenty years and the Big C took her, but not until it kicked her ass, made her so sick and weak she was begging to die. Horrible. Horrible."

"And your parents died when you were little more than a girl," Lou reminded her as if she needed reminding. She was twenty-two and her parents, both in their late fifties, died so close together, both of cancer. That had been forty years ago. Cancer treatment had come a long way since then, but still, it had taken her best friend ten years ago. "That was a dark time for you. We weren't friends then," she added. "I wasn't there for you."

"I didn't even know you then. You've been through a lot since I've known you," Carrie said. "But you never indulged self-pity. You grieved hard, but never felt sorry for yourself."

"Ginger has a right to feel sorry for herself," Ray Anne said.

"This isn't about rights," Lou chimed in. "You had a right to self-pity, too. But you're a survivor. And you're a damn good role model. Your cousin is doing a smart thing, sending his daughter to you."

Ray Anne looked at Lou in surprise. "I didn't think you liked me enough to say something like that," she said.

"It's those shoes I never understood," Lou said. "And you did steal all my boyfriends until I started keeping them secret from you. But I always admired your strength. You're a woman on your own, alone, except for a couple of girlfriends and your recent boyfriend, but we don't count on boyfriends. Women alone have to be smart, strong and durable. We don't bruise easy. And we can't waste time and energy feeling sorry for ourselves. We might want to collapse, but we don't. Probably no one would pick us up!"

"You, too," Ray Anne said. "When Mac's wife left him—"

"Ach!" Lou barked. "Alone with three little kids— the smallest nine months old! Practically no money, two low-paying jobs and his only relative was me. I was a full-time teacher. I don't know how we got through it. And he was a mess! A pathetic, broken mess. Talk about self-pity! Sometimes when you have someone to lead, it's easier to be strong."

"What am I going to do?" Ray Anne asked.

"Be yourself," Gina said, smiling. "Be your wonderful, loving, strong self. Let her talk, push her a little bit, like my mother pushed me when I was a sixteen-year-old mother with no one but her. Get her a little counseling help, bring her around your friends, prop her up with example. Let her see we don't give up, we work. Sure we cry, sometimes scream, but we take it one day at a time and make every day a little better than the one we just left behind. You're really one of the best people for the job, I know it."

"I had no idea you all thought that way about me."

"Pfft. The only thing I feel sorry for you about is that you just can't dress yourself properly. You should be in double knits and wedgies like the rest of us over-sixty broads," Lou said.

"Don't listen to her," Carrie said. "The best part about you is you're unique. As long as you don't make me dress like a cocktail waitress I won't make you dress like a gray-haired grandmother."

Ray Anne couldn't answer. She felt the emotion in her throat. She'd give anything to be a grandmother. "You really think I'll be able to help her?"

"If you have trouble…if you have frustrations, we'll get together and hash it out. We've all been through the bitter side of life. It comes with breathing. Giving up was never an option," Carrie said.

"I have a confession to make," Ray Anne said. "It's not like I didn't feel sorry for myself sometimes. I've cried my heart out. Sometimes I cried till I couldn't stand up straight. It's just that I never cried like that in front of anyone."

"I know," three voices replied together.

Carrie was having trouble falling asleep. She heard the front door open and close. Then she heard the soft drone of the TV and she rolled over and looked at the clock. Almost one in the morning. She got up and found her robe and opened her bedroom door.

"Did I wake you up?" Rawley asked.

She shook her head. "I was tossing around, not sleeping." She gave her neck a stretch, tilting her head from side to side, trying to touch her chin to each shoulder. "This is so late for you."

"That Cooper. He thinks he's a kid. They went to some party up in North Bend with some of Sarah's old Coast Guard pals. Sarah had to drive him home."

"He'll pay for that."

"I hope so. Why aren't you sleeping?"

"I think too much," she said.

"Come here, girl," he said. When she sat beside him on the couch, he turned her so he could rub her shoulders. "Kids okay?" he asked as he massaged.

"They're all fine. It's Ray Anne's kin that's having trouble." She told him about Ginger and her need for a change of scenery. "Brings to mind how I always complained so much about how hard my life was when I never lost anything that dear."

"You lost a husband," he reminded her.

"Exactly as I said. Nothing very dear."

He made a sound that was almost a laugh. "Now you got some old vet taking up space in your house."

"You fit in so well, too. You hardly ever visit that house in Elmore anymore," she said.

"I almost never go to that house. I keep it as insurance for you."

She looked over her shoulder at him. "What does that mean?"

"Means I don't want you to worry none if you start to feel crowded and need your space—there's a place I can go. But I ain't got hardly a shirt left over there anymore. I never thought I'd end up living in some woman's house. Who'd a thought there'd be a woman could put up with me?"

"You're the easiest man I've ever known."

"No one ever accused me of that before."

"Rawley, I've been happy." She patted one of the hands that massaged her tight shoulders. "You're a good man."

"I'll do my best never to be a burden."

"I'm the burden!" she said. "Bad knees, sore back and neck, a family that just seems to grow, friends who count on me, a demanding business!"

He leaned forward and kissed her cheek right below the ear. His lips were dry and his face whiskery, but she leaned back against him for a moment.

"We get along fine," he said. "And you just tell me when you need something. I'll help if I can and get out of the way if I can't. Since we don't have all that much time, might as well enjoy it."

"I hope there's plenty of time!" she said. "I might be getting creaky but I'm not ready to give up. Especially now that life's gotten so sweet."

"Maybe I should've said, there ain't likely to be enough time. I know what. Let's find the lotion and I'll give you a proper rubdown. Get some of those creaks out."

"That sounds lovely."

Carrie went to her bedroom; the lotion was on the bedside table. The television was turned off and Rawley padded into the bedroom in his stocking feet. Carrie lay down on her side and, after just a minute, Rawley lay down behind her, rubbing lotion between his leathery palms. She lifted her pajama top all the way up, almost over her shoulders, baring her back and most of her front.

"My hands are gonna be a little cold," he said.

"I think maybe you should consider renting that house in Elmore. You could let it bring you some income."

"You in need of money, girl?"

She sighed. "No, Rawley. For the first time in my life, I think I have everything I need."

"Then maybe we'll sell that house. Put the money against retirement." He put a hand on her shoulder and pulled a little, rolling her toward him. "How many houses we need?"

"Only one, as far as I can see," she said. "Think anyone really notices?"

"In this town they notice everything," he said. "Think I really care?"

She laughed with him for a minute, then she rolled back so he could rub her back. He had strong, kind hands, the sort of hands she'd never expected to feel on her bare back. "That's so nice," she murmured.

Eight

Troy parked his Jeep behind the flower shop and called Grace. "I'm done at Cooper's. Is it too late for me to come by?"

"I'm with one of my other boyfriends," she said.

He grinned at that. "Can you ask him to step aside for a little while?"

"Is this a booty call?"

"No, it's not, as a matter of fact. I wanted to tell you something, but if you turn it into a booty call, I probably won't fight you off."

She laughed. "When will you be here?"

"I'm parked in the alley. And it's not really so late."

"Come up!"

He was already standing at the top of the stairs when she opened the door.

"You didn't work very late tonight," she said, pulling him inside. She put her arms around his neck, kissing him. "You know what? I really like this boyfriend stuff. It's very convenient. I was just think-ing about a kiss."

He pulled her closer. "You were, were you?" He nuzzled her neck and pressed against her. He fit so well against her soft curves, even though she was much shorter. He put his hands under her butt and lifted her, lining them up even better. Then he kissed her again.

"I thought you wanted to tell me something," she whispered against his lips.

"Right," he said distractedly, kissing her again. "No rush." Of course he began to grow against her enticing form.

"If you keep this up, you'll forget what you wanted to tell me," she warned him.

"No worries. It'll come back to me. You okay?"

"With you? Always okay."

He kept kissing, then touching, then gyrating. "Aw, Gracie," he moaned. "Let's talk a little later, all right?"

"All right."

"Bed? Sofa? Table? Floor?" He swallowed. "Wall?" She giggled.

"I could rip your clothes off right here," he said.

"Oh? And do you sew?" She pulled his hand from her breast and led him to the bed. "It will be more practical if we just undress. Ripping and tearing could be fun, but problematic."

"What if I'm feeling a little wild?" he asked, smil-ing into her pretty eyes.

"You can get a little wild when we're naked," she

said, dropping her jeans and shedding her denim shirt.

"I can do that," he said, getting rid of his clothes even faster. She was down to her tiny panties, so sheer and small they almost weren't there. He followed her onto the bed and reached for those panties with one big hand. "Oops," he said, ripping a short seam.

"You're very hard on my underwear."

"I'm surprised you have any left," he said.

"I love my panties."

"Not as much as I do! God, Gracie, I think you were expecting me," he said, covering her mouth with his and separating her knees with one of his. "You have no idea what you do to me."

"Just as long as I can do it to you again," she whispered. "And again…"

Even with all the romances Grace had read, just dreaming about true love, nothing had prepared her for what it would really feel like. As she lay naked in Troy's arms, enjoying postcoital bliss, catching her breath, ready for sleep, she sighed his name.

"Right here, baby," he said, pulling her tighter against him.

"I think you spoil me."

"That's my intention. You feel good?"

"I'm ruined for other men."

"Good. I can't think about you ever being with another man."

They were quiet for a few seconds. "You said *ever*," she said.

He rolled her over until she was on top of him, her hair a mussed canopy around their faces. "I did. You bring out some feelings in me that I don't recognize. I don't want to think about you ever being with anyone else. I don't want to be with anyone else." He brushed back her hair. "I should slow down, right? Because you're not ready for talk like that. Your other boyfriends never try to hold you down like that."

She shook her head. Pretend boyfriends rarely did—they were both all too aware of that. Here was the first flesh-and-blood boyfriend to hold her, love her, possess her. She didn't want anything to change.

"We both know what's missing from this perfect relationship," he said.

"Missing?" she asked.

"What you've told me about yourself, about growing up, wouldn't fill a chapter in one of your romances, Grace. Even your paper boyfriends would have questions."

"But you haven't asked me any questions," she said.

He shook his head. "I told you, you can trust me. And when you feel safe you'll tell me."

"You think I'm hiding something." It wasn't a question.

He nodded. "It's all right. I'm hiding a few things, too. Just things I don't talk about a lot. Iraq. I hate talking about Iraq, except sometimes with my boys—we laugh about terrible things that aren't really funny. There were youthful scrapes here and there. Trouble in high school, but nothing worse than the kids I teach now run into. We have years. We have plenty of time to learn everything about each other. I hope we don't take too long."

"But what if I say something that changes everything?" she asked him.

"See, that's the other thing missing—you know me, Gracie. You think I'm that kind of guy? That I'd measure you? Judge you by something in your past? You're an amazing, beautiful, kind, wonderful woman. I dare you to try to change my opinion."

She chewed her bottom lip. *Do it*, she told herself. *Do it* now.

But she couldn't. Not naked!

"Is that what you wanted to talk to me about? Is that why you came over tonight?"

He looked startled for a moment, then he started to laugh. He rolled with her again so that she was beneath him. "No, no. Gracie, the second you put your lips on me, you empty my brain! Don't you understand—I can't stay away from you? If I'm alone with you, I can't think of anything but getting busy. Then I want to do it again. Then I want to eat."

"Does everyone make love this much?"

"I don't know. They should. I think we're getting better, don't you?"

She nodded and smiled.

"I wanted to come over and tell you—a friend

of mine is coming to visit in a couple of weeks, if it works out. And I have to ask a favor—can I stay with you while he's here? I don't have an extra room or bed. If it was just Denny, I'd take the couch, but he's bringing his wife and she's pregnant. I think they could use a decent place to sleep and a little privacy."

"You stay here half the time anyway," she said.

"Will you check your calendar, because if you have a wedding or something, we'll change dates. He's a farmer, see, and he either comes before the planting gets serious or he has to wait till after harvest."

"A farmer?" she asked. "You never mentioned a friend who's a farmer."

"He's a buddy from the Marines and he stumbled on this organic farm down in California. He was just helping out while he was looking for a better job and it turned out he liked it. His wife is a teacher like me, that means it's weekends or nothing."

"A farmer and a teacher?" she asked. "Wow, that's so...*normal*!" With normal childhoods, no medals or stalkers, going to school every day, going to the prom, getting speeding tickets or into fights or falling in love like normal kids...

"Wait till Denny tells you about his farm—it's pretty far-out. So—can you check for weddings? Because I know you have to keep the shop open, at least a little bit, but I was hoping we could have some fun with them."

"If I don't have any big events I can post a notice that I'll close early on that Saturday."

"That would be great, Gracie. If you wouldn't mind too much, if it doesn't cost too much. Because we could have fun. And with Becca pregnant, it won't be anything too adventurous."

"So, you're not going to risk your life this time?" she asked.

He snuggled closer. "Gracie, sweetheart, wiggle up against me...yeah, just like that. Move those perfect little hips, aah. You're a witch, aren't you?"

"Tell me about Denny's farm," she said.

"No, we're not talking about him anymore. He's a buzzkill." He grabbed her legs at the backs of her knees, lifting them, tilting her upward. "God, you're magic. I'm glad I taught you how to do this."

She couldn't help but laugh at him. "Don't you think I'd have caught on eventually? Are you really going to take credit?"

"It makes me feel manly," he said. Then his breath caught. "God," he said when he felt her hand on him, gently stroking. "Gracie, Gracie, you're a witch... You're going to kill me, that's what you're going to do. Please, kill me."

She directed him into her, felt him fill her, dug her heels in and pushed against him. Then she wrapped her legs around him and rode with him, stroke for delicious stroke, just like they'd been doing it for years. She came first. When she felt him let go, she held on. He liked it when she did that. And when he was coming down she whispered, so softly he might not have heard, "I love you."

He didn't say *I love you, too.*

* * *

Troy was in a daze when he went into the bathroom in Grace's loft. He was thinking about her beautiful smile, her perfect laugh, the body that welcomed him so naturally, as if they were experienced lovers when they were really new. His fulfillment was always complete, leaving him weak and grateful. And she'd said she loved him. His heart was so full he was tempted to push the issue then and there, tell her what he knew, force her to come clean with him so they could get on with their lives. But it would be better if she came to him with the truth, trusted him.

He went back to bed, crawled in beside her and pulled her into his arms. He pulled her hair aside and kissed the back of her neck.

"Hmm. I thought you were hungry."

"Honey, we have to get you on the pill. Soon."

She rolled onto her back and looked at him. "Huh?"

"I think it's time for us to stop messing around with just a condom. They're not a hundred percent."

"So, what are you getting at?" she asked.

"We should be better protected. Is there any reason you're not on the pill?"

"It never occurred to me before. Before you."

"Yeah, of course. You should see the doctor. Or Peyton—Peyton could take care of you if you prefer a woman. We don't want to have to deal with complications like pregnancy."

She gasped. "You mean I could be pregnant?"

"You shouldn't be—we've been careful. But it's not worth the gamble. It would be a bummer to get pregnant—that's not the plan. That could put a serious damper on our fun."

"Our fun?" she asked softly. "You can say pregnant and fun in the same sentence?"

"Well, I'm not in the market for a baby, are you?" he asked. He grabbed her small waist. "At least it would be a few months before your belly got in the way of our good times." Then he laughed at his own joke.

"Did you just say that? Really? That it would get in the way of our good times?"

"Sorry. I shouldn't joke about it. Listen, can you do it? Check with the doctor and see if you can take the pill?"

"Sure," she said.

Then she rolled away from him and closed her eyes and her mouth before she screamed.

Grace didn't stir when Troy got up early. She feigned sleep while he dressed, kissed her cheek and left to go back to his apartment to get ready for work. When her loft was quiet, she rolled over on her back and blinked. She wasn't sure why she felt so emotional. He was right, after all. This was no time to get caught. But she was a hopeless romantic—she wanted love, marriage, children, happily ever after. Weddings were a big part of her job, after all.

It was just that when a guy you'd whispered love words to talked about the possibility of an accidental pregnancy, shouldn't he say something tender? Something like *Please don't worry—I'd never leave you to deal with it alone.* Or maybe, *You know how much I care about you.* Or how about a real stretch? *It'll be okay, Grace, because I love you.*

Then she asked herself, was she expecting him to do it all when she still hadn't been completely honest with him? After all, the secret of who she was wasn't shameful. It was just weird and complicated. She had no idea how he'd react. Would he let it out? Would Grace Dillon vanish as she became Izzy Banks all over again?

She opened the shop a little early, tidied up and made herself a list, and the top of the list was a visit to the clinic. She refreshed the water in the flowers in the cooler. She'd go see Peyton as soon as the clinic opened to get it over with. When she heard the bell to the shop's front door jingle, she peeked out and almost had a heart attack. There stood Peyton! She had a sudden irrational fear that Troy had called her, told her to go take care of Grace.

"Are you all right?" Peyton asked. "Did I startle you or something?"

"I just… I mean, I was just going to walk down to the clinic to see if you were available. What a co-incidence!"

"I'm totally available," Peyton said, smiling. "Scott's covering for me. What's up? You feeling okay?"

"I'm fine," Grace said. "But why are you here?" she asked.

"Well, Scott and I plan to get married on my folks' farm in late April. Everything will be blooming and there will be a lot of fruit blossoms involved. Is there enough time to talk about some other wedding flowers?"

"I'll have to check my book—I have a couple of weddings in April. But there's plenty of time to order and make up arrangements and bouquets," she said happily. This was her comfort zone. While she talked flowers, she'd work on her confidence. After an hour of flower talk, she'd be ready. "What have you got there?" she asked, indicating a flat box Peyton held under one arm.

"Some pictures. I know—usually the florist shows the bride-to-be flowers. But a wedding on the farm is unlike anything you've ever seen before. The pear trees will be in full bloom. If it's a warm winter they'll start early and if it's a late spring they'll just be starting. My mother's gardens will be blooming and so will my aunts' and cousins'. When a Basque girl gets married, everyone brings flowers and food." She laughed a little. "Even when the *girl* is thirty-five!"

"It doesn't sound like you need me," Grace said.

"But yes, I do. Let me show you."

"Come on back," Grace invited. The worktable was still clean because it was early. Grace only had a couple of orders to make up later, to be delivered tomorrow.

They sat at a corner of the large table and Peyton leafed slowly through a lot of loose pictures, describing them as her brother's wedding, her oldest sister's wedding, her youngest sister's wedding. "She got married quickly—no pear blossoms for her. We had to order from the flower growers. I thought my mother would have a stroke over that—her baby, getting married off the farm. To add to the insult, she married a chef and he insisted his restaurant cater. The fact that I'm finally getting married, in late spring, on the farm—it goes a long way to helping her get over it."

"These pictures are gorgeous. They should be published," Grace said. The trellises were adorned with blossoms, and the women wore flowers in their hair. The tables sitting outside for the reception had arrangements on each one. The women carried beautiful bouquets and the buffet table that held enough food for an army also displayed roses, gardenias, cherry and pear blossoms, hydrangea, roses, baby's breath and rich, dark fern. It was a fortune in flowers, and a great deal of work. More than Grace could possibly manage alone. "You're right, I've never seen anything like it. Who did the flowers?"

"My family," she said. "I'd like to do a few things differently."

"I can't imagine why," Grace said, flipping through picture after picture.

"Well, I certainly can't find any fault with it, except for two things—my mother works too hard and every wedding in our family looks the same. Everyone contributes so much. I know they love it, but it becomes almost a competition." She shook her head. "Not almost. It *is* a competition—in the kitchen, in the garden, everywhere you look. We're going to change a few things. For starters, we're going to get married in a very old church in Mount Angel in an ecumenical service, not outside with the orchard as backdrop. The Catholic Basque relatives will be a little put out, but they won't boycott. There are too many of them anyway. There are so many of them, we're thinking of renting actors to play the parts of Scott's family—his family is so small by comparison. But our friends from Thunder Point will make up the difference. I want to supply some flowers, the bouquets, altar arrangements, boutonnieres and corsages. My mother and aunts can decorate the tent…"

"Tent?"

"My father likes the men to dance under the stars. I want to rent a tent, a dance floor and a bandstand. I'm hiring a Basque band from San Francisco. I'm sure they'll step aside long enough for my father, my brothers and uncles and others to have a turn, but I want my parents to celebrate with me. If it rains, and rain in spring is not at all unusual in north Oregon, we'll be covered. And I want Scott's mothers to have a good time. If possible."

"Mothers?" Grace asked.

"His mother and his late wife's mother. The grandmothers. If you pay attention, you'll hear him complain about them, but I have a mother, grandmother, a million aunts and cousins all over the place, all the way to Spain and France. The Basque people are the only ethnic group to come from two countries, Spain and France, and the tradition and ritual in the old country, even though there is no old country anymore, is rigid and colorful and often troublesome as they argue over control. His mothers can't hold a candle to that!"

"So there will still be pear and cherry blossoms?" Grace asked almost weakly.

"Thousands," Peyton said. "I grew up on that farm. I'm committed to a zillion flowers and fruit blossoms and bees!" she said, laughing. "The sheep are not invited!"

"Oh, God, it sounds amazing! I hate bees," Grace added.

"I'm sure Scott will be packing an EpiPen if you have a reaction. Because, of course, the reason I'm asking you for flowers is because I'd like you to attend if you can. I'm kind of hoping you'll bring some of the flowers. I realize it's a very long trip for a delivery."

"Invited? Me?"

"Of course! I love the flowers my mother and aunts bring, but I'd like a few different blooms this time. Day lilies, calla lilies, hybrid roses, maybe some more tropical blossoms, an orchid or two. If you don't count my younger brother who is divorced, I'm officially the last Lacoumette to marry. I've already talked to my mother about the flowers and the food…"

"The food?" Grace asked.

"She'll be cooking and freezing for weeks, but I'm holding her back. I wouldn't celebrate without her more famous dishes but my brother-in-law, the chef, owns a five-star restaurant! I want him to participate. He's gifted and he's honored to be asked. If you want to really compliment a Basque, praise their cooking, dancing, music making or children raising. My mother is being very stoic about this, that Lucas would provide some of the food. At least he's family." She laughed and shook her head. "They won't share recipes with each other, it's hilarious."

"Peyton, this sounds huge. Maybe bigger than I am. I don't want to buck tradition."

"We *have* to buck tradition," she said. "I'm Basque but my fiancé isn't. He's getting married, too! Although…he can't get enough of them, of that farm. He's so happy when he's there. I can't take him there too often or he'll grow big as a bull! No one loves to eat like Scott."

That made Grace smile. "Troy could probably give him a run for his money."

Peyton's dark eyes twinkled. She was silent for a moment. "How's that going? You and Troy?"

"Nice," Grace said. "Tell me about your family. About how you met Scott. About the farm and the culture and the traditional Basque wedding."

Peyton explained that she was the oldest of eight and, no, she hadn't been dreaming of a big family! She had been determined to be single for a long while but now that she'd found Scott and his two kids, she was very anxious to have one, maybe two, to add to the pack. She described her parents, her siblings, nieces and nephews, talked about Scott and how he was the last thing she ever expected. She explained the Basque people as best she could, how she worked in a Basque clinic in the south of France for a while after graduating from college, getting to know the old country. Grace couldn't wait to do a little online research about the culture. Almost two hours had passed before they got around to blooms and stalks, number of guests and colors.

"It's spring. I'm dressing my bridesmaids in all the spring colors—lavender, pink, baby blue and yellow. I want a colorful wedding! I want their bouquets to match their dresses and mine to represent all of them. I want spring colors in the altar arrangements, then we'll take them to the farm for the reception. The groom's dinner is Scott's responsibility and he's chosen a hotel in Portland that can cater in a banquet hall and I offered flowers, which his mother snapped up immediately. There will be at least thirty people at the dinner.

"There will be about two hundred people, all arriving in cars, RVs, trucks with camper shells and fifth wheels. My mother thinks the tent for the reception is uppity, and my father complains it will block the sky, but he already contacted cousins in the old country to send him crates of their best wine. We always have to rent tables so at least no one is complaining about that. But I want a waitstaff and bartenders for this event, if only to help with the cleanup. My family should celebrate and enjoy the fruits of their labors."

"It sounds positively wonderful," Grace said somewhat dreamily. "I can't imagine having that many family members around to celebrate."

"Oh, there will be arguing, too," she said. "Fights,

even. Big families—big control issues. They're very opinionated, very strong, very nosy. There is always lots of laughter, lots of yelling."

"I'd love to do this," Grace said. "But I'll be honest, I've never done a wedding this big or this far away. The people I worked for before coming here to open the shop are in Portland. I know they could do it…"

"Get them to help you, if you want," Peyton said. "I only want two things from you—flowers and to see you dance at my wedding. I hope a lot of people from Thunder Point will be there."

Grace gave the situation some thought. There were many different ways this could be accomplished. She could order the flowers and even make the bouquets and arrangements and drive up with them—the van was refrigerated in back. Or, she could transport the flowers and make them into bouquets and arrangements once there. Or, she could have Ross and Mamie order the flowers and she could go up a day early, visit with them and make up the flowers in their shop. They'd be thrilled. She ran over all these possibilities with Peyton and Peyton left the final decision in her hands.

"And now, what can I do for you?" Peyton asked.

"Oh. That." Grace cleared her throat. "A checkup, I guess. I haven't had one in a while, like too long. Oh, don't make that face—it's only been a few years!"

Peyton's black eyes grew huge. "A few *years*?"

Grace leaned toward her a little. "I've had lots of

physicals over the years, all with good results, but only a couple of *those* exams. But now it seems I need to be on the pill."

"Ah," Peyton said. "Gotcha."

"Your first thirty-year-old virgin?" Grace asked with a smirk, though she was not thirty yet.

"No," Peyton said, laughing. "I'm very happy to oblige." She glanced at her watch. "Can you come down to the clinic this afternoon at around two? That's a really slow time. Scott will be at the hospital and I can arrange with Devon to get you in right away so we don't take too much of your time. But I'm going to want to do a blood panel to make sure everything is in order."

Grace hadn't been exaggerating—she'd had a ton of physicals. A competitive skater had to be in peak condition, couldn't risk anemia or vitamin deficiency or, God forbid, some lurking condition like a heart or kidney problem. But this was different.

"I can do that. Two o'clock."

Nine

Although they didn't talk about it, Grace realized that she and Troy were having a standoff. She wanted to hear some words of love before she told him the whole story of her life and he wanted the story of her life before there could be words of love. She might be very vulnerable to the promise of first love, but she wasn't an idiot.

She had kept her appointment with Peyton.

When Grace had visited Peyton and asked her about birth control pills, she told her they'd only been using condoms for protection. "I'm not worried about it," she said. "But Troy is getting a little nervous about depending only on that when the pill is safer."

"Perfectly understandable. Are your periods regular?" Peyton asked.

"No, unfortunately. I'm pretty sure I'm due any day now. Seems like it's been a while."

"Well, let's do a physical exam and blood work and then I'll give you a prescription for birth control pills. You can start taking them the first day of your period, but stick with your other protection until two weeks on the pill. I'll also give you a pregnancy test to take home just in case that cycle doesn't arrive— you can check to be sure you're not pregnant."

Troy hadn't even asked her about it. She decided she was going to tell him everything about her past before his friends visited on the weekend. If there was anything about her he no longer liked, he could just sleep on his own couch while they were in town.

She put the morning mail on her desk, went about her work, put together a few floral arrangements for Justin to deliver later. She went upstairs to fix a sandwich for lunch, then cleaned up the shop, made a list of flower orders for the week and visited with customers. It was late afternoon and Justin had already picked up his deliveries before she went through the mail. She leafed through the usual ads and bills, then came across a letter. Her name and address were typed on the envelope and she expected an offer of cheap insurance or something similar. But inside was one folded slip of paper. She opened it and read what was typed across the page.

"I dream of you every night. B."

She stared at it, mouth open. Her hands began to shake. She looked over her shoulder left, then right. Her breath came in short gasps. She locked the back door. She wanted to go upstairs and lock her loft, but she was afraid to go outside. She grabbed her cell phone and then spoke aloud, to calm herself. "Stop. Stop. You're alone here. He's not here."

But she checked every nook and cranny, in the cooler, the office, even under the desk. She looked into the alley and saw nothing unusual. She didn't know who to call. Not her mother, who would only say *I told you so.* Not Mamie and Ross in Portland—what could they do? She finally speed-dialed Mikhail's cell phone. She had no idea where he might be; he could be anywhere in the world. She usually got his voice mail and was constructing the message she'd leave him when he answered in Russian.

"Mikhail, he found me! I just got a letter. It says what he used to say, that he dreams of me every night. It's Bruno! Oh, God."

"Sons of bitches!" he barked into the phone.

"It's not addressed to Izzy. It's addressed to Grace Dillon. Here at the shop. Where I *live.*"

"But he is in hospital," Mikhail said. "I will call them now. Then I call you. Stay where you are," he instructed as though she'd leave the phone if she left the room.

"Thank you. I couldn't make myself call them."

The first note had come when she was twelve, just a little girl, but her parents hadn't shared it with her. At twelve she was already a skater with enormous promise and a winner in her age category. Her parents screened everything that came near her, but she saw one of the notes lying on her father's desk a year later. She got a little excited at first—someone loved her? Dreamed of her? But her mother said, "Don't be ridiculous! It's another nutcase! We reported him to the police."

She didn't think another thing about it. Then, not long after her father's death, after an early morning practice with Mikhail, her new coach, she took off her skates in the arena where she'd been skating and walked toward the exit where the chauffeured town car waited. A man she didn't know and couldn't remember ever seeing before stepped out of a dark hallway, grabbed her, put his hand over her mouth and ran down that dark hallway with her. She struggled and fought and he babbled that he was going to take care of her, rescue her from the people who were exploiting her.

He held her in a maintenance closet with a broken lock on the door. She huddled in the corner, sitting on the cold floor, while he paced and babbled about foreign countries using children to spy for them, that the beautiful children should be freed, on and on with nonsense that had no meaning. He hadn't been armed that she could see, but he was a large man. His hair was thinning on top but long on the sides and back; she found out later that he was twenty-four. She tried to get up and run for the door of that small space but he smacked her right down and threatened her, told her he'd have to hurt her to protect her if she didn't follow his rules.

It took a little over two hours for the police to open the unlocked door, wrestle him to the ground and remove her. It was much later that she learned he was delusional and had to be hospitalized.

After that incident there were a couple of other stalkers that were handled quickly, efficiently and with restraining orders. Those two later perpetrators were not delusional but appeared to be aficionados of the young female sporting scene and seemed to move on with little argument. Who knew who they bothered after her?

Once Grace understood exactly what had been going on she also understood there were predators out there, people who preyed on pretty young athletes, male and female. They usually began by giving small gifts or flowers and praising their talent, but too soon they'd be seen at every practice and competition, always trying to get closer, to chat it up with the coaches or athletes.

It was very likely a combination of her own close calls and the tearful words from that young skater, Shannon Fields, that caused Grace to fire such rash and destructive accusations at the coach, Hal Nordstrom, suggesting he'd been inappropriate. Poor little Shannon had said to Grace, "You don't understand! I gave him *everything* he asked for. *Everything*, even if it was horrible!" Grace believed, in her gut, that Shannon had been talking about something other than, *more than*, practice. She had no evidence. But he did have a sleazy, lecherous look in his eye and he did way too much fondling and butt patting.

What did she know about it? She had Mikhail Petrov, that cold, angry, often silent little Russian who never touched her, not in anger, not in praise. Since his compliments came in the harsh, brittle Russian tongue, she had no way of knowing, for years, that he was sentimental on the inside. Looking back, she could see that Mikhail had almost become the man of her small family; both Winnie and Grace had depended on him. He was always present, completely devoted.

Mikhail also had strong opinions about Hal Nordstrom. He used one phrase whenever he referred to that particular coach. "He is piece of shit."

Winnie had told her to keep her mouth shut and when she hadn't, Nordstrom sued them for defamation and Winnie had settled with an undisclosed sum. When, a few years later, Nordstrom was arrested for molesting several young skaters, Grace felt vindicated. But did Winnie apologize? Just the opposite. "You could have saved me considerable money if you'd just kept your mouth shut. And he would've eventually been found guilty anyway."

It was a long couple of hours before Mikhail called her back. "He is out, *moya radost*," he said, his Russian for *my happiness*. "But he is with family in Florida. They swear on bibles he is safe and taking medicine. I'll get this verified to my satisfaction."

"Oh, Mikhail, what if they're lying? Making excuses?"

"I have called police. I want they should answer me. We shall see. Are you safe?"

"I think so," she said weakly, looking around again. "Why would he even want me now? I'm not on the ice or in the news! He shouldn't even want me anymore!"

"Ach, I can't know the head of a crazy man! If there is doubts, you must take steps. Call police. Or," he said, hesitating briefly, "call Winnie. She will not abandon you."

A nervous laugh that was almost a sob escaped her. The last thing she wanted was to be controlled by her mother again. She talked to Mikhail while she walked to the front door, put up the closed sign and locked it. They talked for just a few minutes. She learned he was in Chicago for some exhibition skating and then would be heading to Southern California, which had become his home base.

Mikhail was over sixty. He was once a competitive skater but gave that up in his early twenties, knowing he was not good enough to be great. But he had the potential to build champions and had been coaching ever since. He'd had only one brief marriage because, *Is not the life for family man.* Grace wasn't quite sure how much or how little that influenced her decision to get out. *What do I care?* Mikhail would say. *I make winners, that is what I do.*

Grace wanted more. Or less, as the case may be.

"I would like to see you sometime," she told him before hanging up.

"You have to find me," he told her. "We would have good meal, laughs, old times. Maybe you skate for me once!"

"Maybe," she said. "For old times only."

"I was better making rules, telling you when you will skate and what you will do. I don't follow so good."

"I know this," she said, laughing through nostalgic tears.

After they hung up, she dimmed the lights in the shop. *When you're closed, you're closed.* She didn't have the courage to go upstairs to her loft. She had an irrational fear that he was waiting for her up there. He was really a kind of tragic, pathetic man who was completely out of reality, left in the care of an older sister who wasn't married and promised to always guard him closely, a woman who really cared about him and was traumatized by the reality that he could possibly hurt someone.

She heard from Troy every day. If he didn't call her after school, she called him. She'd give him till six or so, then she'd text him and ask him what he was doing after work.

In the meantime, she thought about Mikhail and she cried. The truth was, she missed skating for him. She even missed competition and the raw nerves of it. She had no regrets about leaving it—she'd accomplished everything she could and the strain was sometimes debilitating.

It was funny that the girl who was her fiercest rival, who hated her more than anyone on the circuit, an American named Fiona Temple, hadn't ever made her mark. Fiona, who had her own posse of mean girls, spread more dirt about Grace than anyone else, making sure everyone knew that while most hardworking parents got up at four to take their kids to training and borrowed against the mortgage to pay for it, Rich Bitch Izzy's mother put her in a town car at dawn to be delivered to the rink. Fiona, who celebrated the most when Grace walked away, hadn't done anything significant since. She had believed the only thing that stood in the way of gold medals was Grace, yet with Grace gone China and Russia wrapped up the medals.

The pressure to stay in the competition had been fierce from all quarters, from Winnie, from her team, from her country. "You do what you have to do, but until the day comes, say *nothing*!" Mikhail had warned her. "Telling is losing."

Any other coach would've dumped her. In her circles, winning was everything. World-famous coaches don't waste their time on competitors who want to quit. But he stuck with her, gave her everything he had and she worked her ass off for him. Mikhail wasn't warm and fuzzy, but he loved her like a daughter, protected her and challenged her and to this day had not abandoned her.

So she went to her last competition, the biggest in the world, angry and determined to strike one final blow for everyone who depended on her. And she took it. Took it *all*. She took it home by a mile. Winnie had her gold medal. Fiona hadn't even made the cut.

The back door to the shop rattled as someone tried to get in. She nearly jumped out of her skin. She had to take a couple of deep breaths and wipe her eyes before creeping to the door to see who it was.

"Gracie, what's wrong?" Troy said. "You're crying."

"Don't ask me why, just please go upstairs and

make sure no one is up there, ready to jump on us and kill us," she said.

"What?" he asked, aghast.

"When it's safe, we'll talk up there. I'm not sure if I locked the door, but some days I don't. I've gotten so relaxed…"

"Grace, what the hell?"

"Please," she begged. "You'll understand as soon as I can talk about it. I was going to explain some things anyway. Before your friends came to visit, I was going to tell you so it wouldn't be vague anymore…but for right now, can you please check? And be very careful!"

Troy shook his head and went upstairs. He looked around her loft thoroughly, but nothing seemed out of place. He was back down in less than two minutes. "It's okay."

"Did you look everywhere?"

He nodded. "Even in the kitchen trash and the refrigerator. Come on."

She clutched an envelope in her hand. When they were sitting across from each other in her tiny kitchen she started to explain. "My real name is—"

"I know," he said.

"You *know*?"

"Sorry. I wasn't going to tell you, but I can't fake surprise. You're all over the fucking internet, Gracie. I don't know how you felt, how you feel, but I know who you are. And that you won it all and walked away."

"Do you know about the rumors? That I accused a

coach of inappropriate sexual behavior with a minor? That I was *sued*? That there were stalkers? That everyone hated me?"

He shrugged. "I got most of the facts. I don't know how anyone could hate you. Most of all, I don't know why it's a secret."

So she started at the beginning, born into figure skating, the daughter of a champion and coach, the bullying from jealous girls, pranks aimed at hurting her skating, the exhausting training and travel and no friends.

"The coaches demanded everyone behave nicely toward each other, but when the coaches weren't looking... The rest of them were all so close," she said. "They shared hotel rooms to save costs and I stayed alone. My mother would rent big town houses that came with domestic help and everyone thought because of that, I had it so easy, why wouldn't I do well? It came up in every interview and article—as if all we had to do was write a check and first place was mine. All I wanted, the whole time I was growing up, was to be like everyone else."

"Nothing nastier than jealous teenage girls," he said. He gave her cheek a little stroke.

"If I cried or pouted they called me poor little rich girl."

"And yet there were millions of girls all over the country who watched you skate with envy and adoration."

"But I never met them. The happiest day of my

life wasn't winning the gold—it was handing it to my mother and walking away."

"Where did you go?"

"To Mamie and Ross. They were a couple without children who had worked for my mother since she was a girl—over thirty years. He was a driver and she was a housekeeper. They were always so good to me and when they left my mother's employment they opened a flower shop in Portland. They trained me in the business."

"Is there no other family?"

"Remember I told you about a cousin who wrote me asking for a loan?" He nodded. "That wasn't a cousin and it wasn't a loan. That's a half brother, Barry, who is twenty years older than me. My father and his first wife divorced years and years before my mother knew him. He supported his ex-wife and Barry until Barry was twenty-one. He's forty-eight now and has been asking for money his whole life, but I don't remember even three times he visited. My dad gave him money sometimes—my parents fought about it. When my father died, he didn't leave Barry anything. I don't know where he is. Last I heard from him, when I told him there was no money, he was in Texas."

Troy immediately smelled an ill wind. "Maybe Barry is still butt sore about that," he said, tapping the envelope in her hand.

She handed it to him. "I never had a relationship of any kind with him—he was grown when I was born. No, this is just like the note I remember from years ago. The only one I saw before I was snatched."

"Could he know exactly what was in it?" Troy asked, opening it up and looking at the typed sentence. *I dream of you every night. B.* "It's signed 'B.'"

She shook her head. "That's Bruno. Bruno Feldman. The man who held me in a supply closet until the police came. He's been in a psychiatric hospital and I'm told he's out and with family somewhere in Florida. Barry doesn't know that's what the notes looked like. No one knows—just me, my mother, Mikhail…"

"Mikhail?"

"My coach. One of my coaches. We keep in touch a little bit. Of course he was there at the time. Things got pretty crazy because the first notes came while my father was sick, then he snatched me after my father had died. So much happened at once."

"*One* of your coaches?"

She nodded. "There was a team and several different coaches and instructors and trainers. Endurance training, ballet, ice work. For me there was also yoga, sports therapy, and then the tutors and homework."

"How many hours a day was that?" he asked.

"I don't know. Every one of them, I think. It started early, ended late. That's not even counting fittings for costumes, choreography, music…and did I mention homework? How about the number of nights I went to bed with bags of ice wrapped to my ass or calves?"

He smiled at her. "You earned those medals, Gracie. It was a lot to give up. But are you happy now?"

"I was," she said, her eyes glistening again. "Until that came." She sighed. "What kind of jollies does a person get out of just scaring me to death?"

He shook his head. "It's not normal, you know. It's sick and twisted. And from what you tell me, not entirely his fault."

"I don't know what to do," she said. "I feel like I should run and hide."

"That's because you're scared and upset. But it's going to be all right. You'll have to think things through a little, ask yourself some questions…" He got up and opened the little fridge. He didn't find what he wanted, so he looked in the small wine rack on top and pulled out a bottle of Merlot. He opened it and poured a small glass for her. "Have a little of this and take a few deep breaths. I'm not going to let anything happen to you."

"I really don't expect you to—"

"You don't expect me to help protect the girl I love?" he asked.

She stared at him. "You love me?"

"Of course I do, Gracie. Couldn't you tell?"

"You never said anything about love…"

"I was waiting for you to trust me, to be honest with me. Look, I understand how you could want to escape that old life, as difficult as—"

"No, Troy, you don't! I don't want to be that person anymore! That friendless person so many people talked about and hated! Do you have any idea how painful it is to be the constant object of everyone's jealousy? As if I had something that belonged to them? As if my mother's money could buy anything—well, it can't buy safety or a family or love!"

"And so many people admired you, also," he said. "But, no matter what name you decide to use, I'm always going to think of you as Gracie. Everyone loves you. You're not an overworked, abused, over-exposed teenage girl anymore. And the first thing you have to let go of is all the secrecy. Your friends can't watch out for you if they don't know anything. When you let the cat out of the bag, people are going to wonder why in the world you'd keep an accomplishment like that a secret."

"Because they don't understand how hard it is to be in that life!"

"You're not in it anymore, honey." He laughed a little and grabbed the last cold beer out of her fridge. "I have to admit, I had trouble understanding why you'd hide that. Gracie, I get that a lot of it was hard, worse than hard, but it's also an achievement. No one's going to hate you for it."

She sipped her wine. "We don't know that for sure."

"Yes, I know it. First thing we're going to do is get you a couple of things for protection. I think we can find 'em online real easy and get them sent overnight. Maybe some pepper spray. How about a stun gun? A Taser."

"I have to admit, there are a few people I'd like to zap…"

"That's my girl. Only bad guys, okay, baby? Then

we're going over to see Seth. He needs to know there's been this contact. I don't know if you'd call it a threat, exactly, but it's creepy and he's the law around here. Besides that's a good time for you to unload all this on your best friend. You know you can trust Iris to accept you as exactly who you are, no kidding."

"I guess," she said.

Ten

Iris's house was the scene of quiet domesticity. It almost brought tears to Grace's eyes, she was that envious. It wasn't quite seven and apparently they were just getting around to dinner. Seth had changed out of his deputy's uniform into a pair of jeans and a sweater. Since Troy had called and asked if he and Grace could stop by to have a word with them, Iris had added two plates to their dinner table.

"Oh, you shouldn't have," Grace said.

"But of course I should have! And I apologize—it isn't much. I was just about to put in a frozen pizza and since you wanted to stop by, I pulled out a second. To my embarrassment, I have a good supply of frozen pizzas! I doctor them a little—extra pepperoni, cheese and mushrooms."

"That's almost like cooking, right?" Seth said. "Come in. Let's toast whatever you have on your mind."

"I don't think this is toastable, but it's definitely

drinkable. Grace has something to tell you. Then we could use a little help," Troy said.

"Absolutely," Seth said. "Let's sit in the kitchen."

"I hope nothing's wrong," Iris said, pulling out a chair for Grace.

"Something's wrong," Grace said. "I'll try to give you the short version. I haven't been entirely honest with you about my past. My life. I'm not exactly who you think I am. I'm sorry—it's not that I didn't trust you."

By now it was getting a little easier to talk, since telling Troy was the hard part. She got the whole story out without *all* the details about daily life as a competitor, in about fifteen minutes. Iris, stunned by this new information, punctuated the story with *Seriously? You're kidding me!* and *Holy crap!*

"My God, you're famous," she finally said. "I thought you looked familiar but couldn't place the resemblance."

"Only famous at certain times and in certain places, but I'm not that competitor anymore. Which is why I didn't say anything. And it's also why this freaked me out. This guy was obsessed with me." She slid the envelope toward Iris while she explained what had happened with Bruno.

Iris passed the note to Seth, who frowned when he read it. "Is this the only contact?" he asked.

"There hasn't been anything since he was put in the hospital. And only my parents and the police knew about the way the note was written—that one typed line and the initial *B*. Could he still be obsessed with me?"

"Anything is possible," Seth said.

"Can you find out if he's still secure with his family in Florida?" Troy asked.

"I'll make some calls. I'll get in touch with the police department there. Do you know the name of the psychiatric facility?"

She gave it to him. "When my old coach checked, he was told he wasn't a patient any longer, that he lived with his family."

"Grace," Iris said. "This envelope has no postal stamp on it."

"Huh?"

She gave the envelope to Seth. "It wasn't postmarked," she repeated. "It must have been slipped into your mailbox."

"Oh, God," Grace said weakly. "He's *here*?"

"Let's not make assumptions," Seth said, reexamining the envelope and then slipping the note inside. The envelope went in his pocket. "I'm going to look into this. Iris, get those pizzas in, okay?" He immediately turned his attention back to Grace. "Let me tell you something, Grace. If there's an odd stranger lurking around Thunder Point, he's going to stand out like a wart on my nose and even without telling anyone I'm looking, someone's going to tell me. Especially on the main street that runs through town, past all the businesses. Gina never misses a thing, I miss less. Waylan was robbed about ten years ago and he's still talking about it, still checking every face on the street. In fact, this whole mystery will be easier to solve if some stranger came around and slipped the note into your mail slot."

Iris put a glass of wine at her place and Grace's and asked Troy what he'd like. Then a couple of beers appeared in front of Troy and Seth. After sliding the pizzas into the oven, Iris sat down again.

"But," Seth went on, "I'm going to tell my staff and the business neighbors that a suspicious note was left in your mail slot and I'm looking for who could have done that to be sure you're safe. In the meantime, put a note on the door to ring the bell and lock the front and back doors. I'll find out about your former stalker, but I may not hear back from anyone until the morning. Listen, I don't know if you'll take this as good news or bad, but I would be very surprised to find some mentally ill patient from fourteen years ago is still obsessed with you and made it across an entire continent, made himself invisible and shook you up with a copy of an old note. I think this is something else altogether."

"But no one knows about this," she said.

"That's seldom the case, especially after so long. I have no idea what the motive could be, but I doubt this is still a closely held secret."

"But who would do this? Who could possibly care?" she asked.

Seth shook his head. "I don't know. Yet. But I'll be looking for a reason. And you have to think about it, too. Maybe an enemy? Someone who thinks you

have money? Have you ever been followed by re-
porters? A jealous family member?"

"Your mother?" Troy asked. "She's not happy
with your decision to leave competition and you said
she's really controlling."

"I can't imagine," Grace said. "She's been impossible and demanding but, to her credit, she's never
been underhanded."

"Maybe you should contact her," Seth said. "Try
to get a read on her."

"I'd hate to do that. We've been estranged since
I left competition."

"Well, give it serious thought," Seth said. "And
keep the doors locked."

"I won't leave Grace alone," Troy said. "I'll make
sure she's safe in her shop before I go to school tomorrow. And we're going to get some self-defense
things. You know—pepper spray and a Taser."

Seth groaned. "God, I hate when people do that.
People get hurt. Waylan got himself a Taser—the
kind that shoots out the prongs. He accidentally
Tasered his cat."

"I have guns," Troy said.

Seth groaned again, louder. "I assume Grace is
not trained in firearms."

"I am," Troy said. "But they're for hunting. And
you're right, she's so small I'd be afraid it would only
put a shotgun or rifle in the hands of someone who
shouldn't have it."

"Hey," Grace interrupted. "Am I a part of this
discussion? Because I kind of like the idea of hav-

ing some kind of weapon! The bigger and scarier, the better!"

"Are those guns in a safe place?" Seth asked Troy.

"They're in my apartment and there's a great lock on the door. I replaced the apartment lock with a couple of good dead bolts because I have some expensive equipment in there. They're not loaded. Like I said, I do a little hunting."

"Make sure they stay unloaded," Seth said.

"I can keep her safe until you're back on duty tomorrow," Troy said.

"Yeah, I've seen you in action," Seth said with a chuckle. "That takedown at the high school a few months ago, that was dramatic. You were showing off, but it was helpful."

"Helpful," Troy said sarcastically, speaking of the day Iris was threatened by a very big, very angry and abusive student and Troy happened to be there at the right time. Seth was there *second*.

The men talked about that incident while Iris took the pizzas out of the oven, let them sit on the counter for a few minutes to cool. Then Grace and Iris stood at the counter, cutting up the pizzas.

"Iris, I can't eat. I'm sorry," Grace said.

"I know it's not chicken soup, but you should have something. A bite or two. Don't be afraid now—Troy and Seth are on this."

"He didn't say anything about staying with me until we came over here."

"Grace, don't you know how he feels about you?

He's crazy about you! And I can't believe you were this famous person and were afraid to tell me!" Iris said.

"I wasn't afraid. I just wanted you to like me for who I am—a flower girl."

"How could you doubt that? You're the best flower girl this town has ever seen."

"Oh, jeez, what am I going to do?" Grace said. "I have weddings in April! I can't shut down! I can't run! You know brides—they're all on such a weak string to start with. Every small thing that goes wrong turns them insane. Their flowers have to be on time and perfect."

"You don't have to shut down. I can't explain how this would be possible but I bet this note is some kind of ugly prank. Seth will find out. He's not only very good at this sort of thing, he's committed. He's a good cop."

Grace and Troy took a swing by his apartment so he could gather up some clothes, his backpack and laptop so he wouldn't have to go home in the morning before work. Grace was restless through the night, even with Troy beside her. She tossed and slept little and had one terrible dream, but it was not about Bruno. She was skating but her costume wasn't covering her body and her legs wouldn't move. She couldn't see the audience but she could hear them laughing. There was one face—her biggest rival, Fiona, laughing at her, pointing, howling.

In the dream, Grace worked harder. She tried relaxing and focusing and her legs began to move, but something about what she was doing was horribly difficult. She realized she was trying to skate uphill; the ice was slanted sharply upward. Her heart was pounding and her stomach ached, but she strove for poise. She looked down at her feet and the skates were gone, replaced by her Ugg boots. All the pressure of performance crippled her; all the fear of failure brought that lump back to her throat and she knew she couldn't do it, that it would be a disaster. Worse than that, she looked like a fool. She tried to skate in boots while covering her breasts where the costume had fallen away. And what costume was that? Some purple tulle thing that looked ridiculous!

Her heart raced and she woke up with a sob, gasping.

"Hey now," Troy whispered. "You're okay. You're safe."

She curled into him and tried to slow her pulse. She wanted to tell him she hadn't been afraid—she'd been back in that stressed place, the weight of performance anxiety bearing down on her.

Troy's arms were around her and she came back to her senses—it was just a silly dream. Nothing like that had ever happened to her. But she had felt those feelings before—the fear that she'd biff it and go slamming into the ice. Her mother would harp on it for ages, pointing out every flaw. In fact, even her best skating seemed not to be good enough.

She had so loved skating, yet every day of her life had been filled with the burden of anxiety and desperation.

Troy's lips were on her neck and she turned in his arms to meet his mouth with a kiss so hungry she all but consumed him. He growled deep in his throat and his hands were urgently moving. She parted her legs for him and with a deep groan he rolled her onto her back. He reached for a condom and then he reached for her. His fingers massaged her roughly; she was slick with desire. She pulled him to her, her hands on his butt. He was quickly inside her, pumping expertly. She couldn't be quiet. Her sighs turned to soft moans as she met him thrust for thrust.

This is the only place I want to be, she thought with a mixture of gratitude and despair. Her orgasm was so tight and hard Troy stopped breathing for a second. Then he slammed into her and pulsed with incredible power, making her come all over again.

They lay panting, clinging to each other. They were silent for a long time before Troy spoke. "That should help you sleep."

"I don't want to sleep," she said, gently stroking his back. "I just want this."

"Do you now?" he asked with a chuckle. He brushed her hair back from her face and kissed her again. "Sometimes you make me wonder if I have any control at all."

"It seemed like you had plenty."

"No, sweetheart. I definitely lost my head. Gracie, if we're going to get ahead of this thing with the note, you're going to have to be very brave. You're going to have to get back some of that feisty girl. Like the little witch I met on Halloween night—full of attitude. You're going to have to trust some people to help you."

She was quiet for a moment. He had no idea how strong she'd had to be! Since she was just a little girl.

But then she remembered she had won the gold by being pissed off and single-minded. She had decided to give it everything she had. "You really haven't seen me in action yet," she finally said.

In the morning, they proceeded as planned. After showering and eating a light breakfast, Troy made sure she was secure in the shop behind locked doors. At midmorning, Seth rang the bell and she let him in.

"Well?" she asked.

"I hope you consider this good news because I do. Your stalker, Bruno, is safely monitored in a group home in Hillsboro County, Florida. He takes his meds and visits his sister regularly and has not been out of contact with his sponsors for even twenty-four hours since entering the group home. According to his sister, he has not had delusions about you for over a dozen years, thanks to his medication."

"And that's good news?" she asked. "Then who's trying to drive me insane?"

"Easy, Grace. It's a mean prank. But there was no threat."

"What are you going to do about it?" she asked.

Seth frowned, she couldn't miss it. "I'm going to be vigilant. I'm going to tell Gina, Carrie, Waylan and Dr. Grant that someone left an anonymous note that frightened you and we don't know who or why.

I'm going to ask them to watch for strange or suspicious persons. That's about all I can do."

"Can't you do something more? Like check it for fingerprints or something?"

"No, Grace," he said. "I know you feel vulnerable and I'm going to keep my eyes open for this joker, but there hasn't been a crime. Your shop or residence hasn't been broken into, no one has threatened you. I have no reason to think you're in danger. I think you should be cautious and alert—definitely let me know if there's further contact—but even though it's suspicious and suggests a link to an old, resolved crime, at this point it's nothing more than an innocuous note. In itself, the note isn't even malicious. In fact, it could be a coincidence that the wording is the same."

"It's not a coincidence," she said.

"Stick with the locked doors for the time being, all right?"

"And look over my shoulder a lot?" she asked.

"Look, Grace, when those notes were originally sent by your stalker he had a plan that put you in jeopardy. He hasn't delivered this note. Do you have any reason to believe anyone means you harm?"

She thought for a moment before she shook her head.

"I think it's mean, doing that to you. I'll keep my eyes open. I'll watch the shop when I'm in town. I'll tell the other deputies to watch. But it just doesn't follow that whoever did this wants to hurt you."

"Of course you're right," she said. "But someone did do it to scare me. I can't imagine why."

"That's the mystery, isn't it?" he said. "You going to be all right?"

She shrugged. "I guess. I'm not going to let something like this beat me. It really pisses me off."

"Good. It should. Call me if anything happens that worries you. Anything at all."

"Thanks, Seth. I understand there's nothing much more that can be done. I appreciate the time you put into this."

He touched his forehead in a salute. "We'll be on duty, Grace."

When he left, she stepped out onto the sidewalk behind him. It was a sunny early April day, but the front of the shop wasn't as exciting as usual. She hadn't put out her sidewalk displays because some asshole had forced her in behind locked doors with a stupid little note. She turned, stomped back into the shop and dragged out her big wooden bunny for Easter. She cranked out her awning. Next, she pulled out a wicker basket filled with plastic daffodils and a sign that read Spring Sale! Then she unpacked her yellow, pink, mint-green and pale blue banner that read Easter Flowers! Order Now! She fixed it over the door. And finally she tore off the note over the doorbell.

Seth was right, she thought. It's mean and creepy but it's not an open threat. She would be cautious and safe. She refused to be insanely paranoid. If anyone crazy came at her, she'd beat him over the head with her ceramic tulip sculpture.

However, she did keep the back door locked, just to be sure.

* * *

Ray Anne painted her second bedroom, bought new linens for the bed and reupholstered the window cornices with matching fabric. She did it all herself, as she always had. Although she knew every handyman within a hundred-mile radius, she was also adept at home repairs and decorating. She knew how to hang wallpaper, install crown molding, replace wallboard and a dozen other things. In preparation for Ginger's arrival, she removed all her clothes, shoes and purses from the closet in the guest room— she had used it for her overflow wardrobe.

There was a small bath and shower in her bedroom and a larger bathroom with tub and shower beside the guest room. She cleaned under the sink and stocked it with bath gels, bubble bath, scented soaps, lotions and sponges. She put candles on the back of the commode and on the side of the tub.

She was nervous as a cat, waiting for her Gingersnap. She didn't know how she could help her get beyond this dark patch. *How does anyone get past it?* Poor Al had spent over thirty years trying to move beyond the death of his own baby son.

"I must have held on to that pain as stubbornly as an old bull," Al told her.

Ginger was driving down from Portland on Monday. At noon she still hadn't arrived and Ray Anne started to worry. She called her cousin and Dickie said she'd gotten an early start and should be there. Ginger didn't answer her cell phone when her father called or when Ray Anne called. At two, just about the time Ray Anne was thinking of asking Seth to check with the state troopers to see if there'd been any accidents, Ginger pulled up in front of Ray Anne's little house.

Ray Anne had seen Ginger four times in the months since the baby died. She hadn't been looking good then. She wasn't looking any better now. As Ray Anne walked toward Ginger, who was pulling her suitcase out of the trunk, she thought perhaps the girl was steadily deteriorating. She was far too thin, that was obvious even while she wore her coat. She was pale under her freckled complexion and her expression had become permanently downcast. Her hair was pulled back in a ponytail; the beautiful strawberry blonde locks had gone dull and dark. She obviously hadn't done a thing to it in months.

"There you are!" Ray Anne said cheerily. "I was starting to get worried!"

"I stopped to look at the ocean," Ginger said.

"Well, of course! I should have thought of that! But now you're here, let's get your things inside."

"I've got it," Ginger said, snapping up the pull handle.

"Is that all you've got? One bag?"

"It's all I need," she said.

"Well, I guess you'll be doing laundry then. Come on, let's get you settled." Ray Anne took the handle of the suitcase and pulled it up the walk and into the house. "I cleaned out the guest room and the bathroom, so it's all yours. I put some pampering things in there for you—soaps, lotions, candles. Did you bring a hair dryer?"

"I don't need one."

No wonder her hair was so flat and thin looking. She must be washing it and letting it dry any which way. And she wasn't using any product! "We can share mine. Or maybe we'll get you a new one."

"Really. I'm fine."

"Right in here," Ray Anne said briskly, pulling the suitcase into the newly painted and decorated bedroom. "Voilà!" she said, throwing an arm wide to showcase her decorating.

"Thanks," Ginger said, not noticing how pretty it was. "I'll just lay down for a while."

"No, ma'am," Ray Anne said, lifting the suitcase onto the bed. "We're going to unpack, hang and put away your clothes." She unzipped the suitcase and found the items inside had shifted because it wasn't even full. Or maybe they hadn't and Ginger had just haphazardly tossed them inside. She lifted out the first pair of wrinkled jeans. Then a second. Then a long-sleeved T-shirt. Then an old sweatshirt that she might have used when she painted something…years ago. And her underwear—pathetic.

"Oh, brother," Ray Anne muttered.

Ginger just sat on the bed. She didn't respond.

"Are we even related?" Ray Anne asked her. She lifted a dingy pair of granny panties and let them dangle from one finger. "Do we share any DNA at all?"

Ginger shrugged. "Just wasn't a priority, Ray. Why bother?"

Ray Anne sat on the edge of the bed and took one of Ginger's hands. "I'll tell you why we bother. Because there are things you can do to try to get beyond devastating pain. They might be small, stupid things, but they actually help a little. Things like fixing yourself up so you look better than you feel. Getting out helps—you have to live in this world. Work helps. Meaningful work, if possible, and that's something different for everyone, but keeping busy instead of lying in bed and making constant love to the hurt—that can help. Tell me something—are you taking anything?"

"Like what?"

"Like tranquilizers or antidepressants or anything?"

"Not anymore," she said. "They weren't working. And I kept thinking about swallowing the whole bottle."

Ray Anne gasped. "Jesus," she muttered. She wondered if she should hide all pills from Aspirin to hormones. And sharp objects. She stiffened her spine resolutely. "All right, I have to run a quick errand I put off while waiting for you to get here so you wouldn't find me gone when you arrived. I want you to put away your clothes in this chest and the closet. Then put the empty suitcase in the closet. Do that before you lie down. From what your daddy tells me, you've perfected napping and I'm willing to bet you're all caught up on sleep. I'll be back in fifteen or twenty minutes."

"All right," Ginger said, standing.

When Ginger hung her coat in the closet, Ray Anne noticed her jeans were sagging off her flat butt and her tennis shoes were beat-up. The girl was a complete mess. Her attire and body language were such a put off, holding back any well-intentioned person, it was as if she longed to go it alone and wallow in grief.

"Do you have my cell number?" Ray Anne asked.

"Probably," she said.

"Where's your phone?"

"I don't know. Probably in my purse. It's turned off."

"Why is it turned off?"

Ginger flashed her an angry look. "Because no one's going to call me! And there's no one I want to talk to!"

"Is that so?" Ray Anne asked without flinching. "Well, your father and I were trying to reach you to see if you'd had a problem on your drive and we went straight to voice mail, worrying us even more. Now, I can understand if you're avoiding calls, but is it either fair or kind to ignore people who love you and are concerned about you? If you want to do this to yourself forever, I don't suppose anyone can convince you otherwise, but your parents suffered a painful loss, as well, and I don't think they can deal with another one. I'm going to call them and tell them you arrived safely. Meanwhile, please turn on your phone. Charge it. Whatever. I'll be back in twenty."

Ray Anne, who never walked anywhere and was always seen in her little BMW, walked down the street, down the hill and into Carrie's deli. Carrie and Rawley appeared to be cleaning up. Customer traffic was usually at its lowest in midafternoon, heaviest for lunch and dinner. When Ray Anne walked in, Rawley automatically disappeared into the kitchen in the back of the deli.

"Well, hello," Carrie said.

"Call Lou and cancel dinner. Ginger just arrived and she's not fit to go out."

"Is she sick?" Carrie asked.

"She's horribly depressed. She can barely speak. The only thing more depressing than her personality right now is her wardrobe. Apparently it feels better to dress in poorly fitting rags. It's like sackcloth and ashes." She shook her head in misery. "I should have listened to myself. I can't help with this. She is way outside of my experience. I don't know what to do with her." She took a breath. "Can I please have a to-go dinner? Since we're not able to go out?"

"Sure. Now tell me what happened."

Ray Anne explained about Ginger's gaunt appearance, horrible clothing, turned-off phone and so on. "I was already very sad for her and about the baby. Of course I held that baby—he was a perfect baby! But it's been months and one look at her and you'd think it happened this morning. She's in terrible pain. Just terrible."

"She'll have to work through it, Ray. Everyone's grief time is different. Maybe you can get her into some kind of counseling or something."

"We'll look at that," she said. "First, I have to clean her up and feed her."

Carrie stood back from the deli case. Feeding people was her specialty. "What's your pleasure?"

"Something with carbs. And a big salad for me. God knows, I don't need fattening up. If my ass gets any bigger I won't be able to stay up on these heels."

Carrie laughed. "The chicken enchiladas are pretty irresistible. And I have some chips, salsa and guacamole."

"Perfect. And a salad. I can eat a little Mexican food and plenty of salad and she can eat a lot of chips and enchiladas and a little salad. And listen. Would you ask Lou about counselors?"

"I can do better," Carrie said. "When Ashley was on that downward spiral a couple of years ago, Lou found Gina a great counselor for Ashley. She specialized in young adults, but she might know someone to recommend for Ginger. Would you like me to ask Gina to give her a call?"

"Please," Ray Anne said. "I don't know if I'll be able to convince Ginger to go, but really—something has to be done to move forward. I don't know what else to do. And her daddy is right—she hasn't gotten any better."

"What have you done so far?" Carrie asked as she dished dinner into containers.

"Not much. I told her she couldn't take a nap until

her clothes were unpacked and she'd better turn on her phone or else. And…" She looked down somewhat shyly.

"I bought some lotions and stuff for her bathroom. I always feel better if I'm a little nice to myself. Baby steps," Ray Anne said.

Carrie smiled. "Just do what comes naturally to you, Ray. You're not a professional grief counselor but you know a lot about managing your own grief. And you're very sympathetic."

"Thank you," she said. "I'm trying not to mother Ginger, but I'm thirty years older than she is and even though I haven't been a mother, it kind of comes naturally."

Carrie passed the food across the deli counter. "Be yourself. You're a good woman and you love her."

"I do love her. She was my little angel." She dug around in her purse for money.

"Ah, on the house, Ray Anne. Tell her I'm sorry we're not going out tonight, but this is my contribution."

Eleven

Grace had always been capable of focus and discipline. She had amazing willpower and she thought with a clear head about what Seth had said. She reminded herself it was a note and not from the person who had threatened her fourteen years ago. She would be careful. Perhaps she'd be overly cautious for a while, but that was all right. She was not going to melt into a sniveling little girl.

In years past, when she was a teenager and the exhaustion or the other competitors or even her mother got the best of her, when she broke down, it got her nowhere. When that happened, when she *cried*, the abuse was even worse. The only thing that had ever worked for her was strength and grit. So she relied on that again. She focused on her abilities. She was small but very strong.

Troy was at the shop as soon as he was done with work. He had to knock on the back door because, feisty or not, she wasn't an idiot.

"I called Coop and told him I couldn't help at the bar this week because there's stuff going on."

"Let's not do that," she said. "Let's not panic and run scared."

He frowned. "You shook and had nightmares all night."

"Yeah, I hope I don't do that anymore. I'm much stronger and more sensible than that. Go help at the bar—I know how much you enjoy it. I think I'll get something from Carrie to warm up for dinner. If it'll make you feel better, I'll text or call you when I've closed the shop and gone upstairs. If you want to come by later, that's okay, but really, you don't have to. I think I'll be fine. I'll lock the back door and even slide a chair against it."

"This is a pretty sudden shift. What did Seth say to you?"

"Nothing so much—just that Bruno is not a threat and it was only a note, not a crime."

"Are you sure you're not in shock?"

She took a deep breath and leaned one hip against the worktable. "Sometimes I forget about my greatest accomplishments growing up because they weren't medals or ribbons or plaques. Do you know what one of the ESPN commenters said about me when I was fifteen? He said, 'That little girl is one hell of a fighter. Don't mess with her.'"

That made Troy smile. "You must regret leaving it sometimes."

"Never. I was done with that life. I did everything I could do. You can't imagine what it was like—I don't even expect you to try. No," she said, sliding her arms around his waist. "I like this life. And if I ever figure out who would try to screw it up with a scary little note, I'm going to make his life miserable."

"When I said I wanted you to be brave, I didn't mean that you should take any chances. I'll watch the shop while you go get some dinner for later. I want you to call me tonight. Then I'll come over when I'm off work."

"I love it when you come over. But you don't have to babysit me. You had a life before all this, a busy life. We can talk on the phone later, if you want to go home."

"I think I'll come over, if it's all the same to you. At least tonight."

"Then go home and change, bring your work clothes and laptop...you know the drill."

"Are you faking brave? Because of what I said last night?"

"No," she said with a laugh. "I'm faking brave because I just remembered it's how I get control. It's how I begin to feel brave. Now stay put—it shouldn't take me ten minutes to walk down to Carrie's."

Two days later, Troy decided to stop by the deputy's office after school before going to the flower shop. As luck would have it, Seth was there, sitting behind his desk, one foot propped casually on the desk while he talked on the phone. Another deputy, Charlie, seemed to be working at the computer on the desk behind Seth's. When Seth saw Troy he made excuses into the phone and disconnected.

"Hey," Seth said. "Everything all right?"

"Fine. I just thought I should tell you—that stuff I ordered came today. Grace texted me that she got it at the flower shop. Pepper spray and a Taser."

"Really," he said, standing up. "Mind if I look at it?"

"No, of course not. But it's completely legal."

"Sure. But I'd like to know what you could buy so easily and have delivered in just a couple of days. If you can, anyone can. I'd just like to know."

Troy shrugged. "Come on, then. There's a DVD with the package. Should be instructions and safety measures. I'll feel a lot more comfortable knowing Grace has something handy she can use to protect herself if...well, you know. She had that scare years ago."

"I don't think we're dealing with the same set of circumstances, Troy."

"I get that, but wouldn't you feel better, if it was Iris, knowing she had some kind of self-protection?"

Seth laughed. "Have you met Iris's left hook?" he asked. "I'm not sure I'd arm her on top of that."

"Grace needs a little something, if only for her confidence."

"Yeah? Well, be careful. Don't sneak up on her," Seth advised. "I wouldn't mind having a look at the DVD after you've seen it. If you don't mind."

"Not at all." He opened the shop's front door and yelled, "Gracie?"

"Troy! Come and see! You're not going to believe how cool this is! It even comes with a *holster*!"

He walked into the workroom and the box stood open on the table. Scattered about was packing material, extra Taser cartridges, two small pepper spray cartridges, a DVD and a catalog.

"Look at this!" she said, turning to one side so he could see the Taser affixed to a leather belt that was far too large. She took a gunfighter's stance, arms out at her sides. Then she did a fast draw, popped the Taser off the belt, pointed and...

Shot him.

She screamed and dropped the Taser while Troy felt the jolt go through him. He stiffened, trembled and down he went. His hearing was fine, even if he couldn't move his body. In fact, his hearing was a little too good—Grace wouldn't stop screaming.

"Troy! Troy! Troy! Oh, my God, Troy!"

All he could do was twitch on the floor.

Suddenly she stopped.

He heard her talking into her phone. "It's Grace at the flower shop! Send the doctor and hurry! I shot Troy! I electrocuted him! He might be dead!"

As the stinging shock passed, he lay still and pain free, except for the back of his head, which had hit the floor pretty hard. And his right thigh, where the Taser prongs hit. A few more inches and he'd have been a eunuch.

Seth crouched beside Troy, grinning. "Well. That works pretty good."

"Shut up."

"Great idea, Troy. Get a figure skater a stun gun."

"I said, shut up."

"Good thing it wasn't a Magnum." He chuckled. "I don't think she watched the DVD. What do you think?"

Troy groaned and struggled into a sitting position. There was a small amount of blood, very small, where one of the prongs stuck into his jeans, his flesh. He reached for it and Seth grabbed his wrist.

"Leave it, since Grace called for a doctor. Or I could take it out for you."

Then she was there, kneeling on his other side. "Oh, my God, Troy! It just fired itself!"

"Because you had your finger on the trigger! Don't you know you can't put your finger on the trigger?"

"I didn't! I mean, I didn't think I did. Oh, Troy, I'm so sorry! Scott's coming."

"Do you see where this is? I'm lucky he isn't going to pull it out of my dick! Didn't I tell you not to open the box? You could have neutered me!"

Seth smothered a chuckle as he stood. "I guess you turned it on, right, Grace?"

"The instructions said it wouldn't fire just because it was armed. You have to turn it on because it runs on batteries, but… Oh, never mind. I didn't mean to, I promise." Grace added some tears to her apology, hovering and begging for his forgiveness.

"All right, all right," he said. "I think you're perfectly safe from any potential attackers. Might want to work on your aim so you don't kill the poor bastard."

"Troy, really, I thought it would take a little pressure to make it fire! I can't believe I shot you! Oh, God, I'm so sorry. I would never hurt you!"

The shop door crashed open and Scott Grant, breathless, ran in carrying his medical bag.

"Take it easy," Seth said in a calm voice. "It was just a Taser. He's fine."

"*Just* a Taser?" Troy said. "It came a little close to the next generation of schoolteachers! Grace obviously has a shaky trigger finger."

Right behind Scott was Peyton and their office manager, Devon. Behind them was Carrie, who shouldn't be able to move that fast with her bad knees. Then crowding into the little shop was Waylan from the bar across the street and at least two of his customers and, in addition, every person who happened to be outside or even driving by when Scott Grant was seen running down the street with his medical bag.

Scott, panting, stopped in the workroom doorway to catch his breath. "Jesus, you took ten years off my life. I thought you shot him!"

"I did, but I shot him with this," Grace said, reaching for the Taser that lay on the floor where she had dropped it.

"No!" at least four people shouted at once.

Troy grabbed her and pulled her toward him. "Gracie, it's still got voltage. If you accidentally pulled the trigger again, you'd give me another blast."

"Oh, God! Troy, this isn't going to work. I can't be trusted with one of those things. I'm going to kill someone. I'd be better off with a road flare."

"Ever hear of the great Chicago fire?" Seth muttered to Scott.

"Shh, I forgive you already," Troy said. "Just don't touch it again until we figure it out."

Scott Grant crouched next to Troy, his open bag beside him. "Why didn't you take these prongs out?"

"Seth told me not to."

"We usually have to call medical for that," Seth said. "Not that I think it's necessary, but I figured…"

"Not complicated," Scott said, moving one slightly so it slid right out. They were shaped like small apostrophes and pulling it straight out could make it bleed a little, but wasn't likely to even require stitches. He then removed the second prong. "There. Feel better?"

"I'm fine," Troy said.

"I'm not," Grace said. "I'm not fine. I almost killed my boyfriend."

"Nah, not even close," Scott said, standing. "Want a Band-Aid for that, Troy?"

"Funny," Troy said, standing. "Let's joke around after you've taken your hit."

"I don't know how much physical damage was caused, but your mood is definitely affected," Scott said, smiling.

That's when Troy heard all the voices from the shop. *She shot him with the Taser. Worried about that note, so he bought her a Taser. It's just a Taser. Yeah? You ever been hit by a Taser? Damn near killed my cat with one of those! At least something interesting finally happened. Let's have a beer on that, should we?* And there was laughter all around as the shop emptied of everyone but Seth.

"Damn," Troy said, giving his leg a shake as if to bring the feeling back into it. "That sucker packs a punch!"

"I'm going to leave now if you think you can manage the situation without further injuries," Seth said.

"You're going to tell Iris, aren't you?" Grace asked.

Seth nodded. "I'm thinking of quitting early. I can't wait to get home."

"I'm never going to hear the end of this," she said. "I guess everyone knows about my note."

"They don't all know what it said or how it was written out. Just that it upset you and we're looking for a prankster. If gossip works like usual around here, I think you're probably safe." Then he smiled. "Have a nice evening."

Seth was home by five o'clock and Iris walked in right behind him. Iris laughed so hard at Seth's tale that she could hardly stay upright. "Oh, she's right, she's never going to hear the end of it. Poor Grace. How does that thing work? Let me see yours, Seth."

"Ah, no thanks, Iris. You never touch my weapons, right? Because that wouldn't be good. You don't know anything about them."

"Maybe you should train me," she suggested, then giggled again.

"You're doing just fine not touching."

"Aw, come on," she said, moving closer to him, sliding her arms around his neck.

Instead of arguing with her, he kissed her. Then he kissed her more seriously, sliding his hands over her butt and pulling her close. After a little more kissing, he said, "I have an idea…"

"Before supper on a Wednesday afternoon? Why, Deputy…"

"Are you expecting company?"

"Only your mother," she said. "But ever since she caught you in your boxers, she calls ahead if your car is home."

"Good. Troy said something interesting. He told Grace that a few inches to the left and she could have wiped out the next generation of schoolteachers and I thought, don't we have work to do?"

"I wouldn't call it work, exactly."

"Wouldn't it be easier to do naked?"

"Absolutely," she agreed. "But then we have to stay in bed for a while."

"I can do that. I'm very good at staying in bed with you. Are we making any progress on the next generation of deputies and school counselors?"

"I don't know, Seth. We've only stopped using protection for a few months and Peyton said to check with her if we have no results in six months. I'm doing my best. And you are definitely doing your best."

He kissed her again. "I love when you talk dirty."

She laughed. "I haven't started talking dirty yet. I just said you were doing your best..."

"I can do better," he said, and his voice had grown husky.

A half hour later, as they lay tangled in the sheets, Iris said, "That *was* better."

"That had to make a baby. That was good," Seth said. "Maybe two babies."

"I only want one at a time, if it's all the same to you."

"Are you hungry?" he asked.

"Yes, but I'm staying in bed for thirty minutes to give those little guys time to swim. Then we can get up and eat."

"We don't have to get up. I'll be right back." He found his boxers and disappeared.

Iris snuggled into the sheets, her head against the pillow. There were so many times, like now, that she couldn't believe her life had worked out the way it had. She'd loved Seth since she was just a girl, but they'd been estranged for seventeen years while they took different journeys. Hers took her to university and a postgrad program in counseling to bring her back to Thunder Point as the high school counselor. Seth had gone from the football field to a long recovery from injuries he sustained in a terrible car accident, but in the end his choice of law enforcement brought him home. And now he was hers again. All hers.

It wasn't very long before he was back. Iris had actually dozed a little. Seth held a tray with one plate that held two grilled cheese, bacon and tomato sandwiches, pickles, a glass of wine and a bottled beer, a bag of chips held tenderly under one arm.

"Here we go," he said. "It's not much, but it was fast and I bet it's good. Scoot over," he said. He put the tray between them and sat on the bed. He passed the wine to her hand and lifted his beer. "To us."

Iris brought the wine to her lips and to Seth's dismay, she sniffed. He took a big swallow of beer and when he looked at her again, tears were running down her cheeks. "Iris?"

Her nose turned a little pink. "This is all I've ever wished for," she said. A small sob followed.

"Grilled cheese?" he asked.

"You. You and me, together, in love, trying to make a baby. I didn't even hope for a baby. I thought that was impossible. Just you and me, that's all I ever wished for. I love you so much."

He frowned. Then he took her glass of wine from her. "Congratulations. I bet anything you're pregnant."

"What do you mean? You don't know anything."

"I do so. I listen to men talk about their wives. I don't want to—I hate all that talk—but it happens all around me. First their wives cry, then they throw up, then they get grumpy, then they nest, then they whelp." He put the wine on the bedside table. "Bet you anything," he said.

"Whelp?" she asked with a sniff.

"You know," he said, taking a big bite of grilled cheese. He chewed and swallowed. Then he grinned at her. "Bet I nailed you last week. I was *outstanding.*"

"You're an arrogant know-it-all," she said, reaching for a tissue.

"And you're pregnant." He pushed the tray toward her. "Have a sandwich, honey. And if you're still hungry, I'll make you another one."

Scott was working late so Peyton got the kids ready for bed and settled them with their tablets and movies in their beds. Then she collected the tablets and turned them off and kissed the kids. She cleaned up the tent the kids had made with blankets over the dining room table. She'd been in the tent with them for a little story time earlier.

She had her shower, put on soft lounging pajamas that were nice and warm. She lit a couple of candles in the darkened living room. She put wine-glasses out next to a bottle chilling in an ice bucket. But she turned on the lamp beside her on the couch to read for a while before Scott finished up in Bandon. It wasn't very late when he texted her. On my way. Need anything?

Just you, big boy.

Fifteen minutes later he came in from the garage and left his bag in the kitchen. When he took in the darkened room, the ice bucket, glasses and candles, he smiled at her. "Are you planning to seduce me?"

"Could be. Are you covered with blood and guts?"

"Nah. I washed up. Let's get on with the seduction!"

"No one ever accused you of being shy, did they?" Peyton said. She lifted the bottle out of the ice bucket, poured and handed him a glass. "I do have something to tell you. You know how we decided that I'd go off the pill but we'd use protection for a couple of months until my body got used to the idea?"

"Uh-huh. I might've gotten carried away once," he said.

"Actually, five times. At least. So, cheers," she said, clinking his glass. "I really don't mind when you get carried away. It's kind of fun."

He sipped. "Peyton, I think this wine is bad. It tastes sour."

"It's sparkling cider," she said. "You did it, you brute. You knocked me up before the wedding."

He grinned stupidly. "Peyton! That's wonderful!" Then he was stunned silent for a moment. "Crap," he finally said. "Your father is going to kill me. I'm a little terrified of your father, did I mention that?"

"Paco? He's all bluster. But, I think we won't tell him. Or Mama either, for that matter. Do you think you can keep your mouth shut around the grandmothers?"

"Oh, sure. I don't tell them anything. They're a pain in my ass. But it's going to be hard not to tell some of the guys. You know—Spencer, Coop, Seth."

"Try. Because at least two of those three have big mouths and they're coming to the wedding. It would be just like one of them to toast the bride and groom and baby. However, when I don't drink, someone's bound to ask."

"They know we're together. You can tell them you're five minutes pregnant. Just how pregnant are you?"

"Five minutes. I haven't missed a period yet but I peed on a stick."

"You did?"

"Uh-huh. Iris came in to set up a prenatal appointment. She's five minutes pregnant and it made me just wonder."

"Good for Iris! They want a baby! And by the way, we want a baby. This isn't going to screw up your plans, is it? I mean, the big wedding, the dress, the flowers, all that stuff? You're not going to get morning sickness at the altar or anything, are you?"

"No."

"And you're still planning to seduce me tonight?"

"Yes, Scott. I put your children to bed and when you've lost your mind on the sparkling cider I'm going to strip and make you crazy."

He leaned toward her, slid a hand under her sheet of black hair and pulled her closer. "I do love that. If you haven't folded up the tent, we could do it in there."

"I'd rather do it in bed."

He touched her lips with his. "I love you. Have I told you that lately?"

"Several times a day. And I love you, but apparently you have a real talent for procreation. I'm going to keep my eye on you."

"Thank you, Peyton. I really want children with you. At least a few."

"I agreed to one so far. Let's see how it goes."

"It's going to be great. Your family specializes in big herds. Your grandmother had the last child at forty-six."

"In your dreams, doctor hottie," she said, kissing him.

"Hmm. Do I have to drink this," he said, holding his glass up. "It tastes like shit."

She laughed. "If I have to be off wine for nine months, then shouldn't you? As a sign of solidarity?"

"Absolutely, I'll swear off wine if it makes you happy. Thank God, I'm a beer man. Now come on, enough talk about dietary restrictions—let's get you naked."

Troy asked Grace several times if it would be best to cancel his friend Denny's weekend visit. "No," she said. "In fact, it might be better to have things to do, people around. But, Troy, do you have to tell them I shot you?"

"No, I don't have to, but if we introduce them to anyone in town, they're going to find out."

"Oh, God," she moaned. "Things were so quiet, then…"

"All of a sudden," he agreed. "Well, it still isn't bigger than we are, babe."

The early April weather cooperated. Every day was sunny and bright except when those afternoon showers came in over the Pacific. The days had grown longer and Grace could keep the shop open until six and still close in daylight. The downside was that after Denny and Becca's visit, Troy was going to be needed more at the beach bar—people would start migrating to Cooper's for sunset. The weather was warmer, and more people were seen outside, walking rather than driving.

While it gnawed at Grace that someone could send her a note identical to the ones Bruno sent before capturing her, knowing he was under wraps brought her some peace of mind. And while she was loath to admit it, seeing that Taser take down her boyfriend gave her a little confidence. Aside from the confusion about a motive, she was quickly feeling calmer. She did not, however, wear the Taser on her belt. She handled it very carefully. She carried it in her purse and it was turned *off*!

On Friday afternoon at around five o'clock, Troy brought a lovely young couple to the flower shop to meet Grace. Denny was a tall, handsome man in his late twenties and his wife was a pretty blonde with the sweetest little baby bump. They introduced themselves, looked around the shop appreciatively and thanked her for welcoming them so nicely. And then Becca froze. Her mouth stood open slightly and she covered it with her hand. She stared at Grace, wide-eyed. "Oh, my God!" she said. "You're her! You're Izzy Banks!"

Twelve

It turned out that Becca Cutler had been hooked on figure skating and kept up with all the competitions. She loved it all, pairs, ice dancing, long programs, short programs. When it wasn't Winter Games, she watched national and world championships on ESPN. Becca and Grace were the same age. They literally grew up together. Grace admitted who she was.

After closing up the flower shop, they drove out to Cooper's so Troy could show his friends his other place of employment. "Not too different from your little bar in Virgin River," Troy said. "Just a different landscape."

Cooper and Denny shook hands like old friends. "Jack sends his best. Said to call him if you need anything."

"I need his cook if I'm going to get rich. Tell him to send Preacher," Cooper said.

"Like that'll ever happen," Denny said.

"Take a table, the weather's great. Beer on the

house for my friends. What can I get the little lady with that expectant look in her eye?"

"Just a noncaffeine cola, if you have it."

"Sorry, darlin', but everything here is high-test except the light beer."

"There's green tea in the cooler," Troy said. "I'll get you one."

"Can I have one, too?" Grace asked. "I'll drink along with the preggers, here."

Grace was greeted by a number of people as she and Becca went out on the deck, where it was still cool enough that they had to stay wrapped in their sweaters. The men stayed inside. Cooper brought the women some chips. He leaned down to whisper in Grace's ear.

"You doing okay, Gracie?"

"I'm fine, Coop. Thanks."

"If you need Troy next week, all you have to do is say so. We back each other up out here on the water."

"Thanks," she said. "I forget sometimes how great people are here."

"Never forget," he said, giving her hand a pat.

When he left, Becca was smiling. "This reminds me a little of Virgin River," she said. "Everyone is so bonded. I can see they all love you, Grace."

"I think I took that for granted. But tell me how you knew who I was?"

"Seriously? You were always my favorite. I watched you compete in all the big events!"

"How could I be your favorite?" Grace asked. "I didn't think I was anyone's favorite!"

"You were *everyone's* favorite!"

"No," she said, shaking her head. "I had the worst reputation in the business. People called me rich and snotty. My scores always suffered most because of my facial expressions! I never smiled enough for the judges."

"Really?"

"I thought everyone was rooting for Fiona Temple."

"She was the underdog. Underdogs always get attention, in all sports. But you? You were gifted, people said so all the time. A natural on the ice. And scared. You were just a scared kid. But in the Vancouver Games, you nailed it. You owned that competition—there was no contest. There hasn't been a competition like that since. Every newcomer is compared to you. Fiona was a good skater, but a total poser. They caught shots of her cursing or scowling all the time, showing she wasn't the sweet darling she pretended to be for interviews. I bet she was mean."

Grace was stunned. "As a snake," she said. "People knew?"

Becca shrugged. "I bet they did. Don't you remember what people said about you? Your reviews? Kiddo, you stole the show."

She had to shake herself. She only remembered the very critical comments.

"Why did you quit?" Becca asked.

"It's a long story, but it boils down to this—I couldn't take the pressure anymore. I'd gone as high as I could go and I was exhausted. I like my life better now, hard as that might be to understand."

"Not hard at all," she said with a laugh. "A good life, a good man like Troy? That's more than a lot of people have."

"Tell me about you and Denny," Grace said.

"Talk about a long story!" she said. She launched happily into her tale of on-again, off-again romance that finally stuck after she chased Denny to Virgin River and captured him with a broken ankle. She was getting to the wedding and her decision to stay in the mountains with the love of her life when Denny and Troy joined them on the deck, adding bits and pieces to her story. The sun was sinking in the sky when Troy announced that he'd made reservations at Cliffhanger's for dinner.

"Think about what you'd like to see and do while you're here," Troy said. "The weather is supposed to be good all weekend and the coast is beautiful."

"I can think of one thing I'd absolutely die to do," Becca said. "I'd so love to see you skate, Izzy...I mean Grace!"

Troy put an arm around Grace's shoulders. "Gracie doesn't skate anymore," he said.

"Actually, I do," Grace said. "There's a rink in North Bend where the owner lets me skate before they open in the morning. It's early, though."

"Oh, my God, that would be so awesome," Becca said excitedly.

Troy put a thumb and finger on Grace's chin, turning her face toward him. "You're skating again?"

"Now and then. Secretly. Just because, you know…"

"I *don't* know."

"Because I've been skating my whole life, but for the past five years not for an audience. Except the owner of the rink."

"Why didn't you tell me?" he whispered.

"Because I don't want to coach or compete and I wanted you to believe that."

"Gracie, I believe everything you tell me. So, you'll skate for me now?"

"Would you like that?"

"Only if it feels right to you."

"I think I'd like to. If you promise you can love a flower girl."

He just smiled at her.

That Friday night was more fun than Grace had had in years. Seth and Iris were at Cliff's, sitting up at the bar eating crab cakes, so they picked up their plates and joined them. Cliff teasingly asked Grace if she was packing tonight and the story of the Taser came out to the hysterical laughter of everyone but Grace. After Denny and Becca were dropped back at Troy's apartment, Grace and Troy went to her loft, to bed. But there was no sleeping. They cuddled close and talked late into the night.

Grace was enchanted by Troy's friends; she loved what they seemed to have together. "Do we have anything close to that?" she asked him.

"Close," he said. "If I'm not kidding myself, I think we're building something that could be solid."

"You don't talk about the future with me," she said. "Do you want something like what your friends have? A marriage? Children?"

"Of course I do. But, Gracie, we've been together three months and change. That's not long enough. There are a few things we still have to sort out."

"Like what?"

"Well, let's start with how many more secrets you're keeping."

"Troy, I'm not keeping secrets!"

"I didn't know you were skating. Couldn't you trust me with that?"

"Oh, Troy, that's not a secret. I've only been on the ice a few times since right after Christmas. There hasn't been time! You've kept me too busy. And besides, I only do a little skating now and then to keep in shape."

"But why didn't you mention it? That's something I would have told you."

"I don't know. I guess because I don't want anyone to say I shouldn't give it up. I know it's something I'm good at, but everything that goes with it…"

"Grace, you could have told me that."

"I'm sure there are plenty of things you haven't told me," she said hopefully.

He shook his head. "I can't think of anything. Nothing that has an impact on us. I'm just glad Becca brought it out of you because I can't wait to see you perform. And I think if we're just patient, as we get closer, you'll realize you don't have to be afraid of how I'll react."

She wasn't so sure about that.

* * *

Spending time with pregnant Becca brought Grace back to reality. She was sidetracked, busy, and she realized she still hadn't gotten her period and couldn't start the pills yet. She suddenly realized it must be late. She hadn't thought about it—life had been too crazy. First the note came, then she almost killed Troy with the Taser and then his friends came for a weekend visit…

And now she lay in his arms listening to him whisper his love, as well as his concern that she kept things from him.

Grace dug out her tights and skates before first light. She had a flouncy little blue skirt and pulled her hair back into a ponytail. There was a time she had as many pairs of skates as other girls had shoes, with one pair she loved best. One that brought her luck. That was the only pair she had kept.

Troy, Becca and Denny drove to the rink in North Bend at seven on Saturday morning. Grace took the flower van so she could work for a while after the skating. The rink would officially open at ten. Becca was wriggling with excitement. Grace explained that she had to stretch and warm up before she could do any real skating. "And please remember, I haven't trained in years. I'm not on top of my game. Just a few tricks, that's all I have."

Jake Galbraith met them at the door. "Well, an audience? That holds promise."

"It's just a favor for a friend," she said. "It's still private."

"And I still hope you'll train the younger girls one day. It would be a dream come true for them."

"I wouldn't make a good coach," she said.

"You'd make a phenomenal coach," he said. "You want some music?"

"If it's not too much trouble."

Grace took her time warming up. She stretched out on a mat in the girl's locker room, then laced up her skates and raced around the rink a few times, doing front and back crossovers, a few jumps. The music came on, her Gershwin training music, and she started with a few easy moves, working up to the more difficult jumps and spins. She took a spill but got herself up and carried on. She didn't look at her audience but sprayed the ice in their direction a couple of times. She was lost in back crosses, front crosses, figure eights, spins and axels.

Then Alicia Keys blasted into the arena and Grace put on a show. She didn't think about anything but skating. She could lose herself so easily. She didn't try anything fancy, all she wanted to do was make it pretty for Becca. And for Troy. If she were up to speed there would be triple axels and risky jumps, but she was smart enough to know she'd only hurt herself by taking ridiculous chances.

The reason she kept skating was simple. When there was no competition, she felt free, beautiful and fearless. She loved what she could do on the ice.

She'd been on the ice about a half hour, but steady

and hard. She skated around the rink to cool down, then she made her way back to her audience, smooth and sleek, hands on her hips.

"Not much, but that's all I have without training," she said.

"That was awesome," Becca said. "I would give anything to be able to skate, even a little bit."

"Tell you what—when you're not carrying around a little bump, we'll get you on skates. It would take about fifteen years of hard training to do some of those moves, but there are some easy things I can show you."

"I would love that so much."

Grace looked at Troy and he was smiling. "I guess I understand why people try to get you to skate professionally again. Or coach."

"I think that was a compliment, so thanks. But I really like what I'm doing now. And I have to be a drudge now—you guys go play. I'm going to have to open the shop for at least a few hours today. I can catch up with you later. You're in good hands—Troy is the fun coach."

"Thank you, Grace," Becca said. "I know you wouldn't have done that for just anyone."

"It was time to share that part of me with Troy," she said. "And now I have to get into the flower business."

"Do you need me?" Troy asked.

"Nah. It's a sunny Saturday morning. I'll let you walk me to my van, though."

"We're going to see some more of the coast since

we're this far north. Then tonight I'm cooking for us," Becca said. "Get your flower chores done and this evening you're going to relax and let me pamper you."

"Just a word of warning. When Troy tries to talk you into getting closer to the really big waves, don't do it."

"Enough," he said.

When Grace had her boots on, she left her usual hundred dollars with Jake for his scholarship fund. At the van, Troy gave her a kiss that he didn't seem to want to stop. She liked that so much.

Thirteen

Grace prepared a special order of four expensive centerpieces for a customer. An exclusive golf resort in Bandon had a guest who was throwing a party in one of the spacious cottages and wanted a delivery on Sunday afternoon. She could have told them she was closed on Sunday, but the resort was a regular customer, had an account with her and it was an easy five hundred dollars. She made up the arrangements on Saturday and put them in the cooler, then enjoyed dinner with Troy and his friends at his apartment. After dinner they played poker, and she cleaned house. She told Troy she was going to be closed on Sunday as usual but would make a delivery to the resort in Bandon in the afternoon.

"Becca and Denny are leaving around noon and spring break is next week—I'm off. I'll go with you. I love that place. Someday I might even be able to afford to play golf there. Once, though. I'll only be able to afford it once."

They set out at about one o'clock on Sunday. The resort was a beautiful place with lodges, cabins and rooms, not to mention fine dining and gorgeous facilities that could be reserved for everything from weddings to business meetings. There were three golf courses and it was expensive. People traveled from all over the country to stay there. And they liked Grace's flowers. They didn't use her all the time, but when a guest had a special function that required flowers, they recommended her. She billed the resort and they paid promptly.

She had the unit number for the cottage where the flowers were to be delivered and she knew her way around the country club. As they drove through the property, she had to slow for a couple of deer crossing the road.

"Cottage?" Troy asked.

"I know," she said, laughing. "I looked it up online. Living room, four bedrooms, galley kitchen, fireplaces in every room, plus four bathrooms. And a view."

"I'd kill to live in a house that big," he said.

She backed up to the unit. "You take one, I'll take one and we'll go back for the other two. Try not to gawk too much."

"It'll be hard."

She was proud of the flowers she'd put together— lilies, orchids, bird of paradise, roses, baby's breath and greenery. She balanced her arrangement on one hand and rang the bell. Troy waited right behind her with his flowers. In a moment the door opened.

Grace looked into the blue eyes of Winnie Dillon Banks and dropped her floral arrangement. The ceramic dish shattered and water splashed on her jeans, but the flowers stayed in a lump because she had fastened them into the base with tape.

"Mother!"

"Izzy," she said smoothly.

"Holy shitballs," Troy said.

There stood the indomitable Winnie, small like Grace, ivory skin, black hair and red lips. She could double for Snow White. Except for the expression, which was not sweet. No, he couldn't see Winnie singing to the birdies in the forest. But she was so beautiful. And she radiated power.

Troy noticed that Grace began to tremble a little. She must feel so vulnerable in front of her mother.

"Please come inside, Izzy," she said. "I'll arrange for that to be cleaned up."

"What are you doing here? Why?"

"I need to see you. Talk to you. You can send your helper away. I'll make sure you have transportation."

"He's not my helper! He's my *boyfriend*! What the hell is this? Why didn't you call me, tell me you were in the area?"

"Because you wouldn't have seen me," she said.

"Precisely. Because I am dead to you, remember?"

"Look, I take it back. I take it all back. Izzy, you have to give this a chance. I only want to help you!"

"Fine. You'd be helping by acting like a normal mother. That means you communicate. You call and ask if I'm available to visit with you. And if this is about returning to professional skating, there's no need to waste your time."

"I only want what's best for you. I want you settled! Let me help."

"I am settled!"

"Working in a flower shop!"

"*My* flower shop, my business, that I built on my own!"

Grace stooped and began to pick up the flowers, sans ceramic dish. She stood, holding most of the arrangement, and kicked the broken pieces off the walk and into the bushes. "Where do you want this?"

"The patio?" Winnie said, standing aside.

Grace walked in and Troy followed her. Winnie tried to stop him by holding out her hands for the flowers he carried. "I'll take that," she said.

He ignored her and put them down on the first available surface, the small breakfast table.

A woman stood near the patio doors. She was around fifty, very short reddish-brown hair, casually dressed in slacks and a sweater.

"Thank you, Virginia, you can go back to what you were doing. And you can leave us, young man. This business is between me and my daughter."

"I'm not leaving," he said.

"Just tell me what you want, Mother," Grace said when she came back from the patio.

"I'm not comfortable talking in front of a stranger."

"Oh, forgive me, Winnie," Grace said. "This is my boyfriend, Troy Headly. He came with me to help me deliver these bogus flowers. You might as well spit it out because I'm going to tell him everything we say to each other anyway."

Winnie sank into the nearest chair. "I thought we could have a conversation." She appeared to be near tears. "You're all I have left."

"That isn't my fault. I'm done skating, I haven't changed my mind about that."

"There are other options. I get emails and calls all the time. You could report on the competitions. CBS or ESPN would take you to the Games! You could coach! You could consult! Hell, the committee would be thrilled to have you! There are so many things…"

"No," she said. "No, no, no. I'm done. I don't want to coach, don't want to push young girls the way I was pushed! I don't want to report on the sport, critique and label figure skaters the way I was labeled. I don't want to consult or serve on any related committees."

"But you still skate!"

Grace was stunned. *How did she know?* "For pleasure, to keep in shape, and that's all. I don't want to skate professionally or work in the industry."

"But why? It's what you know!" Winnie said pleadingly. "It was our life!"

"Because I don't love it enough to give so much of myself. I'm very grateful that I had such wonderful opportunities, but it's time to move on. I'm retired from that life. I have a new life."

Winnie stood. "You'll have children," she said, her voice shaking a little bit. "A daughter. She'll be born with it, like you were. Will you forbid her?"

"If I'm lucky enough to have a daughter someday, I'll support her, but I'm not going to ride herd on her twenty-four hours a day. I'm not going to expect her to live out *my* dream. I'm going to tell you for the hundredth time, the only way we can communicate is if you give this up!"

"Are you really happier, Izzy? Living in a tiny room over a flower shop, toiling seven days a week to make centerpieces for people you don't even know? You have a legacy. Your time is nearly up—if you wait many more years, these opportunities will dry up and you'll be forgotten!"

"Only if there's a God," Grace said. She whirled around and left the house.

Troy just watched her go, not knowing what to do. When Grace came back with another floral arrangement, he caught on. Of course, even though this was a ruse, she would leave the flowers and the resort would pay her and bill Winnie. She put her large and beautiful arrangement on the coffee table and went back to the van.

It was as if his feet were glued to the floor. He was mesmerized by Winnie, dressed in a silk pantsuit in a rose color, complete with jewelry that was daunting. Diamonds on her fingers, gold on her wrists. When Grace said her mother was rich, he really couldn't make a mental picture of it, but he was getting there now. It wasn't just the clothing or the classy digs she could easily afford, it was the power she thought she had. Winnie speaks and the world comes to heel.

He had no experience with the wealthy. At least

not that he was aware of. There were business owners in town who must be doing well. Cooper was building houses on the hill, so he must be pretty set. Cliff owned the restaurant and a goodly share of the marina, so he had heard.

Grace looked very much like her mother, but he couldn't imagine her becoming this person. Grace was soft and loving; she wasn't controlling or manipulative. Not his Gracie.

Grace came back with the final floral arrangement. Tears were running down her cheeks. She put it down on the coffee table beside the last one. Then she looked at her mother. "I know what you've done, you know." Winnie stiffened as if slapped. She was clearly stunned by this statement, or maybe by the tears. "You placed an order for flowers that you knew I wouldn't be able to resist and asked for them to be delivered on Sunday, when the shop was closed, when I had no delivery help so I would be forced to come to you. Why, Mother? Why couldn't you just love me for myself? Why did you only love me for the gold medals?"

"Izzy, why do you act like it was a curse? We conquered the *world*!" Winnie said. Her expression was pleading. No, it was *yearning*. "Because of your skill, the training the other athletes couldn't afford, because of the dedication, the commitment I made to training, travel, everything you needed to get to the top, we had the dream. My parents didn't care. They paid the bills but never believed in me the way I believed in you. But together, we did it! We were the most powerful mother and daughter in women's figure skating in the world! It meant everything to me. I couldn't do it, but with my help you could."

Grace shook her head sadly. "I'm so sorry for you, Mama," she said quietly. "I love you, but I'm never going to change my mind."

"All right, then!" Winnie shouted. "Stay. Send him away, stay awhile and let's just talk."

Grace shook her head. "Maybe some other time. Sometime when you haven't tried to trick me or back me into a corner."

Grace turned and went back to the van. Troy followed, slowly closing the door as he left the cottage. *My God*, he thought. *No wonder Grace couldn't trust anyone. The people who should be most protective and devoted, like her mother, used her.* He caught up with her just as she was getting in the driver's side.

"Let me drive for you, babe," he said, reaching for the keys.

She wiped at her eyes. "No. Thank you, but no. I'm fine."

He hurried around to his side, buckling in. "Well, that was pretty terrifying," he said. "I think I understand now."

She gave a little hiccup and had to wipe her eyes again. She started slowly driving away from the cottage. "Poor little rich girl?" she asked.

"I think Winnie is the impoverished one. She has no idea all she lost."

"If you win gold medals in the end, you're not allowed to complain about how hard life is. It's self-pitying. Winning is hard and the cost is high. Even if you throw in a bad reputation, a lawsuit, constant pressure, a couple of stalkers, a kidnapping and—" She stopped talking. Then she slammed on the brakes. Troy braced a hand on the dash just before hitting his head. She turned wild eyes toward him. "Shit!" she said. Then she threw the car into Park, unbuckled, got out and ran down the street, back to the cottage.

Troy was too shocked to move for a moment. Then he jumped out and followed her, leaving the van abandoned in the middle of the road, still running. He chased her right to the cottage. Grace barged in without knocking. Her mother sat in the chair.

"My God," Grace said. "How could you do that to me? Are you really that selfish?"

"Grace, what's going on?" Troy asked.

"The note," she said, but she looked at Winnie, not Troy. "She sent it. To scare me so I'd come home."

Winnie didn't respond. She raised her chin defiantly.

"Are you really crazy? As in, need-medication crazy? Or have you absolutely no shame? Your only child? The child who gave you what you wanted, you would do this to me? I was terrified!"

"Nothing happened, did it?" Winnie said.

Grace shook her head. "I think it might take me a lifetime to recover from you."

"I gave you everything! I gave you my whole life!"

"Well, I'm giving it back to you. Leave me alone."

Grace turned and marched back to the van. Troy had to jog to catch up.

"Okay, I am driving," he said, pushing her around to the passenger side of the van. "You're really in no shape."

She didn't argue with him. She silently stared through her window while he navigated the winding road out of the resort, past woods, oceanfront, golf courses and three large clubhouses. He didn't say anything and heard the occasional sniff coming from her side of the van.

"All right, look, lots of people have crazy families," he finally said. She didn't respond. "Most, I think," he added. "In fact, as dysfunctional goes, most families have bigger and tougher issues than a rich mother who pushed you to win gold medals. So, your heart is a little broken, but you're an adult and can decide for yourself how you want to live your life. Think about what some people deal with—death, divorce, abuse, addiction, all kinds of dark secrets. Your mother pushed you and had her own agenda but she never physically hurt you, right? It's emotional abuse, I get that, but, Gracie, honey, you're okay. You're better than okay. You have your head on straight, you're a good, kind person, you know what's really important in life. So she's a pain in the ass. You don't have to deal with her if you don't want to. And if you do want to, demand your boundaries. You know?"

She turned to look at him. "Do you?" she asked. "Do you have dysfunction in your family?"

He laughed. "My immediate family seems reasonably sane. Or maybe we're just used to each other. We lived on a shoestring. Paycheck to paycheck. We got by. It turned my mom into a really good money manager. But in the extended family we have some real interesting characters. My dad's dad was married five times. If you knew him, you'd find that hard to believe—there's nothing all that special about him. My dad has twelve siblings, none of them full siblings, all halfs and steps. Some of them are real losers—money issues, chronically unemployed. One's a scam man—we give him a wide berth. They're always looking for handouts—makes my dad crazy. One of my mother's aunts is a hoarder and the other one keeps cats. Like twenty or thirty cats. We visited them both exactly once. I think there are some serious mental health issues at work there. There's one of those 'funny uncles' somewhere in the family tree—he was not allowed to visit. I'm told my maternal grandfather smacked around my grandmother—my mother said it could get pretty nightmarish when she was a kid. She said if my dad ever raised a hand to her she'd just shoot him. I take it he never did. My dad is kind of a big, handsome, sweetheart of a guy—I guess he inherited the side of my grandfather women fell in love with, but he's managed to be married only once. My mom, though, was married for a very short time when she was real young. Married for a year or something. She divorced her first husband. She never liked to talk about it. I don't think I even knew until my sister, Jess, got married at nineteen and my mother lost her mind, terrified that Jess was headed down the same path. Jess is fine. My mom didn't marry my dad until she was thirty."

"But you had a normal childhood," she said.

"Well, I guess. I don't appear to be scarred. I don't have any medals, either. And I've never been to Russia or China."

"It wasn't what you think. It was work."

"I know. I'd love to see your passports sometime. You're going to think about this for a while and you're going to realize you can deal with her now. She didn't love you enough and she was selfish. She neglected you in ways that still hurt, but you're whole and strong. You're all right. You won't be like that. Because of that experience, you'll be a completely different kind of mother."

"You sure about that?"

"I'm confident. But I want to suggest one thing. It'll be hard because right now you're bruised. I suggest you think about all the things you *had*. You've been putting a lot of focus on what you *didn't* have. Your mother doesn't love you the right way, but she loves you." He reached across the console for her hand. "You have a chance to write the script here, Gracie. You write the life you want. In fact, I don't really get it—you're completely sane. How'd that happen with that prima donna of a mother?"

"Years of therapy," she said. "It was sports therapy, but you can't dump the phobias and anxieties and neuroses without some good old-fashioned counseling. And there was Mamie—sweet, loving Mamie. She worked for my mother and she coddled me."

"That explains a lot," he said.

"I don't want to do all the things that I, on the receiving end, couldn't bear."

"I understand completely," he said.

"I want an ordinary, happy life," she said. "I am not lazy."

"I like your life," he said. "I like the life you envision."

When they finally got back to town, Troy drove the van into the alley behind the shop. No need to park in the front of the store anymore—there was no danger from the mystery man of the note. His Jeep was back there anyway.

"Troy, I think I need some time alone," she said. "I hope you understand. I feel pretty pathetic right now."

He leaned toward her and gave her a small kiss. "Don't work this too long, honey. Lots of people have superannoying mothers."

"I know. But I need a little time. And there's no need to worry that anyone is threatening me."

"Let's at least talk later," he said. "I'll call you."

Troy didn't have to think about it long. He went back to his apartment, cleaned up and changed clothes and drove back to Bandon. He entered the resort property on a guest pass at about six o'clock. There was no answer at Winnie's cottage and he asked himself where she might be. He drove around a little bit, thinking. There were five restaurants on the property—a couple of clubhouse restaurants and then fine dining. He went to the one with the view of the ocean.

The maître d' greeted him. "I'm here to meet Mrs. Dillon Banks," Troy said smoothly as if this visit was planned.

"I wasn't aware she was expecting a guest. This way, sir."

She had a table near the window and she was alone. Her table was a bit secluded from the other diners. She wasn't eating. She had her fingers wrapped around a drink and she looked pensively out the window.

"Mrs. Banks," he said.

She looked up at him.

"May I join you for a few minutes?"

"I suppose this has something to do with my daughter. Yes, Mr. Headly. Have a seat. Have a drink."

"Thank you," he said, pulling out the chair opposite her. The waiter was instantly beside him. "Bring me whatever Mrs. Banks is having."

"So, is Izzy all right?"

"She's a little rattled, but she's resilient. You'll have to forgive me, Mrs. Banks—it's hard for me to think of her as Izzy. She's Grace to me."

"Grace. Yes," she said, sipping her drink. "What do you do for a living, Mr. Headly?"

"I'm a high school teacher. And a part-time bartender at a local beach bar. Not exactly a high-profile profession, but I find teaching rewarding."

"And your relationship with Izz…Grace? Is it serious?"

"Yes," he said. "I'm very serious about her, though we don't have marriage plans. I'm not rushing into anything. That doesn't mean I'm hesitant. It just means we deserve time. Tincture of time, my grandmother used to say."

"Are you hoping for a big inheritance?" she asked forthrightly.

"Until very recently, I didn't know anything about Grace's family. Until this very moment, inheritance never crossed my mind." He laughed uncomfortably. "By the looks of you, such an event is a very long way off."

She didn't make eye contact. She lifted her drink and took a sip. Her hand trembled and she used her other hand to help stabilize it.

His drink arrived quickly. He took a sip. He made a face. "What is this?"

She actually smiled. "A Manhattan. With bitters."

"Delicious," he said, putting it down.

She chuckled in spite of herself. "Well, let's have it, shall we? Why are you here? What do you expect me to say?"

"I've never seen two women more adept at button pushing, and I have a sister and mother. They've had their share of standoffs. But what I saw a couple of hours ago was brutal. So, here's my question. What's it going to take, Mrs. Banks? Is it possible for you to have some kind of decent relationship with Grace?"

She thought for a moment. "I should be having this conversation with my daughter."

"Of course you should, but you haven't. Grace is unhappy and if I'm not mistaken, you're unhappy. There must be a way."

"Look, I don't expect you to understand."

"That there's baggage? That you have a history of conflict? That finding a compromise is difficult? Try me. I've mediated some legendary arguments in my time. Right now, I have at least fifty teenage girls in my classes. Go ahead, lay it on me."

She took another sip. "I've made mistakes with my daughter, but this time I can't afford to make another mistake."

"Sending her that note…"

"It was wrong. I shouldn't have done that. I want my daughter to come home, Mr. Headly. It's imperative that she come home. But I don't want her to come out of pity."

"For a visit?" he asked.

"For a very long visit. In a rash moment I thought if she felt unsafe on her own she would let me help her. I made a mistake."

"She's safe. And I don't think she needs help. She was pretty clear—she doesn't like the career choices you suggested. She's really good at what she does. And she's happy."

"Mr. Headly—"

"Mrs. Banks," he said, leaning toward her. "My name is Troy. For just a minute, let's pretend we're friends and that we trust each other. At the least, let's assume we both have Grace's happiness and safety as our shared priority."

She took another bolstering drink. Her hand continued to shake a little. "Troy. I have money. Family money. Taking care of it is complicated. With money comes predators. With old money there is responsibility. When that money is Izz—Grace's, I frankly don't care if she spends it, gives it away, puts it to work or does what I've been doing—preserve it and grow it. But I don't want her to be robbed or to lose it because of her inexperience. It's time for Grace to trust me. To let me show her how to manage. She has absolutely no experience in the management of wealth."

"She managed to buy a business and operate it at a profit," he said.

"Please. Don't be naive. Her father left her a trust. She used it to buy that flower shop."

Troy sat back in his chair. "What has that got to do with skating or broadcasting or coaching?"

"I thought it would be best if she chose a career path with some longevity in a field she loved. But she's adamant…"

"You're not going to win that one," he said. "I don't know why you can't open a dialogue about what it will one day take to manage your old money. She doesn't have to coach or work for the media for that to happen. And, for God's sake, this is not urgent."

Winnie Banks pierced him with her cold blue stare. "Mr. Headly. Troy. I wanted Grace to come to me out of loyalty and love. I had planned to tell her once we were talking again—there isn't much time. I'm ill, Mr. Headly. I have ALS. The symptoms are getting stronger every day."

He was speechless. She was a young woman, early fifties, he guessed. She appeared strong, except for the tremor. She was beautiful and willful, but with ALS, the mind would be strong until the body finally gave out.

"You have to tell her," he finally said.

"Of course," she said. "At once. I've written a letter. I wrote it before we had our altercation today. I was going to have my driver take it to her tomorrow but if you're willing, you can give it to her."

A bellman came to their table pushing a wheelchair. "If you're not ready, I can come back anytime you like," he said.

"It's fine, Bruce. I'm ready." She transferred herself into the chair. "Will you? Take my daughter a letter?"

He nodded, numb from the news. "Mrs. Banks, I'm sorry."

"The letter is in my room. Can you pick it up?"

A few minutes later, Winnie was resettled in her cottage. Virginia, who was a maid or assistant or keeper of some kind, was there to assist her, some fresh fruit and cheese put out on her small breakfast table. The letter was on the coffee table, addressed but not stamped. She put it in his hand.

"Are you sure this is ready?" he asked her.

"It begins with an apology," she said, reassuring him. "That's something easier to do in a letter, I've found. Easier than while facing her anger."

Fourteen

Troy hadn't liked the Manhattan that he'd had with Winnie but he could really use a drink. In fact, a drink in a dark bar sounded like just the thing. He didn't feel like running into friends so that eliminated Cliff's and Cooper's. He parked in front of Waylan's and went inside.

"How about a Crown. Neat," he told Waylan. "And then another one."

The letter to Grace was in the center console in the Jeep. There was only one dim light shining in Grace's loft. She needed time alone but he was going to have to go to her. There was no way he could have that conversation with Winnie and not tell her; no way he could be in possession of that letter and not give it to her right away. But he thought it was reasonable that he have a couple of belts for both his nerves and need of courage.

So he sipped slowly, dreading what had to be done. What a complicated mess. There was a lot of rage between Grace and Winnie, and now they were going to throw heartbreak into the mix. Heartbreak and impending death. And an inheritance? This was quickly getting bigger than he was. He was beginning to wish he hadn't made that drive up to the resort to confront Winnie. It might be easier not knowing. But he had thought he could help; he had thought he could be the voice of reason. The way he saw it, Grace shouldn't have such a hot button at the mere suggestion she think about a career in the figure skating industry. And Winnie should drop the subject after being told about fifty times it was out of the question.

Here were two stubborn, pigheaded women.

It was nine-thirty when Troy called her. Grace answered sleepily.

"I miss you. Are you calmer now?" he asked.

"I am. I stomped around and cried for a while, then I think I nodded off. I'm exhausted."

"Let me come over and hold you. I don't know how to sleep alone anymore," he said.

"Okay, but you have to be quiet and sleepy. I don't want to talk," she said.

"I don't blame you."

He drove around to the alley access and parked behind the Pretty Petals van. He used his own key to get in and found the loft was dark. There was an empty wineglass on the coffee table. He took the envelope from his jacket pocket and left it on the small table in her galley kitchen, left his jacket over a chair and went to the bedroom. She stirred and sat up.

"Hi," she said. "Can't stay away from me, can you?"

"I sure can't," he said, taking off his shoes. His pants and shirt quickly followed and he slid into bed. She rolled right into his arms and kissed him.

"Wow. Whatever that is on your breath, it's powerful."

"I needed a stiff drink," he admitted.

"Winnie can have that effect on people. Tell me the truth. Did she make you want to run for your life?"

"No." He pulled her into his arms. "I can see the challenge, however. Close your eyes. You don't want to talk, remember?"

"I'm wiped out," she said with a yawn, snuggling against him. "You are such a good pillow. I don't think I know how to sleep alone anymore, either."

"Just rest, baby. I'm right here."

Troy didn't sleep all that well, but it felt good to know that Grace did. She snored, a sure sign she was deep into sleep. He woke at five-thirty, just like most mornings, and after lying quietly for a while, he got up. He brewed coffee and waited for her to wake up. It was almost an hour.

"Why are you up?" she asked, stretching. "You don't have work today!"

"Grace, I have something to tell you," he said, sitting up straighter. "I went back to the resort after I dropped you off yesterday. To see your mother."

"You what? Why would you do that?"

"Get a cup of coffee, honey, and let me tell you." She was back in just seconds, sitting beside him. "I went because I was really disturbed by the way you

two went after each other. Not that it was unique—
my mom and sister have had a couple of good rows.
But they always patched things up, even if it took a
few days or even a couple of weeks. It looked like
this conflict with your mom has been going on for
years."

"True," she said.

"I went back to see her, to ask her what it would
take to have a civilized relationship with you. You
don't have to like each other, but you're mother and
daughter. But that conversation didn't really happen.
She knows she's made mistakes, Gracie. Big ones.
And she has issues." He tapped the letter. "She wrote
you a letter. She was going to have it delivered to you
if that flower delivery she trumped up didn't result
in a conversation. She asked me to give it to you."

She put down her coffee and snatched it. "Do you
really think that was your place? Going to see my
mother?"

"I don't know," he said honestly. "It looked like
you were both in pain. And it also looked perfectly
ridiculous. I couldn't imagine why on earth you
two had to have such a blowup over your future in
the skating industry. It made no sense to me." He
watched her rip open the envelope. "I get it now."

She started reading. She frowned angrily and
made a grunt of disapproval. But then she read to
the bottom of the page and looked at him with a
shocked expression. She put down that page and read
further. Her eyes glistened and her lips moved as

she read. She lifted her gaze from the page to look at Troy. "Is this true?"

"Does she lie? Because she was taken from the restaurant where I found her back to her cottage in a wheelchair."

Grace shook her head. "She's bossy and controlling and uppity. She doesn't lie. That I know of. Well, except for that note, but when confronted, she admitted it."

"Read it," he said, nodding to the pages.

She read on, getting to the third page. She gave a huff of laughter but had to wipe her eyes at the same time. "This is so Winnie. She thinks I'm completely incompetent. If I don't go to San Francisco and live with her for at least six months and learn everything there is to know about her finances I will bungle it and be completely wiped out in six months after she's gone." She looked at Troy. A couple of tears ran down her cheeks. She gave her head a little forlorn shake. "She really cares about me. In a completely insulting way. If she's so worried, why doesn't she just leave it all to a cat or something?"

"She loves you. She's just used to telling people what to do. It would get on my nerves, too."

"She's a pain in the ass," Grace said with a hiccup of emotion.

"But she wants to make it right with you. Before... you know."

Grace put down the letter. Without explaining what she was doing, she grabbed her personal cell and dialed a number. As he watched, she was pursing her lips. They'd become red around the edges and her nose grew pink and wet. She wiped at her face. Then she spoke into the phone. "Mikhail. Winnie finally found a way to break me. She's dying."

Ray Anne had given it a lot of thought. She couldn't make Ginger less sad; she couldn't help her get beyond her grief and there was no way to replace the life that had been taken from her. But it had been nine months since the baby died and she could get her moving.

When Ginger got up in the morning, she stumbled into the kitchen in her shapeless T-shirt and Capri-length leggings, her hair all lank and flat and ratty. She'd barely gotten down three swallows of her first cup of coffee when Ray Anne challenged her. "Well, buttercup, I'm taking you on an outing. We're going to Eugene for the day. We're going to shop and have a nice lunch and go to the beauty shop."

"Thanks, Ray, but I'd rather just stay here, if you don't mind."

"But I do mind, honey, because we've gotta do something. What you've been doing isn't working. You need a fresher-upper." She smoothed her hand over Ginger's hair and resisted the urge to say *Ack*. "A cut, some color, some new clothes. I'm going to get in the shower while you have your coffee. Make yourself some cereal or toast or both. You'll need your strength."

"Ray, really…I'm just not interested."

"Believe me, it's necessary."

"Look, I don't have money to spend on clothes that don't matter, that I won't wear."

"I'm taking care of that for now, but we have to do something about your money situation, too. Once you're fixed up a little bit, we're going to find you a job."

"I'm not sure I can…"

"I want you to try. It doesn't have to be a fancy job. We can go out to the beach and see if Cooper and Sarah need help in the bar. Spring is here, summer is on the way and the beach gets real busy. Maybe Cliff needs a waitress or one of the businesses in town needs clerical help. But you can't look like a vagrant if you mean to work with the public. Ginger, you have to do something with your time. You can't sit around and think all the time. It's not helping."

"But I'm not staying here!"

"As far as I can tell, you have no idea what you're going to do or where you're going to do it. So we should just act like you need to get your life moving forward and part of that is work. Even if you leave in a few weeks."

"Look, I'll just call my mom, have her pack up a couple of boxes of clothes I left there and—"

"Ginger, honey, I'm sure those clothes you left behind don't fit you any better than the ones you brought. Now, you keep an open mind and come along with me. I promise I won't force anything on you that you don't like. I'm not going to make you dress like me," she added, then laughed.

"I don't want you to do this," Ginger said. "I'm not your problem. I just want to be left alone."

"I know, baby," she said softly. "I know you just want to sink in a hole and die. Want to know how I know? Because I've sort of been where you are. Not as bad, but still… I don't usually talk about this, but when I was real young, way younger than you, I had a baby that didn't live. She was stillborn, so I didn't get to know her, didn't get used to her. Because I was so young my folks sent me to Portland to stay with your daddy and his family until she was born. I wasn't married, still in high school, no reason everyone had to know, right? Way back then, we worried a lot more about reputations. And I wasn't real sure who the daddy was, so… Well, there've been times in my life when I made some hasty choices."

Ginger just stared at her, eyes wide, mouth open.

"I held her for a long time before I let her go and the nurses didn't rush me. I wasn't even going to keep her—I figured she could do a lot better than me! I didn't have much going for myself back in the day. Oh, that was so long ago. But for the longest time after that I just wanted to die, myself. Then my mom and dad both died a few years later and I was so alone. And then I really did want to sink in a hole and die. I didn't know what to do. I still don't know what to do. So you know what I do when there's a tragedy? When my life is falling apart? I try really hard to do the best I can. I wake up in the morning, put my feet on the floor, walk. I put on clean clothes every day. I fix myself to look like I'm getting through life even if everything inside me says I won't make it another day. I mostly pretend, have a good hour here and there, then I collapse and cry because I just can't do it, then I put my feet on the floor again and take another step."

Ginger didn't say anything, but a tear ran down her cheek.

"When you came along, I kind of felt like an auntie. You were a gift to me. We had so much fun playing, dressing up, watching movies, going on little trips together, having sleepovers. We can do this."

Ginger shook her head, another tear sliding down her cheek.

"Now, you don't have to tell me what I already know—getting a haircut and a pair of jeans that actually fit—that won't help much. It's just a shallow remedy. My friend Lou says I invented shallow." Ray Anne smiled. "I think she's secretly jealous I can still walk in those spike heels."

"Ray…"

Ray Anne held up a hand. "I know, I get a little melodramatic. A little pushy, too. I can't fix what you feel, Gingersnap. I know I can't. But I can get you a good haircut, put you in a decent pair of jeans and get you some underwear that's not shameful just in case you ever have to be taken to an emergency room. And don't you worry about the money because if I can look at my pretty Ginger again, it's worth my life savings. And if it makes you feel one inch better, it's the right thing to do. Now eat something for breakfast—you're wasting away. I'll be ready to go in forty-five minutes. And it's going to be a busy day."

If Ginger went along with this refresher idea, she thought it was merely because Ray Anne, who she had loved so much since she was just a little girl, had revealed herself and her own losses. Ginger couldn't imagine being a pregnant teenager and giving birth to a dead baby. Of course, she also couldn't imagine giving one away—that notion was impossible to comprehend. But then she was thirty now, and had waited so long to get married and have her baby. And the right husband had clearly been a delusion.

So, to make an effort and to be kind, Ginger went with Ray Anne. Their first stop was the beauty salon. While Ray Anne had a manicure, Ginger sat in the beautician's chair. The woman, Char, took the rubber tie out of her hair and combed it out. "So, what are we doing today?" she asked.

Ginger stared at herself. Her hair, which had always been one of her assets, looked like it had gotten thin. It was straight, lank, the color of dirty water, and lying against her too-thin face. She thought she resembled an Afghan hound. "I don't care," she said.

"I care," Ray Anne said, jumping up from the manicurist's table. "She needs some highlights, a couple of shades. Maybe throw in some lowlights. Bring out the bright in that strawberry blonde. And for the love of God, let's get some kind of shape in there! Layer it. And when you're ready to blow it out, don't save money on the mousse. Women in our family need a little body in our locks."

Char met eyes with Ginger in the mirror. She raised one brow. "That okay with you?"

"Sure," she said, listless.

Ginger couldn't deny that it felt good to have someone's hands in her hair, massaging her scalp. It had probably been a year since she'd had a color and cut. But she paid no attention whatsoever; she was doing this for Ray Anne. If it made Ray feel that she was doing something to help, fine.

But an hour and a half later her mouth dropped open at the sight of her own reflection. Her hair was shaped along her jawline, a little shorter in the back, and it looked full and thick. The highlights made her look sun kissed and healthy. It was an easy style to maintain—a circular brush, a blow-dryer and some styling mousse. Not that she'd bother.

"Now we're getting somewhere," Ray Anne said, satisfied. "Now, wax her brows back into shape."

From there they went to Macy's to the makeup counters and Ray Anne went straight to MAC. It had not missed Ray's attention that Ginger hadn't packed cosmetics. Nor did she wear any. And every woman, Ray Anne said, can use a little help now and then. "My God, this stuff costs a fortune!" Ginger said. "I just buy my stuff at the grocery store!"

"Yes, I know, precious. I've been meaning to have a word with you about that. That stuff turns you orange. Now, we don't need to buy the full monty at the expensive counters, but there are some things you can't do without. Your moisturizer, base, powder, lip color and mascara. That cheap mascara clumps. You need the right colors for your skin and hair. We can get things like blusher, eye shadow and lip gloss at the grocery store." Ray Anne sat her down in a chair and gave orders to the saleswoman in her black smock. "Do her up."

It was transforming. Ginger didn't exactly feel happier in her heart, but when she looked at herself she didn't feel like a walking corpse. "Amazing," she said to her own face in the mirror.

The image that came to mind was when she was getting ready for the baby's funeral and her mother sat her on the closed toilet lid and put a little color in her cheeks and on her lips, saying, "This is nothing more than a little superficial frosting, but it makes you look a little less like you died with the baby." And Ginger had cried so hard, she couldn't sit still for her mother's ministrations. She had wanted to die with her baby, it was that raw in her chest.

But this was somehow different. All Ray Anne wanted from her was a little attempt to reenter the world of the living. It was so easy to lie in bed, to never leave the house, when every time she looked at herself she saw a dead woman.

Ray Anne's phone rang a few times while they were out and she briskly answered that she was spending a day with her "niece" but would look through her listings when she got home and follow up.

While they were at Macy's, Ray Anne whisked Ginger through lingerie.

"Do you have a preference in bras and panties?" she asked. Ginger merely shook her head and Ray Anne sighed. "I don't want you trying on clothes until you have the right underthings and those baggy granny panties aren't going to lay right under a nice pair of pants." She poked through some brands and types—bikini, high cut, boy shorts. She handed three pairs to Ginger. "Try these on while I have a look through the bras."

Ginger did as she was told. She was a little startled by the difference in her body with silky, colorful panties that fit. By the time Ray Anne arrived in the fitting room with bra samples she was able to say something positive. "I like them all."

"Well, that was easy." Ray Anne handed Ginger four bras to try. Then she took all of the underwear with them to the women's wear department next door. Ray Anne didn't even bother selecting but went straight to the saleslady, who she apparently knew. She asked to see a few things in Ginger's size.

"I'd take that to be about a four," the saleslady said. "Is that right, dear?"

She had been a ten or twelve. Her hips had been wide, her booty a little on the big and round side and she'd always had this issue with her thighs. And that was before she'd been pregnant. She had no idea what size she was now. "Sure," she said.

Ray Anne made her put on new underwear, giving the saleslady the price tags for purchase. Then she took Ginger's old underwear away and Ginger had the feeling she was never going to see them again.

The saleswoman put Ginger in a pair of slim jeans with a plain white silky tee and, over that, a pink denim bomber jacket with silver buttons. She had to stand up on her toes to be tall enough for the hem of the jeans but the effect was, well, shocking.

"You look eighteen," Ray Anne said.

In fact, she did.

Next, another pair of jeans, different brand, a black blouse, a white V-necked sweater. Not a heavy sweater—lightweight for spring and summer. Again, amazing. Then came black pants with a tunic-style long-sleeved top. Sleeves pushed up, it was so pretty. It was something a person could wear out to dinner, if a person ever went out to dinner again in her life. A few more slacks, a few more tops, a few more jackets or sweaters.

Then the saleslady held up a dress. "I wish you'd try this on," she said. "I've been dying to see it on someone with your figure. It's so streamlined." It was dark purple with yellow piping across the shoulders to the edge of capped sleeves and down the side seams. There was a gold, slightly glittery pattern embossed on part of the front. It was diamond shaped and in an abstract design, from right below the mandarin collar to right below the waist. It was the most beautiful thing.

"Oh, I don't need a dress. Plus," she said, looking at the tag, "it's much too expensive."

"Put it on, Ginger," Ray Anne commanded.

It was stunning. Ginger felt a little like a princess.

Then she reminded herself that she couldn't be a princess or feel that beautiful. She was in mourning.

"It's irresistible," Ray Anne said. "Now just don't bring us any more clothes. Ginger, put on those jeans with the white tee and pink jacket. You're wearing it to lunch and then home."

"Ray, don't throw out my jeans."

"Of course not, darling. You might need them for the next time you paint a house. We'll stop in the shoe department and then we'll have a lovely lunch together." She looked at her watch. "Good, the lunch crowd will have passed and not only will it be quiet, it's late enough in the day that we can manage with something light for dinner much later." She examined her phone. "Looks like I'm going to be on the phone and computer after we get back to Thunder Point. For a Realtor and property manager a day with a lot of phone calls is a good day."

They were alone in the dressing room and in a whisper she hoped wouldn't be overheard, Ginger spoke. "Ray Anne, I appreciate all this so much, I do. But you can't rescue me from grief with a few new outfits and a haircut."

Ray Anne gave her a pitying look. "No one knows that better than I do, Gingersnap. But the other thing I know is that you have two choices—you can grieve that useless ex-husband and your precious lost baby forever or you can do what you must to move on and make life bearable. Because, honey, we're stuck with life."

Ginger positioned her arms as though cradling a

baby in her arms. "When I put my arms like this, I can still feel the weight of his tiny head right there, in the crook."

"Sugar, that's not ever going away. You're not going to forget. You're just going to carry on. It's not easy. It's all you can do." She blinked. "Now I think we need some shoes and some guacamole. You get dressed. I'm going to deal with the receipts."

Fifteen

When Grace called Mikhail, he asked for the details of this dying. So she read the letter, though she stumbled from time to time.

My Dear Izzy,
First of all, I'm very sorry about my harsh words when you retired from skating. I didn't mean it, you know I didn't. Shock and disappointment got the best of me. And I apologize about the mysterious note. I knew it would frighten you. I actually hoped it would. I think I must have had a stroke of some kind, that something like that would make perfect sense to me. Then you would come to me and I would pull all the right strings—you would feel safe again with my protection.

A fool's game. I apologize. I wanted you to come home but not because you pitied me.

I am sorry about the years of arguments

about skating and, if not skating, coaching or consulting or reporting or judging. Every time we get through with one of those conversations, with one of those power struggles, I am filled with hate for myself and anger with you. It's the worst feeling and I always pledge never to allow myself to do that again. And yet I have.

There is a reason. Not an excuse, but a reason. I learned a couple of years ago that I have ALS. For a while the symptoms were manageable and it was easy to imagine it would be years before it would matter. And I resolved to use those years to lure you back to your roots. It wasn't so much that I wanted you to compete. It was that I wanted you to be secure. I have always known I wouldn't be alive forever, but never panicked that my time was short.

You are the only heir to this old Dillon money. Your half brother is not a part of my family and your father settled with him generously before and after his death. There is no one else, Izzy. It's only you. And to my embarrassment, I've never acquainted you with the complications and responsibilities associated with this legacy. I've been managing since my parents died, before you were even a teenager. The work is immense. The threat of cons and predators and incompetent advisors is constant. People will take advantage of you. Steal from you if you even blink. Even charities will use you. Frankly, I don't care if you spend it all on something that makes you happy, but I worry that if I don't do my job you could lose it or be swindled.

That's why I want your undivided attention for a few months. It is complex and you'll find there are decisions to be made.

This ALS is hard. The symptoms are coming faster now. I'm an athlete at the core and even when I stopped competing, my body never betrayed me before. I was always competent and confident and now I don't dare cross the street alone. The jitters and weakness and trembling and unbelievable fatigue are getting the best of me. I don't know how much time there is. We should get this thing between us settled once and for all.

It's not important that one of us wins, Izzy. It's very important that we forgive each other. Before it's too late. Before we can't go back.
Love,
Mother

When she was finished, still wiping away the occasional tear as she read, she heard Mikhail curse. She had noticed that Troy wandered into the kitchen for more coffee, lingering at the coffeepot with his back turned to her as if it was painful to listen.

Mikhail said something she didn't understand. "Sheet of the gods. I will come. Where do I come?"

She laughed through her tears. *Shit of the gods?*

When he was himself, when he wasn't pushing her to do more, do better, he could make her laugh and love him. "Why come, Mikhail?" she asked. "There's nothing you can do."

"I can see her one time. She made my life when she gave me you. I am now best coach. I was not best coach before you." He grunted. "But is Winifred. Will be hard. Where do I come?"

"Well, I live in one-and-a-half rooms, but Winnie is in a nice house at a resort in Bandon, close by. She has bedrooms."

"She will not have me," he said. "She is diva. Where is this Brandon?"

"It's Bandon. Oregon."

"Oregon? Did we skate in this Oregon?"

Grace smiled. Mikhail was a Russian immigrant; his US geography wasn't great. They used to study the map before every competition. He was much better with Europe and Asia than the US. "We did not. It's about an eight-hour drive north of San Francisco. She brought her car and driver. Before you buy a ticket, let me be sure Winnie goes for this idea."

"Just make me a place to stay. Some dirty hotel will do. I just need empty room. Bed would be nice."

"How can you get away so suddenly?"

"Did you say someone is dying? Ah, is good time. Best matches are coming in fall. Right now I can be spared. For a little while, not forever. I have only terrible athletes now. Maybe they get nervous and work harder if I ignore them, eh? I can throw a little pout so they think I quit, yes? Then we see what we see! Don't tell Winifred. She hates me."

"She loves you," Grace said.

"That is love? She has the hardest love in my experience."

"Yeah. I know." She sighed. "I think you can fly into Eugene. That could be closest. But really, you don't have to—"

"In Russia, is important to pay gratitude. Otherwise, there might not be a place for me when my time comes."

When she disconnected, Troy came back to sit beside her on the couch. "You okay?" he asked.

She nodded. "I'm going to have to see her. Will you come with me?"

"I'll take you," he said. "But I'm not going to sit with you while you talk to your mother. I think she feels this is personal family business."

"What am I going to do? I'm not going to San Francisco to live with her!"

"You can do whatever you have to do, Gracie. No matter what you decide to do, the sad reality is that it's not forever. Be sure that in the end you don't have any regrets. That's all."

Grace hung a sign on the flower shop door. Closed for the Day. Open Tomorrow 9:00 a.m. She put her work cell number at the bottom for phone orders.

Troy was determined not to be involved, at least not at this point. He dropped her at the cottage Winnie occupied and he left. He said he wouldn't be far away and she could call him. He'd come back when she needed him.

Winnie was comfortably settled on a chaise longue in her bedroom, a soft throw around her shoulders and a pillow under her knees. She had a book in her lap, but it was closed. Virginia let Grace into the room.

"You look very comfortable," Grace said, kissing her mother's cheek.

She lifted the book. "The one thing I thought I'd do with all this godforsaken leisure time was read, but do you suppose I can concentrate?"

Grace laughed and sat on the upholstered bench at the end of the bed. "Skating wasn't the only gift you gave me, you know. I love to read and I suppose a lot of that is because of you. On all those long trips we took, you always had a book going. You packed books. You read during practice and in the car on long rides."

"And now I can't seem to focus."

"You will once we get a few details organized. I wanted to bring you flowers but since I brought you five hundred dollars' worth yesterday, it seemed ridiculous."

"I kept the smashed arrangement and sent the other three to hospitals and nursing homes," she said, having the grace to blush slightly. "They're beautiful, Izz—is it really Grace now?"

"It is. And thank you." She took a breath, shaking her head. "Oh, Mother. The drama. You could have just told me the moment you knew. Instead of fighting we could have planned how we'd manage the time. I didn't quit skating because of you. I competed as long as I did because of you. And I don't hate skating—I love it. But I was done with so many aspects of the trials. They were right—Izzy Banks couldn't take the pressure."

Winnie sighed. "They say the mind is not affected by ALS. They're wrong. I've made some foolish decisions in the past couple of years. I've snapped at you in anger and lived to regret it. But that's not all. I've flown as far as Switzerland for a miracle cure when my specialist assured me all along the research hasn't caught up with the power of this disease."

"Well, I guess you're lucky you had that option to fly to Switzerland. Does your specialist do anything for you?"

"I've been taking a drug to slow the progression, but it's not going to cure me and there comes a time... Grace, you'll need genetic testing. You should be prepared."

Grace nodded. "What is Virginia's role? Nurse?"

"She's an assistant. She's been with me for three years and now she does far more for me than she bargained for. I hired her as a secretary but she exceeded my expectations. She's a genius with the computer."

Grace tilted her head and smiled. "Is that so?"

"She's amazing. And she knows she'll be looking for work before long."

Grace knew that anyone who worked closely with Winnie or inside the house went through complete background checks and came with high recommendations. Winnie was a genius at hiring the best people. Just look at what Mikhail was able to accomplish for her. "When you say *before long...*"

"How long will I live? I have no idea. Six months? A year? If I live a year, it won't be a good year. I've already had more time than eighty percent of ALS patients. But Virginia knows her way around files and names and accounts. She can help you with that—she's managed all of my correspondence for a couple of years now. And she will be replaced with a nurse sometime soon."

"In San Francisco?" Grace asked.

"It's where I've lived since you were twelve years old," she said.

"Isn't that big house getting a little overwhelming?"

"What do you mean?" Winnie asked.

"It's just that—doesn't it take quite an army to keep that place going?"

"Indeed," Winnie said with a curl of the lip.

"Mother...Mama...I called Mikhail and he's coming. He wants to see you."

She stiffened in shock. "Why?"

"Well, aside from the fact that he's fond of you? He also believes he owes his reputation to you. It was because you hired him that he had such success. Now, here's what I need to know—how long are you staying here? In Bandon?"

"I can have this cottage for another week, but I was going to go home as soon as possible. Hopefully, you will be coming with me."

Grace shook her head. "I have commitments. For this week, I have lots of orders. After that there's a wedding out of town—one that I've been looking forward to. If I had an emergency, there are several florists who would be happy to take my orders. In fact, for the out-of-town wedding, Mamie and Ross could do the job—they trained me."

"I'm aware," Winnie said, and not happily.

"I want to tell you about my business, Mama," she said. "Let me make us some tea."

Grace started with an idea right after reading her mother's letter and that idea grew as she thought about it. She understood that many people would think running a small flower shop could be a little boutique business, a small-scale and simple operation. And that was true, it could be. But it could be more, depending on who operated the business. Iris had told her that when her mother operated that little shop, they could barely squeak by financially—Rose had done little more than create floral arrangements for the locals who were familiar with her.

Grace had grown the shop significantly, hiring a marketing firm to assist in PR with computer marketing, coupons, specials, advertising in bridal catalogs and in bridal stores, not to mention a website. She'd implemented a creative and complicated computer program to minimize the time spent on demonstrating what was available along with pricing. She was an expert in buying the finest and most cost effective flora and her designs were definitely among the most beautiful. Why else would brides come from towns surrounding Thunder Point rather than going to their own neighborhood florists?

All of her accounting was computerized and she had not run through the trust her father had left. After buying the store and renovating the loft to live in, she had some modest investments that were managed by a wealth-management firm. She hoped the work she was doing would keep her quite nicely for the rest of her life, but it was possible she could actually expand if the notion suited her lifestyle.

"And what about this boyfriend?" Winnie asked.

"Troy? He's the most wonderful man, but I thought we'd talk about my business, Mama. It's really important to me that you know I'm not dabbling to pass the time. I love it, I'm serious about it, I'm good at it. I'm one of the best, Mama. I realize it's not the career you would choose for me, but it's not a waste of time. And depending on how I run it, it can be very successful. Will you come to see it? This week?"

"Of course, Grace," she said. "I'd like to see your store. Now tell me about this man. Does he know you're very wealthy?"

Grace sighed. Well, Rome wasn't built in a day. "Until yesterday neither of us knew I even had the potential to be wealthy. Apparently Troy found out first. I read your letter this morning."

"You must have known that I—"

"Number one, you and I have barely spoken in five years and when we did, it didn't go well and, number two, I have always thought of you as…" Her voice trailed off and, unexpectedly, tears gathered in her eyes.

"Thought of me as what, Grace?" Winnie asked.

"I'm twenty-eight. You're fifty-one. I thought you'd live forever. To at least ninety-five."

"I thought I'd live through at least two face-lifts," Winnie said sourly. "I haven't even had my first yet!"

Grace let go a huff of laughter, but she had to wipe her eyes.

"I was planning to be the best preserved ninety-year-old in the city," Winnie said. "Just tell me about your young man, Grace."

Grace took a deep breath, wiped her eyes and carried on. "The woman I bought the shop from became my best friend—Iris. She's a high school counselor and she's married to the sheriff's deputy in charge of the substation in our little town. I met Troy through Iris—he's a high school history teacher. He makes light of it, as if it's just something he does to fill the days and finance his adventures—he loves everything from river rafting to skiing to rock climbing. I think he's into every sport but figure skating and surfing. But when Iris talks about Troy's teaching she describes him as the most dedicated teacher she knows. He doesn't just teach them history, he keeps an eye on them, paying close attention to any issues that need intervention. He watches for signs of abuse, bullying, drug and alcohol use, any problems teenagers might have. Iris says Troy would make an outstanding guidance counselor—his instincts are right on. There are students whose lives are changed because of Troy's skills as an educator."

"You had good teachers," Winnie said defensively.

"Probably, but it's not the teachers I think about when I look back and examine the choices I've made, when I think about the opportunities and accomplishments. It's the coaches. I've had two of the best."

Grace called Troy's cell and asked him if he'd join her and her mother for lunch at one of the resort restaurants. He was pleased to do that and he showed up at the cottage to push Winnie's wheelchair.

Winnie might not be ready to admit it, but Troy charmed her. He made her laugh and her eyes twinkled. If there was a sweeter, kinder and funnier man, Grace had never met him. And he was completely sincere, Grace felt that in her heart.

On the way back to Thunder Point, she asked him what he would do if money were no object. "Grace, that is such a remote possibility for me, I've never even thought about it. I have no idea. Probably something fun and irresponsible."

"But you're the most responsible person I know. You work hard, you save, you measure every penny."

"That's because in my life, money has always been hard to come by. I learned to be careful at an early age."

Grace and Troy were back in Thunder Point by three, but Grace didn't open the shop. Instead, she made and returned a few phone calls, and then she went upstairs to her apartment and got on the laptop, researching ALS. At six, Troy showed up with crab cakes and salad from Cliff's and a bottle of wine. They talked about all she'd learned in just a few hours of research, how much more she should know, including the need for genetic testing.

"I'm going to do a little more reading tonight," Grace said.

"Would this be a good night for me to spend at my place?" he asked.

"Can you stay? I'm not going to read all night. And tomorrow I'm going to work in the shop in the morning and in the afternoon I'm going to close the shop and drive over to Eugene to pick up Mikhail. He's going to stay at the resort with my mother for two or three days."

"And what will you be doing? Will you spend the evening with them?"

"Maybe part of the evening, but I think it would be best if I let them catch up. Would you like to join us?"

"I don't think so. But I hope I'll meet him before he leaves. Why don't you let me keep the shop open till five or so. I can sell what you have on hand, then I'm due to help Cooper for the next couple of nights."

"Troy, did you plan to go somewhere? Is my sudden crisis keeping you from doing something fun with your spring break?"

"You think I'd run out on you now? Gracie, I think the way you handle this is one of the most important things you'll ever do."

"Because?" she asked, but she knew. She just wanted him to put it into words for her.

"Because you have this one chance to get things right between the two of you. And you should take it."

"Right," she agreed. "I hope I don't really screw it up. And I hope I don't mess things up with you, because you're pretty important to me."

"I'm a big boy, Gracie. Don't worry about me. I'll stick with you while you go through this."

"And after I'm through it?" she asked.

"After? You might be living an entirely different life. Let's see what all this means. I gather there's a fortune involved. And not a small one."

"Troy, that doesn't matter. You can't imagine that it would matter."

"You can't say that yet. That's one of those questions that will have to be answered when it's not just talk, when it's real. But for now, while you try to sort all this out, you can count on me."

That had such an ominous sound, Grace was a little nervous. Concerned enough that she didn't sleep all that well.

When he took her in his arms, everything felt the same—easy and delicious and perfect. But she suspected that Troy, like just about anyone would be, was a bit intimidated by Winnie and her money. Money that she wished to confer on Grace but only after Grace jumped through all the right hoops. What

Troy didn't understand and couldn't until it was, as he said, *real* was that Grace had been happier since she'd been on her own than ever before. And she'd been happier with Troy than she thought possible.

Once she was alone in her shop, when Troy was off doing his own thing, she placed a call to Ray Anne Dysart. Everyone knew Ray Anne was the person to contact for real estate needs. She wasn't sure how to phrase her request exactly. She asked Ray Anne if she had time to stop by Pretty Petals this morning. She wanted to talk about property for rent or sale.

Ray Anne walked in not too long after, and with her was a pretty blonde woman. "Hi," Grace said with a smile.

"Grace, meet my niece, Ginger. Not really my niece, but almost. My cousin Dickie is like a brother to me and this is his daughter. Ginger is staying with me for a while." After the brief introductions, Ray Anne was all business. "How can I help you? Ready for a little more space than your darling loft?"

"Not exactly. I love my little loft. My mother lives in San Francisco and she's up here for a visit. She's staying at the Dunes in one of their beautiful little cottages. And she's handicapped. She's not getting around well and the San Francisco house isn't the best for her disability. She can barely manage the stairs and it's only going to get worse, and soon. Of course I'd like her to be closer. I'm afraid she has a progressive degenerative disease, and we don't know how much time there is."

"Oh, Grace," Ray Anne said, hand to her heart.

"We're doing as well as we can with the diagnosis," she said, making it sound almost as if she'd known as long as her mother had. "Now, when I'd like her nearby, when she's getting worse, I want a house for her. A one-level house. A beautiful flat house. She's certainly not up to looking at houses, but everyone knows you're the best there is. Fortunately, my father took care of my mother—he passed a long time ago. That San Francisco house will bring a nice price and she has a healthy pension. She can afford to spend her last months in comfort."

"Almost anything in San Francisco can fetch a good price. Do you know what kind of house you're looking for besides one level?"

She shook her head. "I don't. It has to be ready. We don't have weeks or months to decorate. Even though my mother isn't getting around much, it should be spacious."

"And will you be staying with her?"

"I'm sure I'll be spending my share of nights there, but let's think of her. I want her to have something to look at—"

"Oceanfront?"

"That would be wonderful, but anything that doesn't feel like a hospital room. She has ALS. The symptoms are coming faster now. I think she'll be bedridden in a few months."

"And your price range?"

"I don't have one. I don't know how much my mother has socked away, but there's plenty. She has old family money and, Ray Anne, I don't want any of it. I want her nearby or else I'll have to close the shop and go to San Francisco until..." She cleared her throat. "If you find something wonderful, I'll look at it and if it's perfect, I'll find a way. My mother has always lived well."

"I assume you want to rent?"

"I'm flexible," Grace said. "If there's nothing stunning for rent but there's a listing that's perfect, I can always sell it..." She looked down. "Later," she finally said.

Ray Anne reached out and touched her arm. "There are some nice properties around. Have you looked online?"

"I haven't. But I could—"

"Don't worry about it. Write your email address on the back of this card," she said, helping herself to one of Grace's flower shop business cards and flipping it over. "I'll get right to work on this. I can see why you're in a hurry. I'll send you some links."

"Is this possible, Ray Anne?" Grace asked. "Because I have to convince my mother that this is a better idea than me moving to San Francisco for a year."

"If it's possible, darling, I can do it. It'll give me a chance to show Ginger a few things about real estate and hunting property in case... Well, my darling girl is with me for at least a few weeks, maybe longer, and we're visiting local businesses to see if anyone needs help. Ginger wants to work while she's here."

"Are you serious? What kind of work?" Grace asked.

Ginger flushed and looked down. "My experience is mostly in retail. I worked in women's clothing, housewares, a little bit in an office. I've done a lot of things."

"Did you work in decorating at all, while you worked in housewares?"

"I wouldn't call it decorating, no. But I did things like bridal registries."

"I'm desperate for help. Especially now, with my mother and all. Do you have any interest in flower design? This is a small boutique, but it's busy. Not crowded, but busy. There are a lot of phone orders and arrangements to design. I spend a lot of time in the workroom, putting them together. Most of them are not originals but created from pictures I have and they're pretty easy to learn. I try new things from time to time."

"I don't know," she said with a shrug. "I could try."

"Would you like to spend a morning with me? Just to see how it feels? It's very messy work."

"Could I? The idea of a small shop appeals to me a lot more than a restaurant or—" she glanced at Ray Anne "—real estate."

"It's okay, babe," Ray Anne said. "Not everyone is cut out for my job, even though they think they are."

"Can you come tomorrow morning? Early? Eight o'clock?"

"I can do that," she said.

"Wonderful! Ray Anne, thank you. Send me pictures, please."

Sixteen

Mikhail Petrov's flight arrived promptly at three in the afternoon and he walked into the baggage-claim area with a duffel over his shoulder. He was sixty-six and his face was whiskery and lined with age, but his hair was reddish brown. *Bad color*, Grace thought. He'd had bad hair color for so many years. But for a man his age, he was fit and strong. Small but built like an ox with his big shoulders and short legs. She held up her tablet upon which she had typed, in very large letters, PETROV. He didn't smile, but she did. He was accustomed to limos or at least town car service. It wasn't as if he wouldn't recognize the best figure skater he'd ever coached.

"I see," he said. "You think you're funny."

"I do," she said, grinning. "Do you have luggage?"

He held out his duffel. "Only this. Two days, maybe three, that is all I have for you."

"Not for me, Mikhail. You came for Winnie, remember?"

"Right," he said. "Lead the way."

Grace directed him to the parking area and opened the back of the van. It was custom painted in pink, yellow, purple, blue with lime-green lettering in script. *Pretty Petals.* "Your luggage, sir."

"What is this?" he said, handing over the duffel.

"The flower mobile," she said. "Jump in front. We have a long drive."

He did as he was told "We'll make one stop, *golubushka*. The grocer, please," he said.

"You won't need food," she said, buckling in.

"Is just for some fruit, if you don't mind so much. You drive this thing?"

"Remember Mamie and Ross Jenkins? Ross taught me to drive. I love driving! Love the control. Tell me, Mikhail, have you been well? You look exactly the same."

"They call it preserved," he said. "I have been six months traveling and now we train in Chicago. There are three assistants and twelve US contenders, from which the US will take a few to the finals, maybe not mine. There is time, but this will be my last Winter Games, if any of my girls are selected. From the look of it, I say there is no a chance in hell. But there is time. And sheet of gods, they need it!" He turned in his seat and looked at her. "Tell me how is Winifred?"

"I spent the day with her yesterday. The first day I've spent with her in five years. She looks very beautiful, but she's thinner and has aged. I think it's the stress of knowing she's battling ALS and is losing. The tremors and weakness are obvious and she said this is just within the past few months. She has no idea how much time she has. She's taking a drug to slow the progression but she's cynical—she doesn't see how it matters. She said, 'What good is three more months?' All she wants to do is clean house, so to speak. Settle her affairs. Get the end of her life in order, but this would mean in order to her satisfaction. It's not as though she can control it from the grave." She bit her lips against the threat of tears.

"If anyone can do that, is Winifred," he grumbled. "I am afraid she has contract with God."

That brought a laugh from Grace. Spurts of laughter through tears had become common the past few days. "We never communicated, Mikhail. She instructed, criticized, praised, but we never talked about our feelings. I talked with my therapist or Mamie. Now I understand that Winnie wasn't ready to retire when I was. It destroyed her."

"There is the thing with athletes and their mothers." He peered at her. "The mother is not doing skating. She can't make decisions like that. She is there for cheering, no more. It is not about Winifred. Unless she wants to take on the ice, then it is not about her. Is about you."

"I wish I'd understood," Grace said.

"You understood," he said. "You knew. You did the right thing. Is time to have life for yourself." He looked around the van. "In flower mobile."

Grace pulled into a grocery store lot not far from the resort in Bandon. It occurred to her that since

Mikhail wanted some fruit, she could pick up a couple of things for later. Troy would probably come over after his evening at Cooper's. They walked into the grocery store and Grace went immediately to the deli and bakery while Mikhail presumably went to the produce section. When she went looking for him he was holding a bottle of vodka and looking a little lost.

"Have you found your fruit?" she asked.

"Where is raisins?"

"Raisins? Let's see," she said, walking down an aisle and around a central counter. "Ah. Raisins."

He selected a big box of plump golden raisins. "Wow. You like your raisins," she said.

"Fruit of the gods," he told her.

"Would you like some apples? Oranges? Bananas?"

"Good to go," he said, heading for the checkout.

"Are raisins your favorite snack?" she asked.

"Put raisins in the vodka, let sit overnight, perfect."

"Ah," she said, laughing at his pronunciation. "And then you eat the raisins?"

"*Nyet!* Drink the vodka!"

She was a little shocked, even though she had remembered that Mikhail liked his *wodka*, especially after the trials or competitions were done. She laughed softly. "Right," she said.

Virginia let them into the cottage and then discreetly left the room. Winnie was standing beside the sofa. There was a tray of hors d'oeuvres on a small table, a couple of wineglasses sitting out and an ice bucket.

Mikhail dropped his duffel and put his grocery bag on the short counter in the little galley kitchen before entering and going to Winnie. "Winifred, this is lie I am told, that you are sick." He put his hands on her face and kissed her cheeks. In high society they stuck to air-kissing, but Mikhail always gave the real thing in loud smacks. "You are beautiful."

"It's all fading," she said.

"Sit down, my dove. You are tired? Weak?"

"Things don't work like they once did but I'm getting by fine. Can we get you something? Food? Drink?"

"Ice," he said. "A glass and ice." He brought his grocery bag to the chair adjacent to her and pulled out his bottle of vodka, putting it on the coffee table. Grace quickly fixed his glass for him.

"As refined as ever," Winnie quipped.

Grace took one of the chairs near them. It had the feel of a reunion, the way these two poked at each other, but the affection between them was so obvious.

"Is perfect," he said. "What do we give you?"

"I'm fine, Mikhail. After you've had a drink, we can order some dinner. Grace," she said. "Will you have dinner? A glass of wine?"

"Nothing for me. I have a drive ahead."

"And your young man?" Winnie asked.

Mikhail peered at her.

"He's working tonight, his part-time job. I'll see him later."

"Grace is in love with a schoolteacher," Winnie said.

"You could not find her a prince or dictator?" Mikhail asked with a smirk.

"I choose my own men," Grace said. "If you don't mind, I think I'll go home now so you can visit. I have to open the shop in the morning, Mother. I have a new employee coming early to train. If you're feeling well, maybe you'll come and look at my little town?"

"Let's see what the morning brings, Grace." Then she shook her head. "This new name. It just doesn't fit you."

"You'll get used to it." She gave her mother a kiss on the forehead. "We'll talk in the morning."

Left alone, Mikhail fetched the tray of snacks and placed it on the coffee table, within reach. He sampled a small toast square with tapenade and hummed his approval. He sipped his drink. "What is your plan, Winnie?" he asked.

"Plan?"

"Do not do this coy with me, it is Mikhail you talk to. You have plan. Like always."

"I want to take Izzy to San Francisco. Home. But she doesn't want to go."

"Then why? Leave the child to have her life. She will visit."

"There's an estate to settle. A complicated estate.

Furnishings, jewelry, art, investments. I can't wave my wand and have it done. It's hers. She has decisions to make. I don't know what she wants to do with all of it. I can't just leave it behind."

"Ah, you will take it with you?" He chuckled and sipped his vodka. "If anyone can, is you."

"I just want to make sure it's all properly dealt with. All the possessions."

"She looks better than I've ever seen her," Mikhail said. "I think it is because the weight of all the world is not on her back. All the burdens of the world—gone. The need to win for her mother, for her team, her country, is done now. Behind her. And she thrives. That is your legacy, Winnie—Izzy. She is your estate. Think on this."

"I have a responsibility…"

"She has had hard life, working to bring home gold when she is only a child. You gave birth to champion, Winnie, and she spent her life to give you what you could not get for yourself. You want her to miss you when you are gone? Set her free. She doesn't work for us any longer."

"That's cruel."

"Is truth."

When Grace was back in Thunder Point, she texted Troy to tell him she was home with food and wine. If there wasn't so much going on, she'd be out at the beach, keeping him company while he served. Instead, she poured herself a glass of wine, got out

her laptop and checked messages. Ray Anne had
sent her a dozen listings to look at and she breezed
through them with disappointment. There was one
with a Pacific view that was spacious and beautiful,
but the kitchen was dated and the bedrooms were all
upstairs. Just like the San Francisco house.

Did her mother really want to die in that house?
That small mansion? The thought made her shudder.
Was that a conversation that had to take place? Two
days after she learned about Winnie's degenerative
disease? She was up to the task of saying, *I think
you should live near me, where we can be close to
each other.* But the subtext of that discussion would
be, *Come to Oregon where I can be available when
the end is near.* That's what this was really about,
wasn't it?

From all she read, she wasn't sure what was involved in taking care of someone with ALS. They
could hire nurses. Hospice seemed to be the end-
stage necessity. But were specialists required? Because Winnie would have to have the best, she'd
demand it. It seemed many ALS patients needed
feeding tubes. IVs. Respirators.

She'd have to see Scott Grant, talk to him. Maybe
he could tell her what she'd need and whether it was
all available here.

She started to cry. It came at the most unexpected
moments and she told herself it was because she was
so tired. She hadn't been sleeping well and the pressure was back, that pressure to do the right thing, to
please. And this time she had to get it right because

her mother was terminal. As soon as she managed to get her crying jag under control, she went back to her internet research.

Finally a text came in from Troy. Nice night on the beach. Won't get there till around ten.

Then she started to cry again, for no reason and every reason.

Ginger got up earlier than she had in months. She showered, blew out her hair, applied a little light makeup and put on one of her new outfits. Just to be safe, she put a pair of her old jeans and a T-shirt in a little bag—Grace had said it was dirty work. She'd ask Grace if she should change before doing anything that might wreck her new clothes.

When she looked in the mirror she admitted to herself that Ray Anne had been right—she needed to be presentable. It didn't make that ache in her heart disappear, but it made her feel slightly less pathetic. Her father had given her some money, just walking-around money he called it, but if she earned a little something she might run over to Target in the next town and buy herself some less expensive jeans and shirts that fit, that she could afford to go to work in.

Ray Anne was in the kitchen, sitting at the table with her laptop open, glasses perched on the end of her nose, clicking through listings. "Well, don't you look pretty," she said.

"I feel kind of guilty," she said. "My mom has been asking me for months to try to do something about my appearance and I blew her off. But I'm here two days and you have me cleaned up and in new clothes."

"I'm very bossy that way," Ray Anne said. "Plus, we have a lot of shopping history, you and me. Are you excited about your new job?"

"Nervous," she said. "What if I just don't have the...energy?"

"Then you'll tell Grace you need a break. Get a soda or cup of coffee. Eat a little something. I think you're going to like it. It's such pretty work—making up beautiful bouquets."

"I've never done anything like this before."

"You helped people pick out their household accessories, linens, dishes, table accoutrements. You have good taste. And if it doesn't prove to be right for you, you'll get a different kind of job. I don't think Grace is going to expect you to take on weddings. She'll probably hand you a broom."

"Probably," Ginger agreed. "I think I'll get going."

"Ginger!" Ray Anne snapped. "Choke down a cup of coffee and a piece of toast! Don't go to your first day without any fuel!"

"Right," she said, going to the coffeepot. "Are you finding anything for Grace? I mean, for her mother?"

"It's pretty tough. I have absolutely no idea what the woman's expectations are. I mean the mother's— would she be grateful just to be near Grace or is she very particular? There are a couple of little duplexes with good views for rent. They're small. I sent pictures to Grace yesterday and last night she emailed back that she was looking for something larger and more *custom*. Something more like the resort facilities but with a full kitchen and deck and view and one level, at least three thousand square feet. And don't worry about the price, she says. When people say that, they mean anything from two hundred thousand or seven-hundred-a-month rent. They don't know how pricey their wishes and dreams can get."

"Are you going to ask those things?"

"Sure. Finding the right house usually takes many conversations, never all at once. Asking again and again, dribbling it out, so it isn't so overwhelming. And I find the answers change over time. Unfortunately, Grace is in a hurry. But lucky for her, I'm good." Then she smiled. "How did you sleep?"

"Very well, as a matter of fact. This house is so quiet. And small—it feels cozy. Plus, I think I'm still recovering from shopping with you."

"I don't have time to screw around," Ray Anne said. "We'll see how you survive the day and if you get through it all right, I'll plan a dinner with my girlfriends for the end of the week. They're dying to get a look at you."

"Oh, Ray, I'm no fun," she complained.

"You don't have to be fun, but I bet you accidentally have a good time." She snapped her computer shut. "I better get on it. I have properties to preview."

Grace was in the workroom of the shop, working on her designs for centerpieces on order. If she got them done this morning Justin could deliver them all this afternoon. She had three orders for church flowers—two in Bandon and one in Coquille—that she really couldn't do before Saturday morning.

The shop wasn't open yet. She was wearing her yoga pants and a long-sleeved T-shirt—the mornings on the ocean were pretty nippy in April. Troy was still upstairs in her bed. Leaving him there hadn't been easy—he'd been facedown, arms stretched over his head, beautiful round booty sticking out of the sheets. She knew if she kissed his shoulder or stroked his handsome butt he would roll over and—

There was a knock at the back door. It was Iris, peeking in the window.

"What are you doing here?" Grace asked, opening the door.

"Grace, why didn't you call me? I can help you!"

"Call you?"

"Seth and I went for a walk on the beach last night and stopped by the bar for a beer. Troy told us about your mother—that she's here in Oregon and she's sick. I mean, very sick. As in trying-to-settle-her-affairs sick."

"ALS," Grace said somberly. "I see her after five years and apparently our reconciliation has an expiration date on it."

"Oh, Grace, I'm so sorry."

"Thank you. But look, try not to worry. I just have to find a way to make sure our last year together is… My relationship with my mother wasn't like the one you had with your mother. It was… God," she said. Then she started to cry again. "I'm sorry. I am out of control. My mother and I had a very difficult relationship, but we loved each other. I thought being estranged was for the best, our time together was so frustrating. But I didn't want this. I thought she'd live to be a hundred and ten. In fact," she said, brushing away a tear. "I thought she'd be a giant pain till a very old age. She's really much too controlling to succumb to this."

Iris stroked her upper arm. "Listen, I can help you. I'm off this week. I'm back to school next week, but I can work after school. And I'm off all weekend, of course. I can help with big jobs. I can clean up and take orders. Whatever you need."

"Can you help train a new employee? I gave Ray Anne's niece a job and she'll be here at eight."

Iris puffed up. "Yes. I can!"

"I don't want to take advantage of you."

"Let me help you get on your feet."

"My mother wants me to go to San Francisco. She wants to get her house in order."

Iris made a sad face. "She probably has no one else to ask."

"Oh, she has an army of people to ask. But she wants me involved. Iris, my mother is wealthy. She has expensive things and complicated finances and I think she believes I'm not up to the job of taking care of her things."

Iris was shaking her head, but she had a kind smile on her face. "It's peace of mind, Grace. Ten years before my mother died she started asking me questions like, 'Before I take this old sewing cabinet to the thrift shop, is it something you might want someday?' and 'Iris, I have all these old Christmas cards—years of them. Do you want to save them so you know the names of all our acquaintances?' I was surprised that it even mattered to her because it didn't matter to me. But it was important to her. And she was the opposite of wealthy."

"Well, when things lighten up a little, I'm going to go for a few days. I'll listen to her tell me what she's worried about, look at her inventory and talk to her lawyers, who I actually already know. I lived in that house for thirteen years. Then she can lock up the house. I'm trying to find her something up here so I can see her often. When it's all over and done, I can go back, take a couple of things to remember her and have her lawyers arrange an estate sale."

"Wow," Iris said. "The difference between rich and poor. Garage sale versus estate sale. You don't want to live in that house?"

"And do what?"

"I don't know. Have a kitchen and a large bathroom?" She rolled her eyes upward, indicating the loft.

At that moment, Troy came in the back door. His hair was errant from sleep and he wore a set of sweats that had somehow found a home in Grace's loft. Hands in his pockets, he shuffled in wearing his docksiders and no socks. He nodded at Iris and went straight to Grace, kissing her cheek.

"I'd rather have this," Grace said, putting her arms around his waist.

Iris, Troy and Grace had a completely unplanned and very productive brainstorming session and it was Iris who provided a solution, if Winnie would go along with it. "Go now," she said. "Go now, while I'm on spring break. Take a few days. Make sure you leave me with your flower orders. Knowing you, you have everything you need for Peyton and Scott's wedding written down somewhere so I can place the order. If your new assistant is good, she'll be available to open the shop next week if you're still gone. If not," she said with a shrug, "I'll post a sign. Closed For Family Business. Leave me your work cell and I'll fill phone orders after school."

"I can help," Troy said.

Grace bit her lip. "I was kind of hoping you'd come with me," she said.

"Me? I don't want to get in the way."

"Even if it's just for a couple of days…"

"You should, Troy," Iris agreed. "All this—Grace's mother, the business of Grace dealing with her will and property—this could affect you."

"She's right, Troy. If you can. If you don't want to, I understand. I know my mother can be hard to take."

"Winnie doesn't get to me like she gets to you," he said. "But you better open this discussion about her relocation right away. She doesn't strike me as the kind of woman who gives in to someone else's ideas easily. And moving out of her home when she's sick and feeling vulnerable—that might be too much to ask of her."

"Moving is hard, but Winnie won't have to actually do any moving. She's been directing traffic her whole life. She'll have other people do it all. She'll board a plane. Her assistant will handle everything from the luggage to the flight. She's the gatekeeper of the records and BlackBerry. When I was young, before I left Mother's house, there was a different assistant in charge and my mother showed me a cataloged inventory of her possessions that was as thick as a big-city phone book."

"Must be nice," Iris said.

"It's how she chooses to live, the same way her parents lived. It's not that it's easy—a lot of energy goes into everything she does. And she does good things. She's a socialite—she's raised millions for charities. But she can't drive a car. I prefer a different kind of life, a much lighter load. I don't want my life to be that complicated." She thought for a second. "This could work except for one thing—the Lacoumette-Grant wedding. I have to be back for that. I *want* to be back for that wedding. It's a big job but I really want to see a Basque wedding in a pear grove! It could be so good for my résumé!"

"Grace, you have a week. And I can keep the shop open for you on that weekend, if you want me to. We're not going. Half the town is going and my deputy is going to guard the town," Iris said.

Grace sank onto the stool at her worktable. "Do you think there's any chance Winnie will go for this idea?"

"What's the alternative?" Iris asked.

"I guess I could fly down to San Francisco a lot."

Seventeen

Ginger started her day at eight that morning and at five she went back to Ray Anne's. To her surprise, Ray Anne was there as if waiting for her. She was sitting on the sofa with her laptop open. Ray Anne had stopped by the flower shop in the afternoon to talk with Grace, but Ginger was too busy to say more than a quick hello. She suspected Ray was watching her, making sure she wasn't going to pieces or running to hide.

"How was your day?" Ray Anne asked.

"Oh, God, it was unbelievable!" Tears suddenly ran down Ginger's cheeks. "The second I walked in, Grace and her friend Iris explained all the complications of the week and how important it was that I get the feel of the shop because they were desperate for help. Iris's mother used to own that shop and Iris started showing me how to make centerpieces and bouquets. She had me watching videos of floral construction right away. Then she helped me do my own—following a picture—and my first two weren't so good, but my third was pretty good and she could fix them. A shipment of flowers came in the afternoon. And Grace's mother and some man came to see her. I had to constantly clean up, run the register, take orders—but I could never get them right the first time so I needed help. I had so much trouble pricing them at first." She sniffed. "Grace's boyfriend brought us lunch that we had to eat in shifts. Iris's husband stopped by three times to see if she needed anything, and Peyton who's marrying the doctor came to check in with Grace about her wedding up near Portland on her family's farm, and I had to learn to write up flower purchase orders, and I think I swept that shop floor more than I've ever swept in my life."

"Oh, honey," Ray Anne said sympathetically. "Was it just horrible?"

"Huh?" she said, and grabbed a tissue to blow her nose. "It was *wonderful*!"

"Wonderful?" Ray Anne asked carefully.

"It's just a little flower shop but it felt like the hub of a big city! I guess word has gotten out that Grace's mother is sick, but she didn't look very sick. She's beautiful and is being chauffeured around with some Russian man who is her escort or something. But people were dropping in all day to check on Grace, ask if there's any way they can help, offering anything she might need and they were so *nice* to me!" And then she broke down and sobbed into her tissue.

Ray Anne moved closer to Ginger. She put a hand

on her back. "Is this normal? To be sobbing because it went well?"

"I don't know," Ginger murmured. She blew her nose again. "Now that I'm home and sitting down, I'm exhausted. And I want my baby, Ray! I want my baby so much."

"Oh, angel."

"But I only thought about him a couple of times today because I was so busy. Maybe it was a few times, but I didn't dwell. I usually think about him from the second my eyes open till I close them again at night."

"I know it seems like such a little thing, but sometimes being busy helps us persevere. Especially if the work feels meaningful. Did it feel meaningful?"

"To the people who chose flowers for special occasions, it means the world to them. Thankfully we didn't make up any funeral flowers. Grace told me if I wanted to go to the wedding to help her, she'd be so happy. And I can visit my parents. I can spend a night with them."

"Do you want to do that, Ginger?" Ray Anne asked her.

Ginger grabbed Ray Anne and hugged her hard, crying on her shoulder while Ray Anne stroked her back.

"Will you do me a favor, Ray?"

"If I can," she said.

"Will you call my mom and ask her to take down the crib? And put away some of those baby things?"

Ray Anne held her away, looking at her in shock.

"Ginger, have you had the crib and all those baby things sitting out all this time? For nine months?"

She nodded and wiped her eyes. "I couldn't let go. I don't know if I'll ever be able to get rid of everything. But I'm afraid if I go to my folks, even for one night, with all his little stuff sitting around like it's ready for him to come back and use it, I'll just spiral downward. I'm afraid I'll crawl right back into the bed and stay there forever."

"Listen to me," Ray Anne said. "You will have bad days. You will get emotional and sad and long for little Josh. And you'll get through it and move on to the next hour, the next day, the next week. And if I hear you're in bed and can't get up, I will drive up there and get you." She gave her hair a stroke. "Don't make me do that. I'm very busy right now."

"I have to get a grip," Ginger said, sniffing. "I think maybe I need a shower. And on Sunday I'm going to run over to Target and get some nice clothes that aren't so expensive for work. I just couldn't make myself change into those baggy old jeans."

"That's my girl."

"I think I fell apart a little bit."

"Ya think?" Ray Anne asked. She gave her a fond pat on the shoulder. "I think I better have a glass of wine. You take a shower."

Troy and Grace were on their way to Bandon to have dinner with Winnie and Mikhail. They were both extremely quiet for the first fifteen minutes. Then Grace reached for his hand and gave it a squeeze. "I know you didn't sign on for this. I really appreciate all your support, but I know how stressful and crazy it is. When you've had enough…I understand. It's too much to ask of anyone."

He squeezed back. "I'm not going to bail out on you in the middle of this."

"We were just dating, seeing where it would go, then the world seemed to explode. Listen, I can do this. I can. I can go with my mother for a few days, get things a little organized, plan how it will go after her… Enough for her to have some peace of mind. Hopefully Ray Anne will find a suitable house and—"

"And if Winnie rejects that idea?" he asked.

"Then I guess I'll be making some trips to San Francisco to visit her, but my life is here. I'm not moving. Not even for six months. The only way we'll live near each other is if she's willing to move here."

"She said you have a trust from your father. Are you actually rich?"

"Nah. I have enough to ensure I won't be homeless or hungry. I could've spent it in one weekend, but I've taken very good care of it."

"Could you live off it?"

"The way I live? In one room? For a few years. But I love working. Listen, I'm never going to live the way Winnie lives. Do you think I'm just saying that? That's one of the two main reasons we barely spoke for five years. I wouldn't compete anymore and I wouldn't come home to step into that life."

"Was it hard?"

"I gave it a lot of thought. I'm not the first person to disagree with her parents or to reject their lifestyle for my own choice. But what was hard was disappointing my mother, letting her down like that. It made her so angry. I might have made a different decision had I known she only had five years. But as Mikhail would say, *die is cast*! I'm sorry this has landed on your shoulders."

"Just do what you have to do and when I can help, I will."

"Thank you," she said quietly. "This isn't what I envision my life to be—one crisis after another."

"Gracie, sometimes that's how it is. We can't plan everything."

"I try. I really try. I like to stay ahead of things, but this…jeez, it's insane, that's what it is."

Winnie had chosen the same restaurant Troy had met her in last Sunday evening. This time when he approached the maître d' he *was* expected. Mikhail stood when they approached the table. He grabbed Grace's face and kissed her on each cheek in his way. Then they sat and ordered drinks while looking at the menu.

"Your flower shop is very cute, Grace," Winnie said. "You must be proud of it."

"Is perfect!" Mikhail said loudly.

Grace looked over the top of her menu. "All right, who are you and what have you done with my mother?"

"If I understood you, it's exactly what you want. Yes?"

"Yes," Grace said. "Why are you being so nice to me?"

Troy grabbed her hand. "Gracie, let your mother be nice."

"Right. Thank you. Troy says we're button-pushing maniacs."

"He would be correct," Mikhail said sharply. "Where is waiter? We should toast something. I don't know what, but something. We are together. Is good enough."

"I have an idea, Mother. Why don't I go to San Francisco with you for a few days. You can tell me all the things you're concerned about. We can make decisions about how you want things to be handled, and you can give me the names of agents and lawyers if you feel like it. Then I'll come home. I already have someone looking for a house for you in Coos County so we can be closer to each other."

"What?"

"I asked a Realtor to look for something nicer than the cottage you're staying in here at the resort, one level with a full kitchen, and I asked for an ocean view. The ocean is beautiful in summer. It's beautiful all year, but we have six months of mild weather ahead. I'll be nearby and can see you all the time."

"What about my house? My things?"

"We'll have Virginia and the housekeeper pack and ship what you want with you. I think I can find a place and have it ready quickly. Let's close up the house. I'll deal with it later. With your instructions and Virginia's help, I'll take care of everything, down to the last crystal ashtray. Right now, I want you nearby. I want to spend more time with you if possible."

"Then come to San Francisco!"

She calmly shook her head. "I don't live there. In fact, with all the traveling you do, you don't even spend six months a year there. I'm willing to do anything you say—dictate your instructions to whomever you like. If I know you, you've already done so. If you don't like this idea then I'll visit you as often as I can. But I'm not going to move to San Francisco. My home is here. But I can move you. I can find you a lovely place and excellent home care professionals if that becomes necessary."

"Is excellent notion!" Mikhail bellowed. "We will toast it."

Heads turned in the restaurant.

"Excellent notion?" Winnie said. "Leave my home for a strange place during the last months of my life? How is this excellent?"

Grace reached for her hand. "Because I don't think I can keep you comfortable in that big drafty urban mini-mansion. It's full of stairs, even in your bedroom and bath. The kitchen is a mile from the master bedroom and when you need assistance with things like getting around, bathing, eating…believe me, you're going to want a little less space and no stairs. Remember that little house you rented in Cabo? One story, nice accessible patio, view of the sea from the window? Hardly a prison, Mama. But I think you'll be miserable stuck in an upstairs bedroom in San Francisco, tended by servants."

She sensed rather than saw Troy's head turn to look at her.

"I don't know…"

"Mama, I want you to be comfortable. I want to be around to be sure…"

"Do you even know anything about this condition?"

"Oh, yes," she said. "I've been up till all hours reading about it every night. I talked to our local doctor about what you might need and if it would all be readily available." She got a little teary. "I think this can work," she said softly.

"Is excellent notion!" Mikhail bellowed again. The drinks arrived right as he shouted. "We go at once! This can happen."

"Don't you have a team to coach?" Grace asked.

"I have family emergency. Excuse me—I will have lovely Virginia make arrangements," he said, standing.

"I'd like Troy to come, if that's all right."

"Certainly," Winnie said, leaning her head into her hand. "But, Izzy…Grace, I meant Grace, we'll be busy with family matters."

"No problem," Mikhail said. "I will teach him poker."

"I know poker," Troy said.

"Ha. You think you know poker. Is too early to tell!"

Before dinner was over, Virginia had flight arrangements for all of them. They were to meet at the regional airport in North Bend for a two-o'clock departure the next afternoon.

Troy took Grace home and stayed the night. He was holding her after loving her. "Are you sure, Troy? You feel okay about going with me? Even though you'll miss a couple of days of work?"

He stroked her hair away from her eyes. "I don't know how we can go forward until you try to fix this thing with your mother. She's not easy, I can see that. But she's your family. And I think if you and your mother's roles were reversed, she'd be there for you. As best she could. And maybe not in the exact way you want her to be—just like you—but she'd do her best."

"Probably..."

"And if you were relying on her, you'd go to her."

"Probably."

"I get real put out with my family sometimes. We have our issues, our fights and standoffs. Then we pull it together. My folks are in their early sixties now, thinking about retirement, and I can't even imagine losing them." He gave her a little kiss on her temple. "When we get through some of this craziness, I want you to meet them."

"I bet they're very nice people."

"You're very nice people, Gracie."

"I know you must ask yourself how you got into this situation."

"Oh, I think it was New Year's Eve." He chuckled. "I'm sure you can't come up with any more surprises now."

"God, I hope not," she said emphatically, then curled up against him and went to sleep.

Grace was a little frantic in the morning, trying to figure out how to get everything ready. She wanted to leave the shop in good shape for Iris and Ginger, her loft cleaned up for her return, and she wanted to pack, shower, look presentable when it was time to go. She threw on her jeans from the day before and dashed down to the shop, leaving Troy in her bed once again. To her surprised delight, Iris and Ginger were already in the shop and Ginger had before her a beautiful white centerpiece.

"Look at *you*!" Grace said.

"I'm getting a little better, but my instructor is right beside me, moving things around, pointing, shaking her head when I choose the wrong stem or stalk, cutting off ends to the right length. I didn't exactly do this alone."

"But she's catching on," Iris said. "In a couple of weeks, she'll be re-creating some of your stock pieces on her own."

"Also, I'm extremely slow and careful," Ginger said. "Iris whips 'em out in twenty minutes."

"Iris grew up in this shop."

"I was helping to make centerpieces and wreaths and bouquets when I was ten. I guess you could say I've had a little practice."

"I'm leaving at around noon today for a two-o'clock flight," Grace said. "Let's go over the schedule and what you need from me before I leave. Iris, there will be a flower delivery today. The vendor will get here at about two and I'll be gone."

"I've done it before, Grace," Iris said.

"Be sure to give him the order for next Thursday, which includes the flowers for the Lacoumette-Grant wedding, and tell him I'll need it before noon. Post a sign that the shop will be closed Monday and Tuesday. I'll be back Tuesday night, open Wednesday."

"I can open Monday and Tuesday," Ginger said. "Don't worry, I won't attempt any extravagant arrangements. If you think it will be slow, I might not even have orders to fill."

"Ginger and I can make up a few stock arrangements so she has some on hand in the cooler to sell if anyone wanders in. And I'll check in after school on Monday to see if we should make anything up for Tuesday."

"You guys," she said. "You're so fantastic."

"We can figure out how to put a sign on the door. When are you headed to Portland for the wedding?"

"Friday morning, first thing. You still want to go, Ginger?"

She nodded enthusiastically. "Are you sure it's okay? Are you sure I won't be deadweight?"

"I'd love for you to come. I'm going to make up a few centerpieces early Friday morning for their Friday-night party but I'll transport the rest of my flowers in the back of the van, which is refrigerated. I'll make up the wedding flowers at my old shop in Portland early Saturday. That way if I'm missing anything Mamie and Ross can probably help me fill in. We're closing the shop for the wedding. That's how it rolls for a big out-of-town affair."

"I'll be around if you want someone in the shop that Saturday," Iris reminded her.

"Nah," Grace said. "When I took this wedding I made a decision—I'd close for a couple of days. What I could earn keeping the shop open is more than offset by Peyton's wedding. Let's not drive ourselves crazy. I can recommend other florists in the area or take orders for Monday pickup or delivery."

"Excellent," Iris said. "In that case, hand over the store cell phone. I'll take it until you're back."

Grace took it off her belt, looked at it and gave it to her. "The charger is on my desk. I think I'm having separation anxiety already."

"Just make sure your desk and computer are just as you want them—I might have to share them until you're back. Then get out of here, get ready to go."

"Right," she said, heading for her office. A half hour later she was hauling some of her spring sidewalk displays outside. When she turned, Iris was standing there, tapping her foot, arms crossed over her chest.

"All right," Iris said. "Ginger and I have this. Go."

"You're sure? I still have time…"

"Go. If I have a question, which I probably won't, I know your number."

"Okay." She looked at her watch. "I'll be upstairs till noon. I'll stop in to say goodbye."

"Great. We'll be fine."

Grace dashed up the stairs and into her loft. Troy

was just tugging up and zipping his pants and she grinned. "Looks like I'm seconds too late."

He pulled the zipper down. "I have a little time to spare."

"I should have learned by now, we don't joke around about sex, since you're a sex maniac. Zip those britches, mister—I have a lot to do. I want to clean up around here and pack. I'm sure you have things to do, too."

He tilted his head. "I'm a guy. My cleaning up and packing will take about fifteen minutes."

"That's great, just don't show up here until noon. It takes me longer."

"Yes, ma'am," he said, grabbing her around the waist and pulling her close to kiss her. "Thanks for last night." Then he let her go and shot out the door.

Grace took just a second to savor the moment. It was so nice having a real live boyfriend wanting her and letting her know it. She never in her wildest dreams imagined this could happen to her, especially not with someone as wonderful as Troy. She thought it only happened in novels.

She shook herself and got busy. It wouldn't take long—this was like living in an RV and she loved it. She changed her sheets and smoothed the comforter over her bed. Then she opened the suitcase on top of the bed but before she packed her clothes, she scrambled around the little loft. She ran the vacuum she kept in the small broom closet, dusted off her wood furniture, wiped off the table, counters, microwave, fridge and left the cleaner in the bathroom for the sink and mirror. She checked the fridge for food that should be thrown out, packed her charged laptop in her briefcase, and then she started on her clothes.

She wasn't taking anything dressy. She folded and packed underwear, a couple of pairs of nice pants, jeans, coordinated tops and a blazer. Shoes were added. She glanced at her watch, proud—there was plenty of time. She'd take a shower, clean the bathroom behind herself and be ready with time to spare. She stepped out of the shower after a nice scrub and shave, dried and moisturized, wrapped herself in a towel and reached under the sink for her makeup. She'd leave her makeup bag, hair dryer, brush and comb, lotion out on the counter so they could go right in her suitcase and—

There it was. Her box of tampons. That hadn't been touched in she wasn't sure how long. And right beside it in a little plastic bag was that pregnancy test Peyton had given her. Just in case... "Oh, dear baby Jesus," she said aloud. She sank onto the closed toilet lid.

What had happened?

Okay, Peyton had suggested the test if her period didn't come.

But instead of getting a period, she'd gotten a scary note that appeared to be from her stalker. The world tipped. She had been consumed with fear, with protection plans that included using a Taser on her boyfriend. She had been filled with frightening memories of being a fourteen-year-old girl held captive in a maintenance closet until police could come. Denny and Becca came for a weekend, and Grace skated for them. Her mother made a surprise appearance and...

Somewhere in there, with one crisis after another, she'd completely forgotten about everything else. She tried counting the weeks since she'd had a period and couldn't figure out the exact number.

The best thing that could happen would be a negative test result now. She unwrapped the test, read the directions quickly and got ready.

And nothing came.

"Come on, come on, come on," she chanted.

She sat and sat and finally, she felt the urge and wet the stick. Then she had to let it sit for a few minutes. She just stared at it. Gradually, after the first minute and a half, a pink shadow began to appear on the yes side. But she stared at it without blinking, because surely it would go away.

But no. It was two lines. A red button appeared and the word *yes* popped up.

Grace felt as if she was going to throw up. She sat weakly on the toilet lid. *Pregnant*, she thought. "Crap."

Eighteen

When Troy arrived back at Grace's place with his packed bag, he saw that hers was sitting at the foot of the stairs to the loft. Sure enough, he found her in the shop, going over last-minute details with Iris and Ginger.

"If Peyton should come in to check on things, tell her we're right on schedule and not to worry about a thing. I think she plans on going to Portland with her sister, Scott to follow with his kids. Even though I won't be here, tell her we're good to go, her flowers have been ordered, rest easy. She might not have my personal cell number so you can give it to her if she needs reassurance."

"Peyton's not the jittery sort," Iris said. "And I didn't think you were, but you seem to be wound up. Is taking the boyfriend home a little nerve-racking?"

She shook her head. "My mother has met Troy, so that's not it. I haven't been home in years. In fact, my last four years in competition I was rarely home.

I was wherever my coach or the competition was and that was everywhere but home. I seemed to be training in LA or Chicago, only visiting San Francisco when my mother happened to be there. I have no reason to be nervous."

"Well, if leaving the shop worries you, relax. Even if I really screw up the next four days, your shop will be here when you get home," Iris said. "And I promise you, I can keep the place standing."

"You will never know how much I appreciate this," Grace said. "I'll make this up to you somehow."

"Just go. Try to enjoy it a little even though it's a heavy burden you're dealing with."

"We'll be fine," Troy said. "I'm anxious to see Grace's home. Come on, Gracie, relax. Iris will take good care of things. Let's go—our flight leaves in a little less than two hours and we have a drive."

Grace gave Iris and Ginger hugs and let herself be drawn away. Troy picked up her suitcase. "Anything else?"

"That's it."

"I hope there's a little time to go into the city," he said. "If you can't, I understand." He hefted the suitcase into the back of the Jeep. "I love the city," he said as he got in the car. He drove out of the alley and reached for her hand. "Are you really jittery?"

"Oh, maybe a little overwhelmed at all there is to deal with. But I'll be fine once we get there."

"It's all good," he said. "Pays to have friends like Iris. Not only is she taking care of the flower shop, she's lining up a substitute for me for Monday and

Tuesday. As much as I enjoy the kids, I'm looking forward to summer." And he proceeded to talk about things he hoped to do over the summer. He realized she might be pretty busy this summer, but he hoped there would be time for a couple of short camping trips along one of his favorite rivers in Idaho. He talked a little bit about some of his favorite river trips in the five-state area. Although Grace nodded a lot, he could tell she was barely paying attention to him. But he thought he was doing her a service by regaling her with stories to take her mind off four days with her mother.

When they got to the regional airport he looked around. "I've never flown out of here. And get this— it appears parking in this lot is free."

She gave him a strange look.

He pulled the suitcases out of the back and Grace took control of hers, extending the handle and pulling it.

"What airline is this?" he asked her.

"Oh, Troy," she said, walking ahead. "I haven't prepared you for this. I'm sorry."

He held the door for her and they entered a small reception area banked by a counter behind which people worked on one side, offices and refreshment machines on the other. A sign pointed to the restaurant. A double door led right onto the runway. There were a few people waiting, and Winnie, Virginia and Mikhail were seated by the door. Mikhail stood up and greeted them. "Good, you are here. We can go."

Mikhail took Winnie's left arm while Virginia

took her right and they carefully guided her out the door and onto the tarmac. They passed through what appeared to be a metal detector but nothing like the usual airport security.

"Where are we going?" Troy asked.

"Air Winnie," Grace said, indicating the small jet straight ahead. There were air stairs, but a uniformed man waited at the bottom with a chair-like contraption for Winnie. The plane was not a little six-seater: it was a private jet.

"Shits of the gods," Troy muttered.

Troy could not believe he was flying on a private jet. Like most people, just affording coach fares was a challenge. And when he thought about rich people, he thought they were very different, not people just like he was. "Did you always travel like this?" he asked Grace.

"No, not very often. We took a chartered jet on occasion. Now, I think my mother indulges this because of her condition. Her days of traveling are numbered."

The jet was midsize, generously spaced with seating for ten, a large galley, large restroom, tables and closet space. The cabin was beautiful, the seats wide and comfortable. And Grace could tell from the glitter in Troy's eyes that he was loving it. "This is shit-hot," he whispered to her.

Hmm. He isn't put off, she thought. Well, that was a good sign.

She wanted to tell Troy about the pregnancy test,

but she didn't dare. Not now, not at the onset of four days with her mother. The second they had this visit behind them, the moment they had some time alone that wouldn't be interrupted by her mother's needs, she would tell him. But the last thing she wanted was for Winnie to find out before she settled things with Troy. She had to know how he wanted to deal with this situation. What if he didn't want it? What if he didn't want *her* anymore? What if everything collapsed because she had screwed up the plan?

The captain came into the cabin and introduced himself to Winnie, saying a brisk hello to the others. "We're ready if you are," he said.

"By all means," Winnie said.

"Our flight time should be just slightly over an hour," he told her. "If you need anything at all, press your call button."

"Thank you," she said.

Once they were airborne, Winnie and Virginia had a little meeting. Virginia had her notebook out and made a list from Winnie's comments. There were many details. Alex, Winnie's driver, had left them at the airport and was driving the car back to San Francisco. A car service had been arranged to pick them up when they landed. Dinner at the house was being prepared and the guest rooms were freshened. There were people Winnie wanted called, household maintenance she wanted done, bills paid. Mikhail pulled out a deck of cards and started playing solitaire. And before long Winnie stopped dictating and nodded off.

"Are you all right?" Troy asked her.

"Sure. Fine. I just have very mixed feelings about going home. A part of me wants to see the place once more but…" She shook her head. "A part of me is afraid I won't be able to leave."

"Because you love it?"

"No, because I'll be trapped somehow."

"Don't be irrational, Gracie. You can do what you want."

"That's always been hard," she said. "Doing what I want instead of what my mother wants."

"Yes, but now you've had some practice."

Just over two hours later a black Cadillac SUV was passing through the iron gates into a Nob Hill neighborhood filled with large old houses fronted by manicured lawns and beautiful landscaping. Their driver pulled into a circular drive and right up to the front entrance of a rich-looking manor house. The driver parked and raced around to help Winnie get out. He was quickly replaced by Virginia on one arm and Mikhail on the other while Troy assisted the driver with the luggage.

"If you'll help me get it inside, I can manage it from there," Troy said.

"Be happy to, sir."

When he passed through the big double doors Troy found himself not in a house but in an impressive courtyard with durable outdoor furniture scattered around, an outdoor sofa and two overstuffed chairs in front of a beautiful hearth. There were two sets of tables and chairs, vines climbing along the walls, small trees, flower beds lining the courtyard, hanging and standing pots filled with plants and a couple of decorative statues.

He brought a couple of suitcases into the courtyard, Grace brought his and her own inside, the driver assisted him with the rest, most of which must have belonged to Winnie. She traveled well, but she didn't travel light. "This is fine," Troy said. "I can get it from here."

"Thank you, sir."

He walked with Grace through the next door, into the house, and he stopped inside the massive foyer with marble mosaic floor, wide curving staircase and huge formal sitting room opposite the staircase. He looked around in awe.

Winnie was four steps up the stairs, grasping the rail on one side, Virginia on the other, Mikhail close behind her. Then she stumbled back a step and Mikhail steadied her. Troy gasped and whispered, "Jesus." He left the suitcases where they sat and went to them.

"Winnie, here," he said, brushing Virginia out of the way. "Let's do this, it's safer." He swept her up in his arms and told Virginia to lead the way.

"Leave those bags, Gracie. I'll come back for them."

But she followed him, pulling her own bag up the stairs. It made her so proud, the way he stepped up to the plate and carried Winnie to her bedroom. He asked her where she'd like him to put her down and she pointed to the chair beside the veranda. He even bent over and moved the footstool for her feet.

"Thank you, dear boy," she said.

He glanced around the room briefly, and his eyes settled on the big four-poster bed. "Winnie, you're not going to be able to get in and out of that bed by yourself."

"Don't worry, I'll stay in the adjoining room," Virginia said. "I'll be able to help her."

"It was where I stayed when my husband was ill," Winnie said. "Grace?" she called, looking past Troy to where Grace stood in the doorway. "Grace, I'm so tired. I might have to miss dinner. I hope you won't be offended."

"Of course not. Let me put my suitcase away and I'll come and help you undress and get into bed."

"Virginia can help me—"

"Let me, Mama. I'll be right back. Troy, let me show you where we're going to be."

"I'll bring up your luggage, Winnie," he said. "It'll just be a couple of minutes."

Grace led the way down the hall to the room that was hers when she lived in this house. She was a little surprised—not a thing had been changed. It looked the same as the day she left. Out of curiosity she opened the walk-in closet and everything was there. She'd even left a comb and brush on the dressing table in the attached bathroom. She hadn't exactly expected Winnie to turn it into a sewing room or anything, but this was almost a shrine. There was a special case for her trophies, medals and ribbons. And there were many.

"Will you be comfortable in here with me?" she asked Troy.

"Will it upset your mother?" he asked. "Us sharing a bed?"

"I hope not, because I can't have it any other way. Seriously? I think she knows I'm no longer a child. She's not a prude."

"If you're sure…"

She left her suitcase standing by the closet door. "I'm sure. I'm going to go help her get comfortable and into that bed. Thanks for offering to bring up her bags. Then you can poke around."

"I might get lost. Grace, I've never seen anything like this in my life. At least not since I toured Hearst Castle."

"Come on, it's not that big. I think it's under ten thousand square feet."

"Right. Four houses. I should take a whistle in case I need to be rescued."

"Don't tease me about it, okay? I know it's a lot of house."

"I can see how something this big can be overpowering," he said, looking around her bedroom. "I think it's hilarious that you live in that little loft."

"And love it," she said. She got up on her toes and kissed his cheek. "Thanks for carrying Winnie up the stairs. That was very gallant."

"I saw a broken hip in her future if I didn't. I'll go get her luggage."

"When the driver is here, he handles things like that. But he probably hasn't even hit Eureka yet."

"Well, you've got me. Maybe I'll come in handy."

* * *

Grace and Troy had their dinner in the kitchen. A caterer delivered and served gumbo, linguini, bread, tomatoes with buffalo mozzarella. Virginia took Winnie a tray and Mikhail joined her, leaving Troy and Grace alone.

They ate in silence while the caterer closed up containers and left them on the work island in the big kitchen to be placed in the refrigerator after they'd cooled. When she left, Grace put down her spoon. "This place isn't going to work for my mother," she said. "I admit, I was being a little selfish when I said we should find her a place near Thunder Point—I didn't want to leave my shop, you, my friends…I knew this house was too big, the furniture and stairs difficult for an invalid, but until now I didn't realize how right I was. This isn't a good place for her now." She shook her head. "If she doesn't fall getting in or out of that bed…"

"You can't leave her here without nursing help," Troy said.

"I won't. Virginia knows everyone. She's like a personal concierge. That's part of her job, knowing where to look, who to call."

"Tell me what you'd like me to do while I'm here," he said.

"I don't know. I'll spend tomorrow with Virginia and my mother. We have to pull together a plan. I better call Ray Anne and see if she's making progress. This is more urgent than I realized."

"Gracie, this is all going to be yours," he said. "What are you going to do with it?"

"I'm going to figure that out. And then I'm going home, where there's a life that's not bigger than life."

"Really, I don't know how you can leave this."

"Do you want it, Troy? All this house, all the up-keep, maintenance, work? All the space? All the responsibility? All the *people*?"

"I don't think so," he said. "But, Gracie, it's damned intimidating."

"In what way?" she asked.

He was quiet for a second. "If you have all this, what more could you possibly need? What could I ever give you that you don't already have ten of?"

"Do you really have to ask?"

Grace had to take on a house she'd never known, not really. It had never been her burden to make sure it was cared for or staffed—that had been something women like Winnie were bred and raised to do. And Winnie was dying.

No matter how much Winnie might want to be in charge, it was no longer practical. Virginia called Winnie's neurologist, the man who initially diagnosed her almost four years earlier. Dr. Halstead came to the house in the late afternoon the very next day. Grace understood that house calls were not typical for him, but he'd known Winnie long before she needed his medical expertise—they had served together on several charity boards over the years. He confirmed that Winnie had hobbled along with her disease for longer than was typical; now it was a matter of finding a team who could help manage her quality of life. When asked how long that life might last, his prognosis wasn't positive. It could be as short as a few months, as long as a year but more likely something in between. Now it was down to staying comfortable and taking advantage of her mental acuity, which would probably be the last to fail.

"I live up the coast in a very small quiet town," Grace told him. "I have someone looking for a place for Mother so I can be on hand, where I can see her every day. I don't want her to have to go to a hospital."

"That's the best way. Most end-stage ALS patients require a great deal of support, but there's no way to reverse the disease."

The first order of business was moving a smaller bed into Winnie's room. Virginia contacted a home health care service and since Winnie didn't go through insurance or require approval, she arranged to pay top dollar for a couple of experienced nurse's aides who would start helping out immediately, taking the burden of her personal care off Grace and Virginia.

And Mikhail.

"You're still here," Grace observed. "When do you plan to return to your team?"

"I think, much later. They're in good hands. If they choose other coach, so be it."

"I'm taking her to Thunder Point as soon as I can," she reminded him.

"Thunder Point," he said with a shrug. "Not so bad."

"Are you planning to stay with her, then?"

"I have nothing so important right now."

He was the perfect distraction for Winnie. He wasn't ready to retire, but he wasn't a young man at sixty-six. "I had no idea Mother meant so much to you," she said. "All the years you coached me, you ran interference between Mother and me. You're the one that kept me working and her in line. I didn't know you loved her."

"Love? Not the love you know, *pupsik*. We understand each other. It could be my life closing, not hers. She would not turn me out. Is family. There should be one person who doesn't hate me on the other side. I'm not long behind her."

But he was long behind her—he was strong, his health good, and this was a sacrifice for him. He was in demand as a coach, his business was still thriving. She knew he would be missed. She also knew that he could stay a few weeks and go back to his team, currently managed by coaching assistants, and pick up right where he left off. "I'm glad you're staying awhile. Don't get underfoot, now. Maybe teach Troy poker or something."

There was a housekeeper who came in weekdays from eight to five. She was fifty-five, of German descent—the woman who had replaced Mamie. She wasn't as warm and motherly as Mamie, but that might've had more to do with the fact that they didn't really know each other. She seemed to have a wonderful rapport with Virginia, who was younger by only a few years.

Gretchen didn't do much housework and only a little cooking. She was the manager of a big house— she hired and supervised a cleaning service, ordered groceries to be delivered and called local restaurants to bring in meals customized to Winnie's needs. Virginia and Grace met with her in the kitchen and Gretchen was more than happy to stay on after Winnie was moved. After all, it was great pay for far less work.

Meeting her mother's two lawyers was emotionally exhausting, but not because it was hard work. Just as Grace had suspected, Winnie had been prepared. She'd known for years that this was coming. Everything in the house had been cataloged, photographed and appraised, including jewelry. As for Winnie's accounts and net worth, it had all been managed and audited—after all, the money was old. It wasn't as though it was a new job.

Grace met briefly with a Realtor. She wouldn't make a commitment and even suggested she wasn't sure what she would do with this property, but she knew exactly what would happen. Whispered feelers would go out and when the time came to sell, there would be an auction. The house was a prime property.

It was all so huge to her. Even flying first-class, going to skate practices in a chauffeured car and owning her own business hadn't really prepared her for the magnitude of her imminent inheritance.

But as Grace began to understand the full weight of it, she felt Winnie's stress. It had been a life's work. "Please don't worry," she told her mother. "I won't let it be abused, stolen or ignored. I promise."

"But what will you do with it?" Winnie asked.

"Just as you did, Mama. I'll take very good care of it."

"And the house and all these possessions?" she asked.

"I want you to be at peace about that. It's all being guarded and cared for. And later, when you don't need it anymore, I'll go through it, claim those things that have sentimental value to both of us and then... Then there will be an estate sale managed by the company you suggested. If it will give you peace of mind, I can meet with them before I go home."

"Grace, do you have to go home?"

"I have to get a place ready for us," she said.

She wanted enough space so that when necessary she could stay the night with her mother, but she wasn't planning to live in the house with her.

"You'll need money. Virginia has some banking cards for you to sign for your checking account. And when you find that house, I want my bedroom rug, the Aubusson. And the antique dressing table. And the china. Not the expensive china, the Audun Fleur. And there's silver that was my mother's—if you don't want to use it, I understand, but if there's a granddaughter someday..."

Grace touched her hand. "I might not use some of my grandmother's and great-grandmother's treasures, but I promise to keep them in case... There could be daughters one day."

"Wouldn't it be wonderful if there were daughters for you?" she said. "You will do so much better with them than I did."

"I hope there are daughters and I hope I can love them as much," she said, even though for so many years she had found fault with her mother's form of affection.

"We got to the top, Izzy," she said.

"Yes, Mother. Thank you for all you did."

"No, Izzy. Thank you for doing it for me."

Grace never thought she'd hear that! "We were a good team when it came to winning," she said. She made a vow. When she had children, she wasn't going to put the burden of her desires on them.

Every day exhausted her. She would see Troy on and off through the days. He poked around the house and neighborhood, went down to the wharf a couple of times and kept himself busy. He made friends with the maintenance men, pestered Gretchen in the kitchen, got lost in the library and spent some time on his laptop. She'd have dinner with him in the kitchen, fall into bed with him at night and sometimes she cried. She was losing the mother she had always loved, tried so hard to please and never really known.

Finally Tuesday came and it was time to go back to Thunder Point. She was so relieved, but frantic at the leaving. Virginia would stay, help get her mother to Thunder Point when the time came. Mikhail was planning on coming to Thunder Point, as well. Then Virginia would return to San Francisco. The house-keeper would remain to keep the house in order and in good repair until it was time to close it up. All the account information and household data was uploaded to accessible accounts so they were easy for Grace to oversee. She could call the accounting firm or lawyers whenever there was a question or request. The neighborhood and the house had private security; the contents had been inventoried, and her mother was in good hands with Virginia running herd on her health care providers.

The plane that Virginia arranged for Troy and Grace wasn't a large plush jet, but rather a small Lear that returned them to Thunder Point in no time at all.

Grace wanted to tell him about the baby. Funny, in her mind it had gone from a positive pregnancy test to a baby. Oh, she was falling in love with the baby already.

But she was so tired after four days of getting things settled, she just fell asleep on the plane. They had a quick bite to eat on the way home from the air-port then Troy helped her get her suitcase up to her little apartment. "I have to go home, babe," he said. "I need to get ready for work in the morning. You going to be all right?"

"I'll be fine," she said. "Thank you for coming with me. Thank you for everything you did."

"I didn't do much. You handled it all. I'll talk to you after work tomorrow."

Nineteen

Troy couldn't count the number of times Grace had said "You don't understand" when she was telling him about her childhood, her life as a competitive figure skater, her parents. Likewise, he couldn't imagine how many times he had replied, "Of course I do, Grace." Now, he realized, he really hadn't. Grace had come from a world so alien to him he wondered if he would ever understand it.

Troy had never been around people with the kind of money it took to rent a jet or live in a mansion with a complete staff to take care of it. But of course there had to be a staff—no one could take care of something that big alone. The closest he'd ever come to that kind of wealth was knowing a guy who had a cousin who was a pro football player and bought himself a three-million-dollar house and a fast car. He couldn't even remember what kind of car because of course he'd never seen it. Troy didn't even read about rich people. He read about rafting, climb-

ing, diving. He was scrimping to make his Jeep pay-
ments. Grace could probably pay it off out of her
allowance.

Did Grace get an allowance?

He left Grace at her place and went home to his
apartment, which was very quiet. It was also very
lonely. He had only rarely spent a night alone since
he started sleeping with Grace and he wasn't thrilled
about being alone tonight, either. Troy had never
lived with a woman and he still didn't, not officially
at any rate. He and Grace each had their own place.
Except he checked in with Grace at least three times
a day and saw her when they were both off work.
And stayed the night more often than not.

But right now he needed a little space and time
to think. He thought he knew her inside and out,
but after four days in San Francisco he wondered if
he knew her at all. He was more than a little intimidated by the magnitude of her wealth. It made him
feel like a failure by comparison. Intellectually he
knew that wasn't the case, but somewhere inside, he
had that sinking feeling of not being good enough.

The next day, during his free period, he went
looking for Iris, whom he considered his closest
friend. She was a counselor and he needed counseling. There was a part of him that hoped she'd be
busy with a student, because he wasn't sure how he
was going to put into words what he was thinking.

"Got a minute?" he asked, standing in her doorway.

"Sure," she said with a smile. "Want to sit?"

"Thanks," he said, sitting in front of her desk. But then he didn't say anything.

"Troy? Problems with a student?"

He shook his head. "Listen, I don't know how to say this, how to explain this, so if I sound like an idiot…"

"Just spit it out. We can rake through the idiocy afterward."

"Can this be confidential?" he asked.

"Of course!"

"It's about Grace. We've gotten pretty close."

Iris smiled. "You two seem great together."

"You know we're not alike, right?"

She made a doubtful face. "You seem a lot alike. You laugh at the same things, you appear to be inseparable, she's an athlete and you're a pretty physical guy. I bet you finally found someone to play with."

"But we come from completely different backgrounds. *Completely.* Did you know Grace is—" He struggled. "She's well-to-do."

Iris leaned back. "I heard that. I mean, she told me. It was pretty recently, when she was telling me about growing up on the ice-skating circuit. She said she had tutors and traveled the world to compete and I asked how expensive things like skating lessons were. Lessons for kids can be as much as ninety dollars an hour but coaching for world champions? It can be any amount, depending on the coach, maybe four hundred a day! Plus expenses. So I asked…"

"Her mother is rich," he said. "*Old* money. Apparently there's a difference," he added.

"She didn't make it on a dot-com," Iris said with a grin. "I assume there's enough so that it keeps growing itself. Not only was Grace born into it, apparently her mother was, as was her grandmother."

"It might be billions," Troy said.

"Billions? Come on!"

"I don't know. How would I know? But here's what I know after spending a few days at her childhood home. The house is bigger than four normal houses, and it takes a full staff to run it so just one person can live in it. There's a full-time driver, even if he's not driving much. I think her mother might have other houses—she likes to spend time in Cabo, in New York, in London. There's art and jewelry and her mother can rent private jets anytime she wants to. I mean, she stinks with it. I'm serious."

"Wow. Incredible. Sounds like the Gettys. You should look and see if they're on the Forbes List."

"I'm afraid to," Troy said.

"Why?" she asked with a laugh. "She'll still be your friend."

"Iris, we've been more than friends. And I can't relate to that kind of money."

"Just as well," she said, laughing. "It's not yours. It's hers."

"Iris, could you please stop laughing. It makes me feel like a poor relation with his hand out."

"You have your *hand* out?"

"Of course not! But that's how I feel! Do you know anyone that rich?"

"I'm not sure," she said. "Peyton comes from a pretty rich family."

"She does?" he asked, shocked.

"Uh-huh. Her parents own one of the biggest farms in Oregon. Huge. They grow pears for Harry & David, potatoes for grocers, have a ton of sheep for the wool and now she says her father and brothers are into Christmas trees. Scott says it's a huge family, almost all of them in the business, and her father has holes in his jeans and drives an old pickup with no shocks. He probably doesn't have a twenty in his pocket, but his net worth is astronomical."

"I didn't know that," he said. "Do they live in a big house?"

"Yes. With one bathroom. Eight kids, one bathroom. Try to imagine."

"Okay, we're not talking about the same thing at all. Grace has money to burn. I think if she started spending it now she couldn't go through it all. Unfortunately for her mother, it's in Grace's near future."

Iris sat back in her chair and chewed on her pen. "Troy, what about this is a problem?"

He shrugged and looked down.

"Spit it out before I start guessing."

"I don't feel good enough."

"Ridiculous," she scoffed. "Your individual incomes have nothing at all to do with your worth. After all, Grace didn't earn hers, did she? She was born to it—that's nothing but luck. You should start playing the lottery, maybe you'll get lucky."

"Tell me how to get past this," he said. "My brain is

telling me it makes no sense to feel this way and I don't know why I can't shake it. I'm a smart person. I don't discriminate against anyone. What the hell is this?"

"I think it's testosterone," she said. "Really!" she said, her tone indicating some disgust.

"Where'd you come up with that?"

"It sounds like just another version of 'let's get 'em out and measure 'em, boys.' Men have this competitive thing, this need for mastery. You have a hard time if you think you're not in control, especially in control of your woman. Something about Grace's family money makes you feel vulnerable and awkward. And yet the girl lives in a tiny loft! She drives a flower delivery van!"

"I've never been like that," he said. "I've never been controlling toward women. If you knew my mother or sister, you wouldn't even suggest that."

"Then what is it?" she asked.

"I don't know. It's just…I wonder what I could ever get her if she has everything. What can I do for her if she can pick up the phone and hire it done?"

Iris stared at him in wonder. She leaned toward him and her voice was disarmingly soft. "Troy, I want you to think about those questions—what could you give her, what could you do for her? When you come up with the answers, you will have solved the problem. I'm not going to be able to answer for you. But can I just tell you one thing?"

"Please."

"The important things Seth gives me never come out of his pocket."

* * *

Grace didn't sleep as well without Troy as she had with him, but after all he'd done for her the past week, she'd never complain. She was up early, not because she was ambitious but because she didn't want to struggle again and again to fall back to sleep. The look it left on her was less than gorgeous. After the past week, including her four days in San Francisco, she had dark circles under her eyes. She used a little cosmetic concealer and hoped she wouldn't yawn all day.

She got into the shop early and found it was as clean as an ICU, her flowers all well cared for and chilling, her desk clear and the front of the store sparkling. Even the scarred, stained worktable had been scrubbed and if she wasn't mistaken, the floor had been thoroughly mopped, something she didn't bother with more than once a week. That workroom saw a lot of action and keeping it pristine was a never-ending task.

Ginger wasn't due until nine but she came in at eight, using her own key. She was clearly surprised to see Grace and her face lit up with a happy smile. "Welcome home! How was the trip?"

"Productive," she said. "And very tiring. I'm going to want to speak to Ray Anne at her earliest convenience. Is she awake?"

"Awake, already left the house and said to tell you she's planning to come down to talk with you today, probably before noon."

"Outstanding," Grace said. "The place looks

great, Ginger. It looks like you were scrubbing all night."

"No, not at all. There wasn't much business. I only tried my hand at one arrangement, which didn't turn out too well, then I stopped. I didn't want to waste flowers on practice."

"Well, we get a new shipment tomorrow and since they're mostly for the wedding, I'll order yet another for Monday. Later today you can feel free to practice. Flowers that have reached their life expectancy have to be disposed of anyway."

"It must kill you to throw away flowers," Ginger said.

"It kills me more to get a phone call from a customer saying their centerpiece lasted two days! Fresh is beautiful, remember that."

"Can I make you some coffee?" Ginger asked, going to the workroom.

Grace thought about it, then lied. "I've already had coffee, thanks. Go ahead, make yourself a pot. The minute we have time, I'll show you how to use the designing computer programs I have."

While they were in San Francisco, Grace had stayed away from wine and caffeine, though she could have used a full tank of each. She'd let Troy pour her a glass of wine, then nurse it. She'd take a sip and complain of being too tired to enjoy it and once she tipped it into a potted plant when he wasn't looking. She poured coffee down the drain. No one seemed to notice. She wasn't sure Troy would question it but since she wasn't ready to confront it, she kept silent.

Tonight, however. Tonight it had to be done. She was afraid, of course. She hoped he wouldn't suggest they terminate to give themselves more time, because in the days since she'd peed on the stick she'd been seeing a real, beautiful baby in her mind. Now there was no direction for her other than to have it, to hold it and love it.

It was late morning when Ray Anne came into the shop.

"I'm so glad you're here," Grace said. "I'm afraid I have to do everything I can to find a place for my mother and quickly. I knew that old house in the Bay Area wasn't going to work for her—everything is a challenge, from the bed to the stairs to the bath. We practically have to have her doctor flown in and she's pretty much captive in that bedroom with no fresh air or—"

Ray Anne was smiling. "We've got the solution. Everything you need, everything you asked for."

"Really? How'd you find it?"

"I'd love to take credit, but Cooper will rat me out eventually. He has three spec houses that can be occupied in three months or less and he's given me the contracts."

Her face fell. "Ray Anne, we don't have three months."

"Not to worry. The exteriors are nearly finished on all three and one of them only needs a little... Oh, listen, come with me, come and see. Ginger can stay here, can't she?"

"She sure can," Grace said. "She left the place better than I leave it!"

Grace jumped in Ray Anne's car and they drove along the beach by the high road that wound behind the houses right down to Cooper's bar. Stairs led from the bar and houses down to the beach, the structures being safely perched on the hill. Ray Anne parked in the drive of the house nearest Cooper's, next door to Spencer and Devon Lawson's home. There were a lot of trucks and construction equipment everywhere and Grace was immediately disappointed. "These houses look far from ready," she said. "And, Ray Anne, they're three levels! Stairs!"

"Oh, they're not completely ready, but Cooper's hoping to get contracts on them before the interior is finished so new owners can choose their flooring, paint, appliances, decorator items like wallpaper. Come inside, you'll see." She led the way and held the door open.

They stepped into a wide foyer that opened right to a large living room and dining room. Very large. "Twenty by twenty," Ray Anne confirmed. Behind the great room was a nice-sized kitchen with plenty of cupboard space, once the cupboards were installed, that is. A breakfast bar divided it from the dining room and there was an island with a small sink. Straight ahead, a triple sliding door led to a wide deck. There was a fireplace on one wall, mantel unfinished. There were no countertops or appliances; the floors were plywood and still littered with construction trash. To the right of the kitchen were matching up and down staircases with crude railings in want of the finished decorator banisters. There was a door into the kitchen from the garage.

"This way," Ray Anne said. She walked to the left down a wide hall. The master bedroom was in front, beach side, with a large en suite bath. French doors led onto the deck. A second bedroom was across the hall. There was a generous bathroom down the hall for the use of anyone on that floor. "Now listen," Ray Anne said. "What do you hear?"

"Hammers and saws," Grace said, again disappointed.

"But not as loud. And I have a solution for that. But consider this. We can get the flooring, appliances and bathroom fixtures in very quickly. Countertops would have to be rushed. You have your choice of cupboards—once you make up your mind about the wood type. They're constructed off-site and installed in a day. Paint on this level would take two days."

"Ray Anne, it's not finished! It's noisy! My mother isn't well!"

"Your mother is quickly becoming wheelchair-bound but she's not feeling ill or in pain—isn't that what you told me? And there won't be any more noise in this property once we get this level finished. And as far as the neighboring houses are concerned— once the exteriors are finished, all the construction noise will be indoors. A good pair of soft noise-canceling headphones can solve that problem easily.

Come back this way." Ray Anne clacked down the hall to the great room in her heels. She stood in the center of the room. "The slab is poured and doors and windows installed on the lower level. The walls for two bedrooms, game room and large bathroom aren't finished, but it's closed up, airtight. There are two rooms and a small bath in the loft. The bedrooms have ocean views. The garage has unfinished walls but it's completely functional. Now use your imagination…" And with that, Ray Anne closed her eyes as if dreaming.

"I'm trying," Grace said. "I've got to get my mother out of that San Francisco house soon, before she goes stir-crazy in that big old bedroom of hers. Before she breaks a hip falling down the three stairs into the bathroom or slips trying to get into the pedestal tub…"

"Grace, if we concentrate on this floor and leave the lower floor and loft until last, we can get you in here in a month at the very longest, but I bet I can do better, lots better, if it doesn't take you long to make your decorating selections. I recommend hardwood floors, shutters for the ocean-side doors and windows—that setting sun can be brutal. I can place all the orders and call in favors—people all over Coos County owe me. And once they start, I know how to motivate. That gives you a finished main level with access to the bath, kitchen, two bedrooms, great room and deck. The other two levels can be left until…" She swallowed and cleared her throat. "Until it's more practical. Devon and Spence moved in when all they had finished was this level.

Spencer worked over the summer and finished the lower floor and loft himself to save money."

Grace was beginning to see it in her mind. She'd been in Cooper's house once when she delivered Mother's Day flowers for Sarah and it was spacious and beautiful. The deck with the fireplace was to die for. She pointed to the deck. "Awning and fireplace?"

"Anything you want. The awning and some comfortable outdoor deck furniture is easy, the fireplace much more complicated, but you're not going to crave an outdoor fireplace for six months. At least."

Anytime she heard six months, it caused her eyes to water, but she'd been very emotional lately. Her mother could be gone in six months. Then again, she could live another year. She could live long enough to meet her grandchild.

"You're close to town. You're close to Dr. Grant and Peyton if you need medical attention for your mother."

"Yes," she said. There was that second bedroom for health care workers who stayed full-time. "Washer and dryer?" she asked.

"In the hall," Ray Anne said, pointing to the two spaces. "Washer and dryer on one side, linen closet on the other. No laundry room, I'm afraid. There is room for one downstairs if a laundry room with a sink is important, but there are a lot of stairs involved in that idea."

Grace walked back down the hall. The master had two walk-in closets and it was, in itself, a spacious room. The bathroom, very roomy. "Could we put a glass block wall in here for the shower? No sliding glass door?"

"I think so!" Ray Anne said. "Not only handicap accessible but very up-to-date decor!"

Grace looked at her. "All right, how much?"

"Brace yourself," Ray Anne said. "It's oceanfront, even though it's a good twenty feet above the beach. One-point-two."

That wasn't thousands, Grace knew that.

"Cooper said because it's you, he'd rent it to you for up to a year, but the rent would be pricey, too."

"How in the world does Spencer do it on a coach's salary?"

"I'm sure he got a great deal. He and Cooper share a son and it was important to everyone that Austin live close to them both. You said not to worry about the money. I know it's a lot, but for what you want…"

"I know. I want my mother to be comfortable and near beauty. And near me, and my shop is walking distance. But I need that loft finished as soon as possible—how complicated is that?"

"Well, there are only floors and paint needed up there, no cupboards or countertops, so that should be quick. But you're going to have to add light fixtures. Light fixtures are simple if it doesn't take you six weeks to decide what you want. Even I know how to install light fixtures."

"Is that fireplace ready?"

"Except for the glass and ceramic logs—accessories. But you won't be cold for…"

"Just thinking about what has to be done to make it ready."

"Take a little time to think about it, Grace. But don't think long if you want to get started. You won't be able to close on it for about thirty days if all goes well, but this is Cooper's property and, given your circumstances, he's willing to start the interior work and even let you in before closing. He didn't ask for a contract for that, but I will. I want him protected in case you change your mind or..." She blinked and made a face. "Or in case something unexpected happens and you don't need the house anymore."

"In case she dies before I get her here? Well, that's not going to happen—she's in pretty good shape for the shape she's in. And we have to move ahead before she gets worse. Where do I have to go to make selections?"

"You want it?"

"Let's do it. Will twenty percent down for a cash sale convince Cooper to take a chance on me?"

"I believe so," Ray Anne said, smiling. "Even better, it'll convince him he made the right choice giving me the listings." She laughed merrily. "I can get this in shape for you, kiddo. You won't believe how good I am at that. If Ginger can watch the shop, I can take you to a couple of places. You should choose countertops, appliances and flooring first. Cupboards and banisters should be next. I can bring you catalogs for fixtures, blinds, shades and shutters, ceramic logs and paint. Given the openness here, you're going to want to match your cabinetry with floors and banisters." She stuck out her hand. "Let's shake on it and go over to Cooper's bar and sign papers."

* * *

Grace had to call Ginger and ask her if she felt confi-dent enough to manage the shop another day and, bless her, she was good with that. She then spent four hours with Ray Anne, first signing the contracts for the house and then heading to Bandon and North Bend to make decorating selections. She didn't screw around pon-dering her choices, but Ray Anne enthusiastically en-dorsed every one.

About two hours into the project, Grace suddenly felt very faint and woozy with a touch of nausea. "Oh, damn, I forgot to eat," she said to her Realtor.

"I have an energy drink in my purse," Ray Anne of-fered.

"Oh, so that's what keeps you going," she joked, but a bit weakly. She used to live on those! But with a bun in the oven, she wasn't sure what was safe. "Pull into the next grocery or deli. All I need is a half sandwich or something and I'll be fine." But it reminded her that she had other important business at hand.

She was just getting back to the flower shop a little after three when she finally texted Troy. Am I going to see you tonight?

He texted back that he was working at Cooper's from four till whenever and if she wanted him to, he could stop by afterward.

If I want you to?

It was usually hard to keep him away.

Please, she responded. I really have to talk to you about a couple of things.

From that point until nine-thirty she wondered what she was going to say. How she was going to say it. When he finally arrived and used his own key to get in, she leaped to her feet and ran to him, throwing her arms around him. Even twenty-four hours away from him was too much.

But he didn't embrace her as wildly. His hands rested on her hips. This was where Troy usually wondered how fast he could get into her. *Counter, table, floor, wall?* And yet there was a sudden distance she couldn't understand.

"Why are you different?" she asked.

"Different how?"

"I don't know," she said. "There's something different. You're not clutching me. You're not trying to get under my clothes. It's like you don't want to be here!"

"No, no, I want to be here. Gracie, we should talk about a few things."

"Yes," she said, drawing him into her little space. "Yes, we have to talk. You first. What's bothering you?"

They sat on the couch together. He held her hands. He gazed into her eyes—all the gestures of impending bad news. "Grace, I'm not proud of this, okay. I have to be honest with you. The money. *Your* money. It was ten times greater than I imagined. A hundred times greater. It kind of blew me away. Intimidated me. Filled me with doubts."

"Doubts?"

"About us, Gracie. I don't feel like we have as much in common as I thought we did. It worries me a little. I'm wondering…what do we do if we find out we don't fit? If we're just too different?"

She was stunned. "Are you breaking up with me?" she asked.

"No. *No*, of course not. I'm just a little…I'm worried about us. I need time to figure out how we go forward together. I don't have anything, Grace. You're as rich as the Gettys. I don't want to live off you. You can't live off me. We have to figure this out."

"Oh, for pity's sake," she said. "Do I look like I'm rich?" she said, throwing an arm wide, indicating her little loft. "I have an idea—how about if I earn a living, you earn a living and neither of us *lives off* the other?"

"And that fortune you're sitting on?"

"I'll do exactly as I promised my mother—I'll take care of it. Troy, I'm not going to live in a big cold stone manor house with a full-time staff. I do need more space than this someday, but…I bought my mother a house today. On the beach. One of Cooper's new houses. Something that would be perfect for her—the warm sun on the deck, the sound of the ocean. I think it could be comforting for her, much more so than the big house in the city. And I—"

"See? See? That was just so easy. You just went

out and bought a house that must have cost, I don't know, a million dollars or—"

"One-point-two," she said, lifting her chin a notch.

"Holy Jesus..." He leaned an elbow on his knee and put his head in his hand.

"Close to my shop, close to the doctor, close to the sound of kids having fun, dogs barking as they play fetch or chase birds along the beach, nice neighbors..."

"Do you have any idea how weird that is? That you can just plunk down over a million dollars and—"

"So much for *You don't have to be afraid to tell me anything, Grace,* and *You don't have to worry about how I'll react, Grace.* It's who I am!" she shouted. "I'm sorry I couldn't be broke and up to my eyeballs in student loans for you, but this is who I am and I'm not a bad person!"

"I never meant to suggest you were—"

"And I'm pregnant!"

All sound and motion stopped. She could tell that Troy didn't breathe. He just held his breath and looked at her. Finally he said, "Whoa." And that was all. After actual minutes had passed, he asked, "How pregnant?"

"I don't know. Not very."

"I thought you were going to see Peyton. I thought you were going to—"

"Take care of it?" she asked tartly. "I went to Peyton. She said I had a few days to see if my period would just come on its own so I could start on the pill. I was supposed to follow up with her."

"And you didn't?"

"A few things happened! I got that note, I tried to electrocute my boyfriend, your friends came for the weekend, my mother showed up with ALS...I forgot. It just slipped my mind. When I realized my period was really late, I used a test and peed on the stick. I wanted to tell you that second, but we were literally on our way to the airport and things were complicated enough. This is the first chance we've had to talk."

"Oh, God," he said.

"You didn't remember, either! You never asked!"

"Grace, I take responsibility and you're right, I didn't follow up, either. But let's not panic. It's early. We don't have to make any decisions tonight. We can process this."

"I don't have any decisions to make, Troy. I have a baby in me. It's just a little seed, but it's there and I'm not making it go away just because it's inconvenient."

"Okay, fine, right. But we don't have to make any irrevocable decisions tonight. There's time to think this through."

"All right. You go think this through. When you know what you want, you know where to find me."

"You want me to *leave*?"

"Yes," she said. "You have a lot of issues. Whether we're right for each other, whether we have enough in common, whether the fact that I come from a family with money is going to be a problem for you, what you want to do about a baby. I have no issues. I have nothing I have to *process*."

"Okay, now you're getting mad," he said. "Be fair, Grace—what can I ever give you if you have everything? If all you have to do is point and it's yours?"

Right, she wanted to say. *The same way I bought the gold medals.* Her hand slid over her flat tummy. "I want you to go," she said evenly. "I want you to process. When you know how you feel about me, about us, about this little seed, you let me know. You'll get more thinking done on your own. Besides, I'm not lying naked in bed with someone who isn't sure. That's too much to ask."

"Gracie, I love you," he said.

"Great. Thanks. Doesn't sound like that's going to do me much good right now. So let's take a break while you decide whether this is all too complicated for you. I have to take care of myself, my little seed, my mother, my shop. I don't have any extra energy to take care of you right now."

"Are you sure that's the way you want it?"

"I'm sure," she said.

Twenty

Early Thursday morning, Peyton stood in the doorway locked in a passionate kiss with Scott while her sister, Adele, waited in the car. When the kiss wouldn't stop, Adele tooted the horn. Peyton laughed against Scott's lips. "I'll see you tomorrow night," she promised. "And you'll bring my honeymoon suitcase."

"And you have your wedding dress and will pick up my tux."

"And you'll take the kids to the grandmothers."

"They want to stay at the farm, which is going to hurt the grandmothers' feelings."

"Talk to them about that your drive up, okay? They'll get plenty of time at the farm, but they do have to visit all the grandparents and take turns and be fair. They know how to share and be fair."

"I'll talk to them," he promised. "But I want to stay at the farm, too. With you."

"Starting Saturday night we will always stay together and I won't have to sleep in your mother's craft room anymore," she said.

"I never understood that," Scott said. "She doesn't do crafts. Not really."

"I love you, Scott. I'm going to marry you."

"I can't believe it. Are you sure?"

"I'm sure. Are you?"

"I was sure the day you walked into my office. The only reason I didn't make a pass right away was because I thought you were a lesbian. Lesbian hearts are breaking all over the world and I got you."

She laughed. "You got me all right. My breasts are actually getting sore already."

He grinned at her. "Then they're going to get big."

Adele gave the horn another toot.

"Think I'd better hit the road?" she asked.

"Call me when you reach the farm. I'll get to my mom's tomorrow. I'll help her with the groom's dinner if she needs it."

"Grace is bringing the centerpieces."

Another quick kiss and Peyton was in the car with her sister. Adele's baby girl was in the car seat in the back. "Are you absolutely sure you don't want to go back in there and maybe have a little more sex before you leave?" Adele asked.

"I've had all the sex I can take for a while."

"Ah. Spoken like a wife!"

"And a mother?" Peyton asked.

"Oh, my God, you're pregnant?"

"Just a little," she said. "I wasn't going to tell anyone, but you're not just anyone."

"This is fabulous! I'll be counting the days! Our kids will be so close to the same age! Have a girl, will you?"

"I'll see what I can do. Now don't tell anyone, all right? Because we should concentrate on the wedding, not the pregnancy."

"Everyone will know the second you say no thank you to a glass of wine."

"It's not like I drink that much wine," Peyton said. "You didn't notice last night."

"You appeared to have wine!"

"No, that was citrus green tea in a wineglass." She grinned. "I can fake my way through this."

"Oh, this is going to be so fun! Thank you for getting rid of that ass Ted and finding adorable Scott. I love him. What ever happened to Ted?"

"Last time I talked to his daughter, she said they had a very nice housekeeper and he was playing grandfather. Apparently he's better with her little one than he ever was with his kids. A transformation, it sounds like. Good for him."

"No regrets?"

"Are you kidding me?" she asked. "Scott is my dream man."

The drive to the farm, near Portland, was four hours from Thunder Point. Adele lived in San Francisco and had arrived two days ago; her husband would be driving up on Friday morning in a catering truck stocked with prepared dishes—he was a restaurateur and would be catering much of the reception, but not all—Peyton's mother, sisters, aunts, grandmother and cousins would not be held back from sharing their special Basque dishes. But Lucas was an amazing chef and wanted to do this for Peyton. He would follow Adele back to the city on Sunday.

Peyton and her youngest sister were best friends. It was odd in a large family how the siblings paired up and there was no formula to it. Peyton was always there for Adele and vice versa. They talked all the way to the farm—about their men, their jobs, the wedding, the other siblings, their parents.

When they arrived, all was as expected. There were vans, RVs, trailers and trucks with camper shells everywhere. The kitchen was full of women, talking, laughing, some arguing here and there. Adele walked in ahead of Peyton, carrying baby Rose, named for her great-grandmother and at least three women on Lucas's side of the family. Peyton followed with her wedding dress hidden by a garment bag so that Scott wouldn't see it.

"We're here," Adele said. "Peyton's pregnant."

Peyton gasped but the women shrieked and came running, fussing over her, hugging her, laughing and shouting, "Way to go, Adele," Peyton said when the din died down.

"It's an icebreaker. They're going to find out within twenty-four hours anyway. It's not like you're a virgin bride. And besides, they're Basque women. They have a couple of pregnant brides every year. We have the passion," she added with a heavy accent.

"Now I'll have to call Scott so he can tell the grandmothers. I'm never telling you another secret."

"Yes, you will," Adele said with a grin. "I'm very responsible. Most of the time."

Grace and Ginger were under way with the flowers by seven on Friday morning. Grace was so glad to be leaving town.

Troy had texted her once in the past twenty-four hours— Are you okay? She texted back one word. Fine. Was she angry? Damn straight. This was all so familiar. Her mother had furs and jewelry, so that made her life simple? Easy? The reverse was also not true—there was family money and that made her tragic, evil and doomed? No. It made her an individual. *We're all very different with our own challenges and joys.*

What could Troy give her since she had everything? Well, she didn't have a father for her baby. *My mistake*, she mused. *I thought he could love me no matter what.*

She didn't betray her feelings, something she'd become an expert at. She'd done it for years, starting when she was a young girl. She could be terrified and her heart breaking, but she could smile for the judges like she had the world on a string. She knew how to cope. Or cover.

She used the time to get Ginger's story. When she gave her the job in the shop, she had no idea what Ginger had been through, the selfish husband, the baby's death. "I think the job at the flower shop has saved me," she told Grace. "It's like a brand-new chapter for me. I haven't been happy in so long, but I get excited to go to work every day. I hope you'll need me for a while."

"Are you kidding? You're doing wonderfully. And my mother will be moving here in a month or so and you know all about that. I want to be able to see about her if she needs me or wants me. It's so nice to know there's someone who can take care of the flowers. I might have had to go to part-time hours, but with you in the shop and Justin to deliver, I'm in great shape. I can give my mother some time. When you get down to it, that's the one thing you can't buy or trade or borrow."

"And you're close to your mother?" Ginger asked.

"Yes and no. My mother was always so proud of me and my father died when I was young, so it was just the two of us, no siblings. But she was also demanding and impatient and sometimes she angered too easily. But now her life is slowly ending and all she wants is to be comfortable and near me. This is our chance to close on a good note."

"A second chance. We should never take that for granted."

"Your husband," Grace said. "You said you should've known. Why did you marry him if you should've known?"

"Oh, it's a long story, but the truth is, I loved the wrong man. I wanted him so much and put up with so much to have him. And in the end he wasn't worth it. Listen, it was very nice of Peyton to invite us to the wedding, but do you think she'd be offended if I didn't go? I'm completely over my ex, but a wedding might just make me very sad. I could go to the reception for a little while, just to see the wedding party with their flowers, but not the wedding ceremony. Would it hurt Peyton's feelings?"

"Not at all. I'm going—she's a friend of mine. But the way we usually service a wedding is to deliver the flowers early, arrange and stage them in the church and make sure the bride and her wedding party have theirs, leave the centerpieces and any other decorations either with the catering staff or if the tables are ready, put them out, then leave. Just that much takes quite a while. When we've done our work and are ready to go clean up, I can drop you anywhere you like."

"And on Sunday morning, you want me to drive the van back to Thunder Point?" she asked.

"I might be going back in the van, also. I don't know if Troy will make it. He has stuff going on. He'd like to, I'm sure, but it's iffy. I can stay with my friends, Mamie and Ross. I'll know for sure about Troy on Saturday night. That okay?"

"Sure. Anything you want."

On Friday afternoon, Troy leaned in the doorway of Iris's office, arms crossed over his chest. She looked up and raised an eyebrow. "What now?" she asked.

"Are men born stupid or does it come over time?" he asked.

"Sadly, I think you're born with it."

"That's what I was afraid of. Think I can still make it right with Grace?"

"I don't know, Troy. How badly did you screw it up?"

"I carefully explained all my doubts and feelings," he said. "I was very articulate. I listed them and suggested there was plenty of time for me to *process* them. I was eloquent! She told me to go away and process. She showed me the door. I thought I had been extremely sensible and sensitive."

"Is that so?" Iris said.

"Turns out Grace is a little bit pregnant. I didn't panic, not me. I said we didn't have to make any decisions about what to do right away. I got the distinct impression that wasn't the best response."

Iris rolled her eyes. "Wow. What an idiot. You're lucky she didn't fire up that Taser."

"I think I'm figuring that part out. I bet you know exactly what I should have said instead. Why don't you tell me and I'll tell you if you're right."

"No, I don't think so, Troy," Iris said. "I think you should puzzle this out for yourself. I don't want to mix you up with my words. You've been whispering in Grace's ear for months now. You know what makes her happy and what doesn't. Get your head out of your butt and think like a hero instead of an escaped convict who's trying to dodge the law. You're not going to be put in prison, you know. If you're smart and lucky, you'll get to share lives."

"Right," he said. "Good advice. I'll let you know how it turns out."

"You do that, Troy."

He left and she looked back at her paperwork. She smiled. Peyton had confessed she was a little pregnant when Iris confessed she was a little pregnant. And now Grace was, too. "I guess we know what everyone was doing the first week in April," she said softly.

Grace was looking forward to seeing Peyton and Scott's wedding reception in the orchard but on Friday night, after putting out her table arrangements at the restaurant where the groom's dinner was held, Grace was so happy for a quiet evening with Mamie and Ross. Although she talked to them almost every week, she had held the news of her mother's health until she could tell them in person. Mamie and Ross had spent twenty years in Winnie's employ. They felt much closer to Grace than to Winnie, but they immediately promised they would be visiting Winnie when she was relocated in Thunder Point.

"I'm so happy you two have reconciled," Mamie said. "For both your sakes."

"We are, too, Mamie. The sad truth is, if Winnie weren't ill I don't know if we'd have this relationship. But I'll do my best to be sure she's comfortable and well cared for. Winnie is making it surprisingly easy and I think Mikhail has a lot to do with it. He came immediately and is in no hurry to leave her."

"Like your mother, he has very few people he's

tied to. For many years they kept each other close. Your mother always listened to Mikhail."

On Saturday, Ginger borrowed her mother's car and drove to Mamie's shop and all of them worked together on the flowers for the wedding. They had the altar arrangements and bouquets at the church by noon and the rest were delivered to the Lacoumette farm. Then Grace went back to Mamie's house to clean up for the four-o'clock wedding. She wore a peach dress and nude sandals she loved and wore her hair down because Troy loved it that way.

But she had not heard from Troy.

Their plan had been that he would meet her at the wedding. They would spend the night in one of the coastal inns and let Ginger take the van back to Thunder Point on Sunday while they rode together in the Jeep, but she had a sense of foreboding. Maybe in the course of all his processing he had decided that getting involved with someone like Grace had been a mistake. Grace came from a different world, a world he wasn't comfortable even thinking about.

It could be worse, she thought. He could try to marry her for her money.

It just felt so hopeless. What could she do? Nothing. It was on him now.

When she got to the church, she was distracted for a while, chuckling to herself when she saw the parking lot. It was full of trucks, RVs, SUVs—all big vehicles, some that family members would be staying in while attending the Lacoumette wedding and reception. If they didn't look like a band of Gyp-

sies, she didn't know what did. There was Peyton's
car, parked in front. She knew that Peyton had rid-
den to the farm with her sister and Scott was driving up here in that fancy Lexus. There were only a
couple of late-model cars. These farmers and fish-
ermen and vintners were hardworking country folks
and although Grace had heard it was a very successful family, you'd never know it by looking at them.
They just weren't showy.

There was no Jeep anywhere and her heart sank.

She turned her phone to Silent, but, ever the opti-
mist, she sat near the back of the packed church and
on the aisle. If he came, he would find her.

The church was so beautiful. She hoped someone would mention the flowers, the aisle drapes, the
bridal bouquets—she was so proud of them. Peyton
had such good taste and when she finally walked
down the aisle and all heads turned to her, she was
stunning in her strapless gown. But Grace watched
Scott. Even from a great distance she could see the
glow in his eyes. He adored Peyton. He worshipped
her. This was what every woman should have on her
wedding day.

The ceremony was not long. It was an ecumenical service performed by both a Catholic priest
and a protestant minister. Grace silently chuckled
as she noticed some of the Basque family members
whispering and she remembered that Peyton had
said some would be disgruntled by her not having
a mass but they wouldn't boycott. The family dis-

agreed often and heartily, but at the end of the day they were one for all.

A large family, Grace thought. Maybe that's the answer to all these issues. A huge family, like the Lacoumette family, so many of them they were like countries tied together by treaties and pacts. *Oh, hell*, she thought. She had a hard enough time functioning in a family of two.

Peyton and Scott spoke vows they had created themselves. They were blessed by both the priest and the minister and then, after less than a half hour, they embraced passionately and cheers erupted inside the church. Down the aisle they fled, followed by their wedding party, then family and friends, out the door, where a receiving line formed and someone from the family released white doves. By Peyton's surprised expression, she had not expected it.

No Jeep. No Troy. She would not cry.

While there were a few pictures taken in the church, most of the caravan headed back to the farm, and it was not a short drive. It was nearly an hour away from this ornate, historical church. Grace was happy to see that Ginger had decided to come to the reception.

By five they were serving wine and tapas in the reception tent and the flowers looked beautiful, as did the plentiful fruit blossoms everywhere. The band was playing and Grace noticed that some of the Basque men had changed into their native dress—trading their suits and tuxes for white pants and shirts, red vests and caps. They were getting ready to party.

By six the bride and groom had arrived, and another cheer erupted. The music picked up its pace, the champagne flowed, all glasses were filled and the noise was wonderfully happy. Caterers brought plates to the wedding party. The rest of the guests, mostly the Basque population of the Pacific Northwest, fell on the buffet like locusts. But the food was never ending, as was the wine, it seemed. And the dancing, even during dinner while others ate, was extraordinary. Paco Lacoumette took the floor and was joined one at a time by his brothers, his sons, nephews, even his klutzy son-in-law, and showed them all what this clan could do. It was like a flash mob, so much fun. The cheers were enough to almost bring the tent down.

Grace sat with a few of the people from Thunder Point: Spencer and Devon and their kids, Cooper and Sarah and little Summer. They asked if Troy was coming and she said she had hoped so, but he wasn't sure. "He had something going on today."

"Well, it wasn't work. Rawley's holding down the fort. I could do that," Cooper said of the men dancing.

"A couple more glasses of wine and I'm sure you will," Sarah agreed.

"Why didn't I come from a clan like this?" Spencer asked. "These people know how to have fun."

"From the looks of this place, they know how to work, too," Cooper added.

Grace took her plate as if she'd be going back for
more, but she put it in the bussing cart and wandered
out of the tent. The sun was setting, the party was
going strong and she walked toward the orchard.
She wanted a good look at it before it was dark.
The house and garden stood between the big party
tent and row after row of blossoming pear trees. She
looked at Mrs. Lacoumette's garden with envy and
crouched down—vegetables, flowers, herbs. Everything was just coming in—the vegetables weren't
even showing their faces yet, but she longed for this.
That's what she would do next—get a house with
room for a garden and teach her child how to grow
things.

"Grace?" a voice called.

She looked up and saw Troy. He looked like he'd
slept in his suit—his tie was crooked and there was
a smear of dirt on his face. His duffel was sitting on
the path behind him. "I thought that was you."

She stood. "Troy. You came? Why weren't you
here for the wedding?"

He waved over his shoulder and a noisy tow truck
pulling his Jeep edged away from the party, leaving
Troy behind. "The car broke down. The tow driver
dropped me here. In all the calls I had to make to get
service, my phone went dead."

"What happened? You have grease on your—"

"What didn't happen?" he said, pulling out a
handkerchief. "I was running late to start with, then
the damn thing just crashed. Transmission. It wasn't
going anywhere. I bet a million dollars the jerk who

sold me that Jeep put a rebuilt transmission in it. I have to go to the guy's garage in the morning before we head home to see what's up. I might have to tow it home, get Eric at the service station to look at it. Jesus, I'm sorry."

"I didn't think you were coming," she said. "I didn't hear from you. In fact, you've been pretty quiet."

"Did you know that when men are in love there's a kind of atrophy of the brain that causes them to do stupid things? Even when they know better?"

"I didn't know that."

"I'm living proof," he said, taking her hand and walking with her along the path to the orchard. "Gracie, can you forgive me?"

"For having doubts?" she asked.

"For not grabbing you and kissing you and begging you to marry me the second you told me there's a baby."

"Oh. That. Well, yes, I guess so. You want to get married? Because you don't have to. I'm going to have it no matter what you say or do."

"Grace, I want to marry you even if there is no baby! I love you. I can't sleep unless you're next to me. And I may not be rich but I have important things. There are a million things I can give you that nobody else can. It appears I can give you children, without hardly trying."

That made her smile. "In fact, trying not to," she said.

"Did I mention I'm good with kids?" he asked her.

"I'm not a teacher for the time off. I love what I do. I get a kick out of the kids. I'd like a few of my own."

"A few?" she asked.

"I get that I'm slightly less than fifty percent of the vote, but I think we'll be good parents. As a matter of fact, I think we have a lot in common."

"A couple of days ago you were worried that it wasn't enough."

"Yeah, I got hung up on things that had nothing to do with us. We have fun together. Really, I've never had this much fun with a girlfriend before, and we don't even have to do anything to laugh a lot. Who would've guessed a picnic in the Jeep would get you excited? Good thing, too, since it looks like that's about all that Jeep's going to be good for. I spend half my time off in that little dorm room you live in and it's not too crowded—that means something. Every day when I wake up if you're not right next to me, I start thinking about when I'm going to see you."

"You've had a lot of girlfriends, Troy. What makes this different?"

He stopped walking and turned her toward him. "You do, Gracie. I've dated a lot, but I've never been this serious about a woman. I've always known I'd settle down when the right woman came into my life and a couple of times I asked myself, *Is this her? Is this the right one?* I never asked with you. I knew. I knew right away. But we had to learn about each other. You had to learn to trust me."

"Yes, and the minute I did…"

"Brain atrophy," he explained. "At least it's not permanent."

"And if you get it again?"

"Try a club," he suggested. And then he pulled her against him and kissed her stupid, a kiss that seemed to last forever. His hands roamed up and down her back. and her arms went around his neck. Their bodies were flush together so that only an earthquake could distract them. "And then there's this," he whispered against her lips. "The way we fit together. The way you can't breathe for a minute after you come. The way I can't stop after once and almost can't after twice. We were made for each other, that's the truth. Sometimes I can taste you in my dreams."

"And what if I want six kids?" she asked very softly.

"Bring 'em on."

"You're the only man I've ever been with. Except for the knight, the Navy SEAL and the vampire."

"You're not going to need those boys anymore, Gracie. I'm going to keep you busy." He kissed her again. "I bought you a ring. It's not flashy. Or big."

"You bought me a ring?"

"You can't have it unless you promise to marry me and get old with me."

"I don't know…let me think…"

"I can promise you hand-holding and picnics and laughter. I can give you children and loyalty and love. I will stick by you through hard times and beside you through good. And I will never again doubt you, I swear. I'll trust you and you can always trust me. I'll be a good husband and a strong father for our kids. Do it, Grace. Forgive me, trust me, marry me. I can't make it without you."

"Okay. But only because I love you so much in spite of your flaws."

He sighed in relief and pulled a ring box out of his pocket. Without letting an inch separate them, he slipped it on her ring finger. It was a lovely solitaire, certainly not too little on her small hand. She thought it was the most beautiful thing she'd ever seen. But it could have been a cigar band and she would have been filled with love for him. "Be my life, be my love, be my wife."

"Yes," she said.

* * * * *

Turn the page for a sneak peek at
A NEW HOPE,
the next book in Robyn Carr's
#1 New York Times *bestselling*
THUNDER POINT *series.*

The Basque really know how to get married, Ginger Dysart thought. She hadn't attended the wedding ceremony and had had doubts about attending this reception, given all the sadness she'd suffered over the past year. Her own marriage had barely begun when it ended in divorce. But she was so glad she'd come to the reception. It was an ethnic extravaganza—the Basque food, the music, the dancing. The bride and groom, Peyton and Scott Grant, had whirled around the dance floor a few times, then parted so Scott could dance with his mother and Peyton could dance with her father. And then there were a series of handsome dark-haired men who claimed the bride—brothers, cousins, uncles.

Paco Lacoumette presided over the party with all the aplomb of a king and was clearly in his element. The couples dancing would cease and the Basque men in their traditional white outfits with red vests and caps would take the floor and put on a show to the wild applause of the guests. Then more couples dancing. Even Ginger was dragged from her chair and pulled out to dance, despite her efforts to decline. She danced with men she knew—Cooper, Spencer, Mac, Scott—and men she didn't know, those good looking Lacoumette relatives. At one point she spied Troy, Grace's boyfriend, who must have just arrived. Grace, Ginger's boss and owner of the flower shop in Thunder Point, had believed he wasn't going to make it and was so disappointed; yet there he was, twirling Grace around with almost professional skill. And by the glowing look on Grace's face, she was completely thrilled.

Wine flowed, food was constantly replenished, dancing and laughter filled the night. Ginger felt pretty for the first time in so long. She wore a new dress, cut to her slim figure. She'd lost a lot of weight in the past several months; men were looking at her in a way they hadn't before, and she actually enjoyed the feel of their eyes on her. Those lusty, dark-haired Basque men did nothing to conceal their appreciative gazes.

The whole atmosphere was magical—teenagers were dancing or dashing about the grounds and orchard, sneaking behind trees for stolen kisses; children were riding on the shoulders of fathers, grandfathers and uncles; women were clapping in time to the music, laughing, singing, gossiping. Peyton and Scott were in much demand on the dance floor, and in between songs many toasts were made.

There were far too many Lacoumettes to remember all their names, but they made Ginger feel welcome and appreciated.

There was one darkly handsome man she'd noticed right away because he was the only one who seemed sulky and unhappy, and he was the one approaching her now as she stood beside her table. He had the swarthy good looks and fierce eyes of a pirate or maybe serial killer. And with such precision timing, he had singled her out when everyone else from her table was dancing.

"Hey, pretty lady," he said, attempting a smile that was off-kilter. His words were slurred. That would at least partially account for the half-mast eyes and pouting expression—he was obviously drunk. Well, this happened at weddings with great regularity, she thought, especially weddings where the wine flowed so liberally.

"Time for a dance!" he said.

"Thank you, but I'm going to sit this one out," she replied.

"Hmm," he said, stroking his chin. "Then we should go straight to the hayloft!"

She was appalled. But she remained composed and confident. "I'm sitting that out as well."

"No, come with me," he said. "You and me—let's do this." And then he reached for her. And grabbed her right breast.

She shrieked, shoved him away. His feet got tangled, he fell backward over a chair and went down, hitting his head on the way. And there he lay, motionless and unconscious.

"Help," she said. Then louder. "*Help!*"

She got far more attention than she wanted or expected. And of course, there were the questions. *What happened? Are you hurt? Did he pass out? Is he dead?*

"He grabbed at me," she said, waving a hand over the area of her breast without pointing or saying it. "I shoved him away and he fell and I think he might've hit his head on the table."

There he lay in a heap, on his back, his legs twisted awkwardly.

In just seconds Peyton and Scott were there, Scott crouching and lifting the man's eyelids, looking at his eyes. "Well, they're equal, but damn...they're big. Does he take anything?" he asked his bride.

"Yes, wine," Peyton said. "He killed a full skin before the dancing."

Then Paco was pushing his way through the crowd, looking down. "I knew it would come to this," he said. "There was no slowing him down."

"I think we call 9-1-1, get a head CT, make sure he didn't crack his skull," Scott said.

"His head is made of wood," Paco said. "It would serve him right, to be carried out of his sister's wedding on one of those back board things and spend the night in a hospital." Paco reached for the ice bucket on the table. Everyone scooted back immediately, as if they knew what was coming. Peyton pulled Scott away while Paco took a bottle of white wine out of the bucket and put it on the table, then doused the man with the ice water.

He sputtered and coughed and sat up.

"See what I'm telling you?" Paco said. "Wood. George! Sal! Mikie! Get Matthew from your sister's wedding! Hide his keys!" Three men moved to action immediately. Paco looked at Ginger and said, "There's always one. I apologize." Then he took in the gathering crowd and clapped. "I think it's time I dance with my wife!"

Grace arrived, pushing her way through the crowd. "Ginger! Is everything all right?"

"I'm not sure," she said, watching as the men were leaving—three of them walking steadily and one weaving dangerously.

"My brother, Matt," Peyton said. "He has issues. Divorce issues. He was divorced a little over a year ago but it appears he's still very bitter. Weddings don't seem to bring out the best in him. He didn't hurt you, did he?"

"He didn't quite connect," Ginger said. "I was about to say good night anyway. I'm going back to my folks' house in Portland for the night."

"I might kill Matt," Peyton said.

"Just enjoy the rest of your party," Ginger said. "No harm done. To me, anyway. God, I hope I didn't hurt him."

"You heard my father—his head is made of wood."

"I'll call you in the morning," Grace said. "Troy had some car trouble on the way up here and we'll have to see where that stands in the morning and figure out how we're all getting home. I've got the van. You take your father's car back to him."

Ginger turned to Peyton. "It was a wonderful reception. You look ravishing. And I was just thinking, the Basque people really know how to get married."

Ginger's parents, Dick and Sue, had waited up. That was definite evidence as to how concerned they were about her—they'd stayed up past ten when their usual bedtime was before nine. And when she walked in the front door, looking perfectly alive, they both stood from their recliners. They looked at her expectantly.

"Did you have a good time?" Sue asked hesitantly.

"I had a lovely time," Ginger said. "The flowers were beautiful, the wedding party was gorgeous and the party was like one out of a fairy tale. You wouldn't believe the fun of Basque dancing and music! And the food? Oh my God, the food was just amazing. And I'm exhausted—I'm going straight to bed."

"Are you...comfortable in your room, Ginger?" Sue asked.

"Yes, of course. And thank you for making it so nice for me."

She kissed them both on their cheeks and went upstairs. Upstairs to the large bedroom and adjacent room that had been renovated especially for her when she'd come home to her parents, pregnant and alone; to the room where she had cared for her little son for the four short months of his life.

Ginger had been staying with her cousin Ray Anne in Thunder Point for the past month. It was through Ray Anne that she'd gotten the job in Grace's flower shop, a job that was really saving her life, hour by hour. Before she came back to Portland with Grace for this wedding and weekend visit, Ray Anne had called Sue and asked her to pack up all the baby things that Ginger had been looking at since his death over nine months ago. The crib and mobile had been taken down, the clothes removed from the drawers, boxed up and stored, the necessary accoutrements like car seat, bouncy chair, bath items and changing table were all gone. She didn't think her parents had given them away, but they were out of sight. Probably stored in the attic or garage. There was only one framed picture of Ginger and Josh, which she found in the top drawer.

She took it out, put it on the bedside table, and changed into her pajamas.

When her father had suggested, rather emotionally, that Ginger go to Thunder Point and stay with Ray Anne for at least a few weeks, she had not wanted any part of it. But it was plain to see her parents needed a break from her grief. Now she was so glad she had gone. When she was in Thunder Point, she at least had the illusion of getting on with her life. She had a new, improved appearance, at Ray Anne's insistence. She had that lovely little job in the flower shop. She had slept well and had an appetite again. Oh, she'd longed for little Josh, like always. But she was marching on.

She crawled in the bed at her parents' house, turned the picture of herself and her baby toward her, left the light on so she could see it, and sobbed.